THE
EVERYTHING
PRINCESS
BOOK

Dedicated to girls everywhere and the
incredible women we know they can become.
—The Familius Family

Published by Familius LLC, www.familius.com

Familius books are available at special discounts for bulk purchases, whether
for sales promotions or for family or corporate use. For more information, contact
Premium Sales at 559-876-2170 or email orders@familius.com.

Library of Congress Cataloging-in-Publication Data
2016940699
ISBN 9781942934653

Cover and book design by David Miles
Edited by Sarah Echard
Public domain stories compiled and edited by Emily Faison
Digital illustrations by Rebecca Sorge. Patterns, embellishments,
sketches, and watercolor vignettes from Shutterstock.com.

10 9 8 7 6 5 4 3 2 1

First Edition

Printed in China

THE EVERYTHING PRINCESS BOOK

BY BARBARA BEERY,
BROOKE JORDEN,
MICHELE ROBBINS,
DAVID MILES

ILLUSTRATIONS BY
REBECCA SORGE

FAMILIUS

My Dearest Princess,

I've worked with royalty for many years now (I won't tell you how many!). By and large, you're a pleasant lot, though I confess I'm appalled at how many *still* can't tell a pumpkin from a squash (and only *one* of those will do for a coach, dear). No matter.

In this volume, you'll find years of wisdom from all the princesses, fairy godmothers, and courtiers across the land. You'll learn to have good manners, learn how to break enchantments, and even find games and activities to do with your fellow princesses.

Most importantly, you'll learn how to become a real princess. Yes, a *real* princess. Real princesses are rare in the world. They're kind, they're courageous, they think for themselves, and they treat others as if they were royal, too. It takes effort to become a real princess, but when you work at it, it's a magic stronger than anything my wand can do (and that's saying something!).

So off you go, darling. Shoo! Your journey begins. Be kind, be smart, and remember that happily ever after starts with you!

Hugs and kisses,

Your Fairy Godmother

P.S. If you make any of those scrumptious fruit tarts, would you send a few my way? The Queen of Hearts pinched the last of mine . . .

Contents

Princess Practices

Being a True Princess

Games & Activities

Things to Make

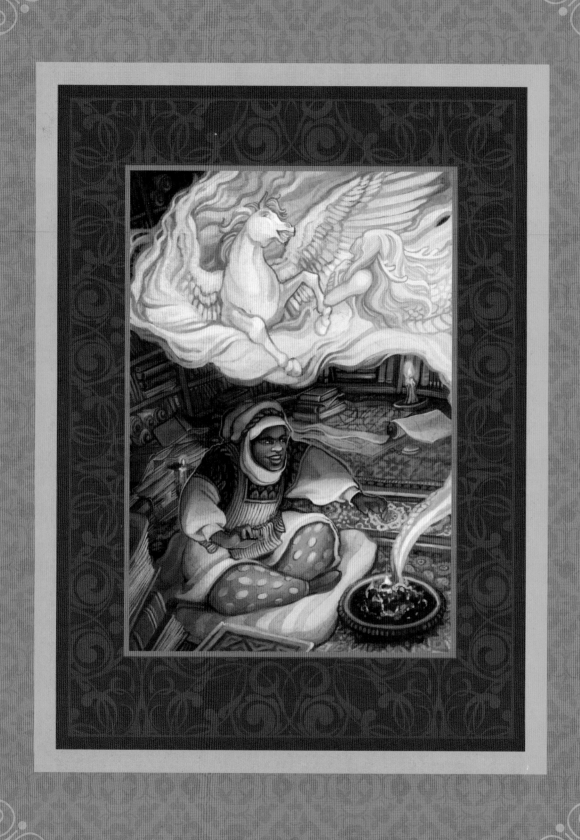

SECTION ONE

Classic Tales

FROM AROUND THE WORLD

The Tale of Thumbelina

HANS CHRISTIAN ANDERSEN

 nce there was a tiny girl who lived inside a tulip. She was only as big as your thumb, so she was called Thumbelina. In the day, she sang as delicately and prettily as no one had ever heard, and at night, she slept in a splendid lacquered walnut shell with rose petals for blankets. One night, a horrid Toad came hopping by. The Toad was ugly and big and wet and hopped right up to the walnut shell inside the tulip where Thumbelina lay asleep under her rose petal.

"She would make a lovely wife for my son," said the Toad, and, taking hold of the walnut shell where Thumbelina slept, the Toad hopped off to a garden with sleeping Thumbelina. In the middle of the garden flowed a big, broad stream, and there the Toad and her son lived at the marshy, muddy edge of the water. There were a great many water lilies growing out in the stream, and the lilypad that was furthest out was also the biggest of all. To this leaf the old Toad swam out and put the walnut shell with Thumbelina on it.

When poor little Thumbelina woke up in the morning, she began to cry, for she couldn't possibly get to land. Before long, the old Toad swam out with her ugly Toad son to the leaf where Thumbelina sat. The old Toad curtsied low in the water before her and said: "I present my son to you. He is going to be your husband, and you will have a delightful life with him down in the mud." The

Toad's son was ugly and horrid, just like his mother.

"Koäx, koäx, brekke-ke-kex," was all he could say when he saw the pretty little girl in the walnut shell.

Then they swam off to prepare the son's muddy home while Thumbelina sat alone on the green leaf, crying. She didn't want to live with the horrid Toad or have her ugly son for a husband. But little fishes, swimming in the water, heard what the Toad said, and it grieved them that the beautiful Thumbelina had to live in the mud with the ugly Toad. So all the little fish swarmed together all round the green stalk that held the lilypad leaf Thumbelina sat on, and they gnawed it through with their teeth. Soon the leaf went floating down the stream, taking Thumbelina far, far away, where the Toad could not go.

Thumbelina was very happy, for now the Toad could not get her. Everything was beautiful where she was sailing: the sun shone on the water and made

it glitter like gold. Eventually, Thumbelina's lily-pad came to a stop on the banks of the stream, near a cornfield. As Thumbelina wandered the cornfield, she came to a Mouse's door, a little hole among the stubble of stalks. There a Mouse lived snug and happy, with a whole room full of corn, a lovely kitchen, and a dining room. Poor Thumbelina went up to the door just like any little beggar girl and asked for a few bites of corn, for she hadn't had anything to eat.

"Poor little thing," said the kind old Mouse. "Come into my warm home and have dinner with me."

As they ate, the Mouse said, "My neighbor visits often, but his house is even better than mine. And he goes about in such a beautiful black velvet coat! Ah, if only you could get him for a husband! You would be well set up." But Thumbelina didn't care much about this—she didn't want to marry the neighbor, for he was a Mole.

But the Mole in his black velvet coat came and visited, and he fell in love with Thumbelina, though he said nothing about it. He had dug a passage through the earth from his house to the Mouse's and invited the Mouse and Thumbelina to walk there whenever they liked.

As the Mole showed the Mouse and Thumbelina the passage, he begged them not to be frightened at the dead bird that lay in the passage—a whole bird with beak and feathers! There was a little hole in the passage that let in light, so Thumbelina could see a very still Swallow with its pretty wings close against its sides and its legs and head down in among its feathers. The poor bird had certainly died of cold, though not very long ago. Thumbelina was very

sorry for it; she was fond of little birds, who sang so prettily.

But the Mole kicked it with his short leg and said, "It must be wretched to be born a little bird! A bird has nothing but its *twit, twit* and is bound to starve to death in winter."

"Yes, what has the bird to show for all its *twit, twit* when winter comes?" agreed the Mouse.

Thumbelina said nothing but stooped down to kiss the poor Swallow when the others were not looking. That night, Thumbelina couldn't sleep at all, so she got out of bed, plaited a warm blanket of hay, and carried it to the bird, so that it might lie warmly on the cold ground. She laid her head against the Swallow's heart. It seemed as if something was knocking inside! It was the bird's heart. The bird was not dead; it was only in a swoon, and now that it was warmed, it came to life again. The next night, Thumbelina crept down to the bird again, who was quite alive but so weak that it could only open its eyes for a moment.

"Thank you, you pretty little child, for warming me," the sick Swallow said to her. "Soon I shall get back my strength and be able to fly about again in the warm sun outside."

"Oh," said Thumbelina, "but it's dreadfully cold outside, snowing and freezing! You must stay in your warm bed, and I'll take care of you." As the Swallow gained strength, he told Thumbelina how he had hurt his wing on a thorn bush and so couldn't fly as well as the other Swallows when they set out to fly far, far away to warm places. All winter, the Swallow stayed in the passage, and Thumbelina grew very fond of him.

Meanwhile, in the Mouse's home, Thumbelina was very unhappy. She rarely saw the warm sunshine, and the tiresome Mole in the black velvet coat had proposed to her. Every evening, the Mole visited, and they always talked about how when winter was over, Thumbelina should be married. But Thumbelina didn't like the Mole one bit. Every evening when the sun set, she crept out to the doorway and thought how bright and pretty it was outside.

As soon as spring came, the Swallow said goodbye to Thumbelina. The Swallow asked if Thumbelina

would not come with him; she could sit on his back and they would fly away into the sunshine. But Thumbelina knew that leaving would grieve the old Mouse. "No, I can't," said Thumbelina. "Goodbye, goodbye, you kind, pretty maid," said the Swallow and flew out into the sunshine. Thumbelina stood looking after it and cried, for she was very fond of the poor Swallow. *Twit, twit,* sang the bird and flew away.

So the wedding was to be. "It's a splendid husband you're getting," the Mouse said to Thumbelina. "A queen herself hasn't the like of his black velvet coat, and a full kitchen and cellar he has, too!" Thumbelina cried and said she wouldn't marry the Mole. "Rubbish!" said the Mouse, and the Mole came to fetch Thumbelina. Poor Thumbelina was bitterly grieved to live with the Mole deep down underground, where she would never see the sunshine or hear a bird's song.

"Farewell, bright sun," she said, stretching her arms outside the door to the Mouse's house. "Farewell!"

Twit! Twit! sounded at that moment above her head. She looked up, and there was the Swallow flying by. He was overjoyed when he caught sight of Thumbelina, and she told him how she hated to have the ugly Mole for a husband and how she must live down underground where the sun never shone. She couldn't help crying.

"Come with me," said the Swallow. "Do fly away with me, you sweet little Thumbelina, who saved my life when I lay frozen in the dark underground."

So Thumbelina got up on the bird's back, and off flew the Swallow high in the air over forest and lake, high above the great mountains where the snow always lies. Thumbelina might have frozen in the cold air, but she crept in among the bird's warm feathers and put just her little head out to see all the beauty beneath her.

At last they got to the Swallow's warm nest. There the sun shone bright, and everywhere grew the loveliest flowers. In the woods grew oranges and lemons, and great playful butterflies flitted about. Under splendid trees, beside a blue lake, stood a shining palace of white marble ruins, built in ancient days, with creepers twining about its tall pillars. At its top were swallows' nests, one of which was the home of the Swallow who was carrying Thumbelina.

Among the broken marble grew large, beautiful white flowers. The Swallow flew down with Thumbelina and set her on one of the broad leaves. But what a surprise for her! A little man was sitting in the middle of the flower, with the prettiest gold crown on his head and the loveliest bright wings on his shoulders, and he was no bigger than Thumbelina. He was the angel of the flower. In each of them there lived such another little man or woman, but this man was the king of them all.

"Goodness, how beautiful he is," Thumbelina whispered to the Swallow. The little king was alarmed by the Swallow, which was giant compared to him, tiny and delicate as he was, but when he saw Thumbelina, he was delighted, for she was by far the prettiest girl he had ever seen. He asked whether she would be his wife, queen of all the flowers.

Here indeed was a husband—very different from the Toad's son or the Mole with his black velvet coat. Thumbelina said "Yes" to the handsome prince, and out of every flower, ladies and lords brought Thumbelina presents. The best of all was a pair of beautiful white butterfly wings, which they fastened to Thumbelina's back so she could fly from flower to flower. There were great rejoicings, and the Swallow sat on his nest up high and sang to them as well as ever he could. ♣

The Tale of the Frog Prince

THE BROTHERS GRIMM

A long time ago, there lived a King with many daughters. All his daughters were beautiful, but his youngest daughter was so exceedingly beautiful that the Sun himself was enchanted every time she came out into the sunshine.

Near the castle of this King was a large and gloomy forest. In the midst of the forest stood an old lime tree, beneath whose branches splashed a little fountain. Whenever it was very hot, the King's youngest daughter ran off into this wood and sat down to play by the cool water of this fountain. She would often amuse herself with her favorite plaything, a lovely golden ball. She was always tossing it up into the air and catching it again as it fell. But one day at the fountain, the Princess threw her golden ball so high into the air that she missed catching it. The ball landed on the grass and bounded away, rolling along on the ground until at last it fell down into the fountain.

The King's daughter followed the ball with her eyes, but when it disappeared beneath the water, she began to cry. The water was so deep that she could not see to the bottom. As she cried louder and louder, a voice called out, "Why do you weep, O Princess? Your tears would melt even a stone to pity." She looked around to the spot where she heard the voice and saw a Frog stretching his thick, ugly head out of the water. "Ah! You old water

paddler," said the Princess. "Was it you that spoke? I am weeping for my golden ball, which has slipped away from me into the water."

"Do not cry," answered the Frog. "I can help you! But what will you give me if I fetch your plaything from the deep water of the fountain?"

Privately, she thought to herself, *What nonsense this silly frog is talking! He can never even get out of the fountain.*

But she wanted her favorite golden ball back. "What will you have, dear Frog?" said the King's youngest daughter. "My dresses, my pearls and jewels, or the golden crown which I wear?"

The Frog answered, "Dresses or jewels or golden crowns are not for me! But, if you will love me and let me be your companion and playfellow, and sit

at your table, and eat from your little golden plate, and drink out of your cup, and sleep on your little bed—if you promise me all these things, then will I dive down and fetch your golden ball."

"Oh, I will promise you all," she cried, "if you will only get my ball." But as she said this, she thought to herself, *He may be able to get my ball for me, and therefore I will tell him he shall have what he asks.*

The Frog, as soon as he had received her promise, dived down under the water. Soon, he swam up again with the ball in his mouth and threw it on the grass. The King's daughter was full of joy when she again saw her beautiful golden ball. She picked it up and ran off immediately.

"Stop! Stop!" cried the Frog. "Take me with you! I can't run like you can." But all his croaking was useless. Although he was very loud, the Princess was already running quickly through the forest to her home and did not hear the Frog. Hastening home, she soon forgot the poor Frog, who was obliged to leap back into the fountain.

The next day, the Princess was sitting at the dinner table with her father, the King, and all his daughters, and all his sons, and all his courtiers, eating from her own little golden plate, when something strange was heard coming up the marble stairs outside.

Splish-splash! Splish-splash! Splish-splash!

When the *splish-splash*ing guest arrived at the top of the marble stairs, it knocked at the door. A loud voice said, "Open the door, youngest daughter of the King!"

The Princess ran to the door and opened it, and there she saw the Frog, whom she had quite forgotten. At this sight, she was sadly frightened and slammed the door shut. She went back to the table as fast as she could and sat down, looking very pale.

The King saw that something had frightened her and asked her what was the matter. He asked her whether it was a giant who had come to fetch her away who stood at the door.

"Oh, no!" His daughter answered. "It is no giant, but an ugly old Frog."

"What does a Frog want with you?" asked the King.

"Oh, dear father, when I was playing by the fountain in the forest yesterday, my golden ball fell into the water. This Frog fetched it for me because I cried so much. I promised him that he could live with me here, thinking that he could never get out of the water. But somehow he has jumped out, and there he is at the door, wanting to come in here."

While she was speaking, the frog knocked again at the door and said:

King's daughter, youngest,
Open the door.
Have you forgotten
Your promises made
At the fountain so clear

'Neath the lime tree's shade?
King's daughter, youngest,
Open the door.

Then the King said, "You have given him your word, and you must do what you have promised. Go and let him in." So the King's daughter went and opened the door. The Frog hopped inside. *Splish-splash! Splish-splash!* The Frog hopped all the way to the chair where the Princess sat at the dinner table.

As soon as she was seated, the Frog said, "Pick me up! Let me sit next to you." She hesitated so long that at last the King ordered her to obey. As soon as the Frog sat on the chair beside her, the Frog jumped onto the table and said, "Now push your plate near me, so we may eat together."

And she did so, but as everyone saw, very unwillingly. The Frog seemed to enjoy his dinner very much, but every bite that the King's daughter ate nearly choked her, she was so unhappy.

At last, the Frog finally said, "I have satisfied my hunger and feel very tired. Will you carry me upstairs now into your chamber and make your bed ready that we may sleep?"

At this speech, the King's youngest daughter began to cry, for she was afraid of the cold, wet Frog. She did not dare touch him, and she especially did not want the Frog to sleep in her own warm, dry, clean bed. But her tears only made the King very angry, and he said, "You must not despise the Frog, who helped you in the time of your trouble!" So she picked the Frog up with two fingers and carried him upstairs to her chamber, where he slept all night long.

As soon as it was light, the frog jumped up, hopped downstairs, and went out of the house.

"Now, then," thought the King's youngest daughter, "at last, he is gone, and I shall be troubled with him no more."

But the Princess was mistaken! When night came again, she heard a *Splish-splash! Splish-splash!* at the door. Then she heard the Frog's voice, again calling,

King's daughter, youngest,
Open the door.

Have you forgotten
Your promises made
At the fountain so clear
'Neath the lime tree's shade?
King's daughter, youngest,
Open the door.

When the Princess opened the door, the frog came in and hopped right into her chamber. She put him in a corner of her chamber, far from her beautiful bed. But as she lay in her bed, the Frog crept up to her and said, "I am so very tired, and your bed looks so very soft. Do pick me up, or I will tell your father." The Frog's speech put the Princess in a terrible fit of anger. She picked the Frog up and threw him against the wall with all her strength, shouting, "Now will you be quiet, you ugly Frog?"

But as he fell, he changed from a Frog into a handsome Prince with beautiful eyes. He told her how he had been transformed by an evil witch and that no one but herself could have had the power to take him out of the fountain.

"You have broken the evil witch's cruel charm," said the prince, "and now I have nothing to wish for but that you should go with me into my father's kingdom, where I will marry you and love you as long as you live."

The young Princess, you may be sure, was not long in saying "Yes" to all this. The Prince became her dear companion, and they were betrothed. Not long after, a brightly colored carriage pulled by eight beautiful white horses, decked with plumes of feathers and a golden harness, arrived at the door of the King's castle. The King's youngest daughter and the Prince said "Farewell!" to the King and got into the coach with eight horses. And they set out, full of joy and merriment, for the prince's kingdom, where they lived happily a great many years. ♣

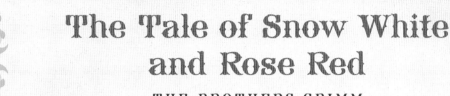

The Tale of Snow White and Rose Red

THE BROTHERS GRIMM

here was once a poor widow who lived in a forest cottage. In front of the cottage was a garden with two rose trees—one grew white roses, and the other, red roses. The poor widow had two daughters who were just like the two rose trees. One was called Snow White, and the other, Rose Red.

Snow White and Rose Red kept their mother's little cottage so neat that it was a pleasure to look inside it. One winter evening, Snow White lit the fire and warmed the kettle. The kettle was made of copper, but it was so brightly polished that it shone like gold. The two daughters sat with their mother round the hearth while the mother read aloud out of a large book. Close by lay a lamb upon the floor, and behind them upon a perch sat a white dove with its head hidden beneath its wings. As they were thus sitting comfortably together, someone knocked at the door, as if he wished to be let in. The mother said, "Quick, Rose Red, open the door; it must be a traveler who is seeking shelter." Rose Red opened the bolt on the door, thinking that it must be a poor man, but it was not! Instead, it was a bear that stretched his broad, black head within the door!

Rose Red screamed, the lamb bleated, the dove fluttered, and Snow White hid behind her mother's bed. But the bear began to speak and said, "Do not be afraid; I will do you no harm! I am half frozen and only want to warm myself a little."

"Poor bear," said the mother, "lie down by the fire." He stretched himself by the fire and growled contentedly. The mother cried, "Snow White, Rose Red, come here! The bear will do you no harm." So they both came closer, and soon the lamb and dove came nearer and were not afraid of him. It was not long before they grew quite comfortable and played tricks with their furry guest. They tugged his hair with their hands, put their feet upon his back, and rolled him about, and when he growled, they laughed.

When it was bedtime and the children went to bed, the mother said to the bear, "You can stay there by the hearth, safe from the cold and the bad weather." As soon as morning dawned, the two

dwarf [ˈdwörf]

These small, stout creatures live deep in the woods with their roommates. No two dwarves have the same disposition, but all have long beards, and nearly every dwarf shares a love of treasure, a lack of table manners, and a soft spot for princesses. Dwarvish parents are not overly creative with names, so dwarves are often named after their defining personality trait. Some common dwarf names include Smiley, Lazy, Picky, Smelly, Hungry, Fearless, and Hairy.

children let him out, and he trotted across the snow into the forest.

The bear came every evening at the same time, laid himself down by the hearth, and let the children amuse themselves with him as much as they liked. They got so used to him that the door was never bolted until their furry friend had arrived.

When spring had come and all outside was green, the bear said one morning to Snow White, "Now I must go away, and I cannot come back for the whole summer."

"Where are you going, then, dear bear?" asked Snow White.

"I must go into the forest and guard my treasures from the wicked dwarfs. In the winter, when the earth is frozen hard, they are obliged to stay in their caves and cannot work their way through the earth. But now that the sun has thawed the earth, they come out to steal. What once gets into their hands, and in their caves, does not easily see daylight again."

Snow White was quite sorry for the bear's going away, but she unbolted the door for him to leave. As the bear was hurrying out, his furry coat caught against the bolt and a piece of his fur was torn off. It seemed to Snow White as if she had seen gold shining through it, but she thought she must have been mistaken. The bear ran away quickly and was soon out of sight behind the trees.

A short time afterward, the mother sent her children into the forest to get firewood. The sisters soon found a big tree which had fallen on the ground. Close by the trunk, something was jumping backward and forward in the grass, but they could not make out what it was. When the children came nearer, they saw a dwarf with an old withered face and a snow white beard a yard long! The end of the beard was caught in a crevice of the tree, and the little fellow was jumping backward and forward, trying to break free.

He glared at the girls with fiery red eyes and cried, "Why do you stand there? Can you not come here and help me?"

"What are you doing there, little man?" asked Rose Red.

"You stupid simpleton!" answered the dwarf. "I was going to split the tree to get a little wood for cooking, but the wretched wood caught my beautiful beard! Now it is stuck, I cannot get away, and you silly things laugh! Ugh!"

The children tried very hard, but they could not pull the beard out. It was caught too tightly. "I will run and fetch help," said Rose Red.

"You senseless goose!" snarled the dwarf. "Why should you fetch someone? You are already two too many for me! Can't you think of something better?"

"Don't be too impatient," said Snow White, and she pulled her sewing scissors out of her pocket and cut off the end of the beard.

As soon as the dwarf was free, he grabbed a bag full of gold that lay amongst the roots of the tree, grumbling, "Uncouth folk, to cut off a piece of my fine beard. Bad luck to you!" Then he swung the bag on his back, and off he went without even once looking at the children.

Some time after that, Snow White and Rose Red went to catch fish for dinner. As they came near the brook, they saw a creature jumping towards the water, as if it were going to leap in. They ran to it and found it was the dwarf.

"Where are you going?" said Rose Red. "You surely don't want to go into the water?"

"I am not such a fool!" cried the dwarf. "Don't

you see that the accursed fish wants to pull me in?" The little man had been fishing when unluckily the wind had twisted his beard with his fishing line. Just then, a big fish bit. The feeble dwarf did not have the strength to pull the fish out, and the fish tugged the dwarf toward the water. The dwarf was being yanked around by the fish and was in urgent danger of being dragged into the water.

The girls had arrived just in time! They tried to free his beard from the line, but all in vain—beard and line were entangled fast together. Nothing was left but to bring out the scissors and cut the beard.

When the dwarf saw that another small part of his beard was lost, he screamed out, "Why, you toadstool, did you disfigure my face? Was it not enough to clip off the end of my beard? Now you have cut off the best part of it. Bad luck to you!" Then he took a sack of pearls that lay on the water's bank, and without saying another word, he dragged it away and disappeared behind a stone.

Soon afterward, the mother sent the two children into the town to buy needles and thread. The road led them across a field where huge rocks were scattered. The girls noticed a large bird hovering in the air, flying slowly round and round above them. It sank lower and lower and at last settled near a rock not far off. Immediately they heard a loud, piteous cry. They ran to the bird and saw with horror that an eagle had seized their old acquaintance, the dwarf, and was going to carry him off.

The children, full of pity, took tight hold of the little man and pulled against the eagle's grip so hard that at last the eagle let the dwarf go. As soon as the dwarf had recovered from his fright, he cried with his shrill voice, "Could you not have done it more carefully? You dragged at my coat so that it is all torn and full of holes, you clumsy creatures!"

Then he picked up a sack full of precious stones and slipped away under the rock into a hole. The girls, who by this time were used to his thankless-ness, went on their way and did their business in the town.

As they crossed the field again on their way home, they surprised the dwarf, who had emptied out his bag of precious stones, thinking no one would be in the field so late. The evening sunset shone upon the brilliant stones; they glittered and sparkled with so many beautiful colors that the children stood still in amazement.

"Why do you stand gaping there?" cried the dwarf, his ash-gray face turning copper red with rage. Suddenly a loud growling was heard, and a black bear came trotting toward them out of the forest. The dwarf sprang up in a fright, but he could not get to his hole in the ground, for the bear was already close.

The dwarf cried, "Dear Mr. Bear, spare me! I will give you all my treasures—look at the beautiful jewels lying there! Grant me my life! What do you want with such a slender little fellow as I? Come, take these two wicked girls, they are tender morsels for you! For mercy's sake, eat them!" The bear ignored the dwarf, giving the wicked creature a single blow with his paw, and the dwarf did not move again.

The girls ran away in fright, but the bear called to them, "Snow White and Rose Red, do not be afraid. Wait, I will come with you." They recognized his voice, but when he caught up to them, his bearskin fell off. There stood a handsome man, clothed all in gold.

"I am the king's son," he said, "and I was be-witched by that wicked dwarf, who had stolen my treasures. I have had to run about the forest as a bear until the spell was broken by his death. Now he has got his well-deserved punishment."

Snow White married him, and Rose Red married his brother, and between them, they divided the great treasure the dwarf had gathered in his cave. The old mother lived peacefully and happily with her children for many years. She brought the two rose trees with her to the King's castle, and they stood before her window and every year bore the most beautiful roses, white and red. ⚓

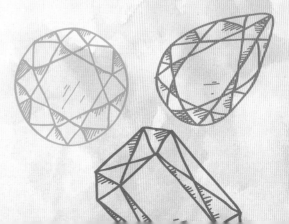

The Tale of Princess Savitri

ADAPTED FROM THE MAHABHARATA

 here was once a beautiful Princess, the daughter of Aswapati, the King of Madra, and her name was Savitri. Her eyes had burning splendor and were fair as lotus leaves, and she had exceeding sweetness and grace.

It came to pass that Savitri looked with eyes of love upon a youth named Satyavan. Although Satyavan dwelt in a small cottage, he was of royal birth. His father was a virtuous King named Dyumatsena. When Dyumatsena became blind, his kingdom was stolen by a nearby enemy. The dethroned king retired to the forest with his wife and his only son, Satyavan.

When Savitri confessed her love of Satyavan to her father, the King of Madra, the great sage Narada, who sat beside him, spoke. "Alas! The Princess has done wrong in choosing this royal youth Satyavan. He is handsome and courageous; he is truthful and forgiving; he is modest and patient and kind; he is possessed of every virtue. But he has one defect. He is cursed with a short life. Within a year from this day, Yama, god of the dead, will come for him."

The King said to his daughter: "O Savitri, you have heard the words of Narada. Choose for yourself another husband, for the days of Satyavan are numbered."

The beautiful maiden answered her father, the King, "I have already chosen. Once have I chosen, I cannot make the choice a second time. Whether his life is brief or long, I will marry Satyavan."

So Savitri and her father visited Dyumatsena, the blind father of Satyavan, in the forest.

"O king, this is my beautiful daughter Savitri. Take her as your daughter-in-law," Aswapati said to Dyumatsena.

But Dyumatsena said, "I have lost my kingdom and with my wife and my son dwell here in the woods. We live a simple life. How will your royal daughter endure the hardships of a forest life?"

Aswapati replied, "My daughter knows that joy and sorrow come and go and that nowhere is bliss assured. Therefore, accept her."

Dyumatsena consented that his son should wed Savitri. Satyavan was glad because his wife was accomplished. Savitri rejoiced because she obtained a husband she loved.

So Savitri lived in the forest and practiced a simple life with Satyavan. She removed her royal garments and ornaments and instead wore bark and red cloth. Her sweet words, her skilled work, her even temper, and especially her love gave Satyavan great joy. But she never forgot the terrible prophecy of Narada the sage. His sorrowful words were always hidden in her heart.

Finally, the time came for Satyavan to pass away. When the sun rose on the fateful morning, her face was bloodless but brave, and she said to herself, "Today is the day." Satyavan then rose, strong and healthy. Taking his axe upon his shoulder, he started toward the jungle to gather food for his wife, whom he loved. Savitri spoke to him sweetly. "You should not go alone, my husband. It is my heart's desire to go with you. I cannot endure being separate from you today."

"You shouldn't enter the dark jungle. The path is long and difficult," Satyavan replied.

"You will be by my side." Savitri laid her head on his chest. "I have decided to go with you." So Savitri turned toward the jungle with Satyavan, her beloved husband. She smiled, but her heart was torn with secret sorrow.

As they walked, Satyavan gathered fruits and stored them in his basket. Peacocks fluttered in the green woodland through which they walked together, and the sun shone in all its splendor in the blue heaven. "How beautiful are the bright streams and the blossoming trees!" said Satyavan. The heart of Savitri was divided. With one part, she happily talked with her husband, but with the other, she waited with dread, though she never uttered her fears.

Suddenly, Satyavan felt weary. "My head aches, and my arms are weak. My body seems to be pierced by a hundred arrows. I would like to lie down and rest, my beloved."

Speechless and filled with terror, the gentle Savitri laid her husband's head on her lap as she sat on the ground. Remembering the words of Narada, she knew that the dreaded hour had come. Satyavan's moment of death was at hand. Gently, she held her husband's head and kissed him softly, though her heart was beating fast and loud. The forest grew dark and lonely as Satyavan slept.

Suddenly, an awful Shape emerged from the shadows. Savitri looked up, her heart trembling with sorrow and with fear. The Shape was tall and dark, wearing a blood-red cloak and a gleaming diadem. He stood in silence and gazed upon slumbering Satyavan. The Shape was Yama, god of death.

"You love your husband, and you have lived a simple life. But I am the god of death, and I have come to take this man away," Yama said to Savitri.

Yama plucked the soul from Satyavan's body and turned to leave. But Savitri's heart grieved, and she could not desert her beloved husband. So she followed Yama, the god of death.

"Turn back, Savitri. You cannot follow me," said Yama.

"I must follow my husband," Savitri replied. "Besides, I have already walked with you seven paces. And according to custom, anyone who walks seven paces with another becomes a companion. And since we are now companions, you must listen. I have lived a virtuous and simple life, and I have been devoted to my husband. It isn't right for you to take him from me."

"You are very wise, so I will grant you one request." Yama said. "Except the life of Satyavan, I will give you whatever you desire."

"Because my husband's father became blind, his kingdom was stolen," Savitri said. "Restore his eyesight, O mighty one."

Yama said, "Your father-in-law's vision is restored. But you are tired from this journey. Turn back now, and your weariness will fade away."

"I will follow my husband wherever you carry him," said Savitri. "But hear me, O mighty one, whose friendship I cherish! It is a blessed thing to see a god, and even more blessed to befriend one!"

"Indeed! Your wisdom delights my heart," Yama said. "Therefore, you may ask me for a second request. Except the life of your husband, it will be granted."

Savitri said, "May my wise and saintly father-in-law regain the kingdom he lost. May he become once again the protector of his people."

"The king will return to his people and be their wise protector," said Yama. "Turn back now, O Princess. Your request is granted. You cannot come farther."

"My heart desires to follow my husband even farther on our journey, O mighty one," Savitri said. "You are great and wise and powerful. I'm lucky to have a god such as you as a friend."

"Your wise words are like water to a thirsty soul," Yama said. "No mortal has ever spoken to me as you have. Your words are indeed pleasing, O Princess. I will grant you a third request; except your husband's life, it will be granted."

"May a generation of children be born unto my husband and me so that our family may endure," Savitri said. "Grant me this third request, O mighty one."

"I grant you a generation of children, O Princess," said Yama. "They will be wise and powerful and your family will endure. But turn back now, Princess; you have come too far already."

"O mighty one, I cannot turn back. You have promised what cannot be fulfilled unless my husband is restored to me. You have promised me a generation of children. Therefore, I ask that you give me back Satyavan, my beloved, O Yama. Restore Satyavan's life so that your word may be fulfilled."

"The more you speak, the more I admire you, O Princess," said Yama. "So be it. With a cheerful heart, I unbind your husband. Disease cannot afflict him again, and he will prosper. You will share long lives together with a generation of children. Your sons will be kings, and their children royalty also."

After he said this, Yama disappeared. Savitri was returned to the place where her husband's cold body lay on the ground. She sat and pulled his head into her lap. Satyavan's eyes opened, and he looked at Savitri with love, as if he had been on a long journey.

Meanwhile, Dyumatsena, the father of Satyavan, had regained his sight. When Satyavan and Savitri reached the cottage, Satyavan's parents were overjoyed to see their son!

The next morning, messengers arrived to tell Dyumatsena that the enemy who had stolen his kingdom had died and all the people of the kingdom were calling for their legitimate ruler. "Chariots await thee, O King," said the messengers. "Return to your kingdom!" So the King was restored to his kingdom, as Yama had promised Savitri.

Savitri bore Satyavan children, and thus Savitri's gentleness and intelligent reasoning rescued her husband and ensured happiness and prosperity in her family for generations. ⚓

The Tale of Princess Kaguya

JAPANESE FOLKTALE

One evening, an old bamboo cutter was going home. As he passed among the stalks of feathery bamboo, he saw a soft light coming from within one of the stalks. He opened the bamboo stalk carefully and found a tiny baby girl inside. She was only a few inches tall, but as beautiful as a fairy.

The man and his wife were glad he had found her, for they had no child, and loved the tiny girl as their own. They called her Kaguya, the Bamboo Princess, because she was as lovely as any princess. In a few years, she had grown to be a young woman. She was as sweet and kind as she was beautiful, and a soft light always seemed to follow her.

People heard of how beautiful she was, and many peered through the hedge that surrounded the bamboo cutter's garden in hopes of seeing a glimpse of her. Among those who came often to the hedge were five princes. Each one thought Kaguya the most beautiful woman he had ever seen, and each wished her for his wife.

Kaguya did not wish to marry any of them, so when each of the five princes asked her to marry him, she asked him to bring her a gift to prove his love. But the gift Kaguya asked of each of them was impossible to retrieve.

The first she asked to go to India and find the great stone bowl of Buddha.

The second one was to bring her a branch from the jeweled trees that grew on the floating mountain of Horai.

The third prince was to bring her a fur robe of mink shining like fire.

The fourth prince offered to bring her the shell hidden in the swallow's nest.

She asked the fifth to bring a jewel from the neck of the sea dragon.

The princes hurried away, each anxious to be the first to return and marry the beautiful Bamboo Princess.

THE GREAT STONE BOWL

People say that far away in India, there is a stone bowl that belonged to the great Buddha. Hidden deep in the darkness of a great temple, it gleams and sparkles as though set with the most beautiful gems. The prince who promised to go to India in search of the bowl was a very lazy man. He asked

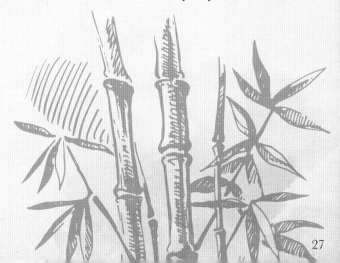

some sailors how long it took to travel to India and back. They said it took three years. The prince could not imagine spending three years looking for an old bowl! So he did nothing. After three years, he went into a little temple and found an old stone bowl. The prince wrapped the bowl in a rich silk cloth and sent it to Kaguya along with a letter describing his long hard journey to find the bowl for her. But the Bamboo Princess was not deceived and sent the bowl and letter back to him.

THE FLOATING MOUNTAIN OF HORAI

The prince who was supposed to bring a branch of the jewel tree was very cunning and very rich. He did not believe that there was a floating mountain called Horai. He did not believe there were trees of gold with jewels for leaves. However, he pretended to go in search of the floating mountain of Horai and its golden, jeweled trees. After three years, he suddenly appeared before the princess, bearing a wonderful branch of gold with blossoms and leaves of colored jewels. Kaguya asked the prince to tell of his journey.

"I let the wind and the waves carry me where they wished," he said. "I passed many beautiful cities. I saw great sea dragons lying on the water and sea serpents playing in the bottom of the ocean. When I thought I would be sailing forever, I saw a great mountain lifting its dark head out of the morning sea . . ."

Just then, three men arrived, interrupting the prince's tale. "Could you pay us now?" they asked. "For three years, we have been working to make this beautiful golden branch. Now that it is finished, we want our pay."

The prince was ashamed, so he left Kaguya and went far away. The princess gave the jeweled branch to the men to pay them for their years of work, and they went away praising the princess for her kindness.

THE FUR ROBE OF FIRE MINK

The third prince was to bring the robe made of the fur of the fire mink. The prince went to every temple, inquiring of the priests if they knew anything of this robe. All the priests knew the legend of the fire mink robe, but they did not know where it was. Only one old priest said, "When I was a child, I remember hearing my grandfather tell about this fire mink robe. It was kept in a temple upon the top of a mountain, hundreds of miles from here."

The prince was delighted at this, and they immediately set out for the mountain temple. When they reached the top of the mountain, they found no temple, only a heap of stones. But among the stones was an iron box. The prince opened this box and found within it a strange, beautiful fur robe. According to the legend, every time this beautiful robe was put into the fire, it came out more silvery bright than before. So the prince decided to put it into a fire once more, so that it would be all the more beautiful for the Bamboo Princess.

So he built a fire and laid the dazzling silver robe over the burning coals. Like a flash, the red flames leapt up, and before he could snatch it from the fire, there was nothing left but silvery smoke drifting off on the wind and silvery ashes dimming the red of the coals. Princess Kaguya never heard from this prince again.

THE SHELL FROM THE SWALLOW'S NEST

The prince who was to find the shell hidden in the swallow's nest was a very proud man. He asked his servants, his gardeners, and his neighbors if they knew about the shell in the swallow's nest. One little servant boy thought that he had seen one once, up on the roof of the kitchen where the swallows nested. The prince ordered his men to go and search the swallow nests on the roof of the kitchen. The men built a rope and a basket so that a man could be drawn up to look into the nests. They spent three days searching but found no shell.

The prince was furious and insisted on being pulled up to see for himself. The men tried to persuade him not to do it, but he jumped into the basket and commanded them to pull him up at once. When the prince reached the swallow's nests, he thrust his hand into a nest. He thought he felt something hard, like a shell, and seized it, but the swallows began to peck at him. They did not care to have all their eggs broken and their nests torn to pieces!

"Help, help!" the prince screamed as the birds pecked at him. The men began to lower the basket, but the prince lost his balance and came tumbling down. Instead of coming down in the basket, he came down with a thump on the hot stove in the kitchen below.

The prince was badly burned and bruised. In his hand, he held a shell, but it was only a broken bit of eggshell, and the egg was spattered all over his hand and face. He decided that he wanted nothing more to do with the shell from the swallow's nest and forgot all about the Bamboo Princess.

THE JEWEL FROM THE NECK OF THE SEA DRAGON

The prince who was to find the dragon jewel was a great boaster and a great coward. He called together his servants and soldiers and told them to ready a boat. They were frightened when they found out that he was seeking a jewel from the neck of a sea dragon. They begged him not to go for fear that the dragon would destroy them.

"That dragon will be afraid of *me*!" boasted the prince.

Once they were at sea, a fierce storm came up. Rain poured, lightning flashed, and thunder roared. Great waves rocked and dipped the boat. The cowardly prince was sure they would drown or be struck by lightning and huddled in the bottom of the boat, seasick and frightened.

"Why did you ever bring me here?" he shouted at the crew. "Get me out of this boat at once or I shall shoot every one of you with my bow and arrow."

The men could hardly keep from laughing, for it was only at his demand they had set sail at all. As for shooting them, they knew he could not lift an arrow, much less use the bow. When the storm died down, the men came ashore on a small island, where they placed the seasick prince on dry ground. When at last he felt firm ground under him, he wept aloud and vowed that he would never leave dry ground again. He was on an island far from home, but he refused to step foot on a boat, so he stayed there the rest of his life.

THE MOON PRINCESS

Years passed, and Kaguya took good care of her father and mother. Each day, she grew more beautiful and more kind and gentle. They understood why she had asked the five princes to do impossible things. She wanted to stay with her parents and care for them, yet she knew that if she refused to marry the princes, they might be angry with her.

When she was twenty years old, her mother died. Kaguya grew very sad. Whenever the full moon dusted the earth with its soft light, she would go away by herself and weep. One evening, she was looking up at the moon, sobbing as though her heart would break. Her elderly father came to her and said, "My daughter, tell me your trouble."

"I weep, dear father, because I must soon leave you," Kaguya said. "My home is really on the moon. I was sent here to take care of you, but now the time has come for me to leave. When the next full moon comes, I must go."

Her father was sad because he did not want his daughter to go away. The nights passed, and each day, the princess grew sadder. The first night of the full moon came. Slowly over the tops of the trees on the mountain rose the great silver ball. The princess went to her father, who lay as if asleep. When she came near, he opened his eyes.

"I see now why you must go," he said. "It is because I am going, too. Thank you, my daughter, for all the happiness you have brought to me." Then he closed his eyes and did not open them again.

The moon rose higher. Drifting down from it, like smoke before the wind, came a silent silvery figure. Silently, he handed Kaguya a tiny cup of water of forgetfulness. All her life on Earth faded from her memory. Once more, she was a moon princess. Rising like the morning mists, the princess rose slowly to the top of Fuji Yama, the sacred mountain of Japan. Up, up, up through the still whiteness of the moonlight she passed, until she reached the silver gates of the moon. People still say that even now, a soft white wreath of smoke curls up from the sacred crown of Fuji Yama, like the beautiful Princess Kaguya floating away from earth. ⚓

The Tale of the Twelve Dancing Princesses

THE BROTHERS GRIMM

here once was a king who had twelve beautiful daughters. They slept in twelve beds all in one big room. And though the chamber door was locked and shut, each morning, the princesses found their shoes to be quite worn through as if they had been danced in all night! Nobody could find out how their shoes were worn down or where the princesses might have been.

The King decreed to all the land that if any man could find out where the princesses danced in the night, then he could have the daughter he liked best for his wife. The man who discovered the secret and married a princess would be heir to the King's throne. But whoever tried would only have three days to discover the secret.

Another king's son soon arrived to try his hand at the mystery. He was entertained by the twelve princesses all day in the King's castle. In the evening, the prince was taken to a chamber next to the room where the princesses lay in their twelve beds. There he was to sit and watch for the princesses to find out where they went to dance. So that no one could pass by without the prince hearing, the door of his chamber was left open.

But the prince soon fell asleep! When he woke in the morning, he found that the princesses had all been dancing, for the soles of their shoes were full of holes. A second night and a third night, the prince fell asleep without discovering where the princesses had gone to dance. So the King ordered the unsuccessful prince to leave.

After this prince came several other men, suitors and princes, but they were all equally unlucky, and none discovered where the princesses were going to dance in the night.

Now it happened one day that a soldier, who had once been wounded in a battle and could no longer fight, passed through the land where the twelve dancing princesses lived and their father was king.

As the soldier was traveling through a wood, he met an old woman who asked him where he was going. "I hardly know where I am going," said the

soldier, because he was not from this land, "but I think I would like very much to discover where the princesses dance. Then, in time, I might become king."

"Well," said the old woman, "that is no very hard task! Simply take care not to drink any of the wine which one of the princesses will bring to you in the evening. As soon as she leaves, pretend to be fast asleep."

Then the old woman gave the soldier a cloak and said, "As soon as you put this on, you will become invisible. Then you will be able to follow the princesses wherever they go."

When the soldier heard all the old woman's good counsel, he was determined to try his luck. So he went to the king and asked to try his hand at the strange task.

The soldier was as well received as the other men had been, and the king ordered fine royal robes to be given to him during his stay. When the evening came, he was led to the chamber near where the princesses slept. Just as he was going to lie down, the oldest of the princesses brought him a cup of wine, but the soldier threw it all away secretly, without drinking a drop. Then he laid down on his bed, leaving the door open as the others had. After a little while, he began to snore very loudly as if he were fast asleep.

When the twelve princesses heard his snores, they laughed heartily. Then they opened their wardrobes and drawers and boxes, took out all their fine clothes, dressed themselves in gowns and ribbons and lace, and skipped about, eager to begin dancing. But the youngest princess said, "While you all are so happy, somehow I feel very uneasy. I feel certain some mishap will befall us."

"You simpleton," said the oldest princess with a laugh. "You are always afraid! Have you forgotten how many princes, suitors, and other men have already watched in vain? And this old soldier would have slept soundly enough even without a sleeping draught!"

When all the princesses were dressed and ready, they peered in at the soldier, but he snored on. He did not stir, not even a hand or foot, so the princesses thought they were quite safe. The oldest princess

went to her own bed and clapped her hands. The bed sank into the floor, and a trapdoor flew open!

With one eye open, the soldier saw them sneak down through the trapdoor, one after another, with the oldest leading the way. Thinking he had no time to lose, the soldier jumped up and put on the cloak the old woman had given him. The soldier quickly followed the princesses down the trapdoor, but halfway down the stairs, he accidentally stepped on the hem of the youngest princess' gown. She cried out to her sisters, "I told you, all is not right! Someone grabbed my gown!"

"You silly creature," said the oldest princess. "It is nothing but a nail in the wall." Down they all went, and at the bottom of the trapdoor stairs, the princesses found themselves in a most delightful grove of trees. Silver leaves glittered and sparkled beautifully. The soldier wished to keep a token of the beautiful place, so he broke off a little silvery branch, making a loud noise. The youngest princess said again, "I am sure all is not right—did you not hear that noise from the tree? That never happened before." But the oldest sister said, "It is only our princes shouting for joy at our approach."

They quickly arrived at another grove of trees, where all the leaves were of gold! And presently, they passed through a third grove, which glittered with diamond leaves. The soldier broke a branch from each grove, and each time she heard the loud noise, the youngest sister trembled with fear.

Soon, they came to a great lake. At the edge of the water there bobbed twelve little boats with twelve handsome princes in them, who seemed to be waiting for the princesses.

Each princess climbed into a boat, and the soldier stepped into the same boat with the youngest. As they rowed across the lake, the prince who was in the boat with the youngest princess and the soldier said, "I do not know why, but though I am rowing with all my might, we are not moving as quickly as usual. The boat seems very heavy today, and I am quite tired."

"It is only the heat of the weather," the princess replied. "I feel very warm, too."

On the other side of the lake stood a fine illuminated castle, from which came merry music of horns

and trumpets. There all the boats landed, and all the princes and princesses went into the castle. Each prince danced with his princess, and the soldier, who was all the time invisible, danced with them too. When any of the princesses had a cup set by her, he drank it all up, so that when she put the cup to her mouth, it was empty. At this, the youngest sister was terribly frightened, but the oldest always silenced her. They danced on till three o'clock in the morning, and then all their shoes were worn out, so that they were obliged to leave. The princes rowed them back again over the lake, but this time, the soldier placed himself in the boat with the eldest princess. On the opposite shore, the princesses left the princes, promising to come again the next night.

At the entrance to the princesses' chamber, the tired princesses moved very slowly up the stairs, and the soldier ran ahead of the princesses. He quickly removed his cloak and laid down on his bed, so when the twelve sisters arrived at the top of the stairs, they heard him snoring in his bed. The oldest said, "All is quite safe," and the princesses put away their fine clothes, pulled off their shoes, and went to bed.

In the morning, the soldier said nothing about what had happened. Determined to see more of this strange adventure, he followed the princesses again the second and third nights. Everything happened just as before: the princesses danced each time till their shoes were worn to pieces and then returned home. However, on the third night, the soldier carried away one of the golden cups as a token of where he had been.

After the third day, the time came for the soldier to declare his secret. He was taken before the king and brought with him the three shining branches and the golden cup.

"Where do my twelve daughters dance at night?" the King asked the soldier.

The soldier answered, "With twelve princes in an underground castle." And then he told the King all that had happened, showing him the three branches and the golden cup he had taken along the way. Then the king called for the princesses and asked them whether what the soldier said was true. When they saw the three branches and the cup, they knew that they had been discovered. It was no use to deny where they had been, so they confessed it all.

So the king asked the soldier which of the princesses he would choose for his wife. The soldier answered, "I will have the eldest." And they were married that very day. ⚓

SECTION TWO

Royal Recipes

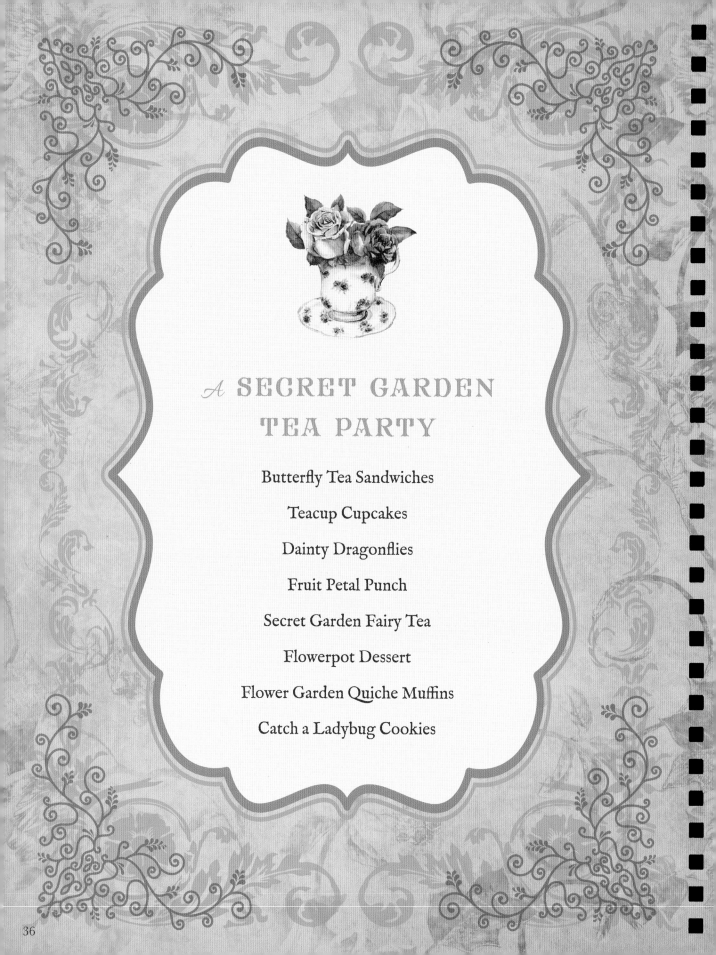

A SECRET GARDEN TEA PARTY

Butterfly Tea Sandwiches

Teacup Cupcakes

Dainty Dragonflies

Fruit Petal Punch

Secret Garden Fairy Tea

Flowerpot Dessert

Flower Garden Quiche Muffins

Catch a Ladybug Cookies

utterfly Tea Sandwiches

1 package (8 ounces) cream cheese, room temperature

1/4 cup mayonnaise

1 drop paste food coloring (pink, blue, or yellow)

1/4 teaspoon garlic powder

1/4 teaspoon onion powder

1/8 teaspoon Worcestershire sauce

Salt and pepper to taste

24 thin slices of sandwich bread

1 medium cucumber, sliced

12 red or green grapes, sliced in half

Shredded carrots

Serves 24

There's nothing quite so nice as a tea party out of doors. Pick a day with perfect weather, find a sunny spot tucked away from the palace among your favorite flowers, and invite your friends from the kingdom next door!

1. In a mixing bowl, combine cream cheese, mayonnaise, food coloring, garlic powder, onion powder, Worcestershire sauce, and salt and pepper.

2. Cut bread into butterfly shapes using a butterfly-shaped cookie cutter.

3. Spread each piece of bread with cream cheese mixture.

4. Slice each cucumber slice in half to form the butterfly wings and place on each bread slice.

5. Place the grape halves between the cucumber wings to create the body of the butterfly and garnish with two shredded carrot antennae.

Sandwich Assembly

Bread · Shredded Carrot · Grape · Cucumber · Spread

Teacup Cupcakes

Assorted china or pottery teacups

1 package cake mix, any flavor

Frosting

Assorted sprinkles and candy decorations

Makes 24 cupcakes

1 Preheat oven to 350 degrees. Spray each teacup with nonstick cooking spray and dust with flour. Set aside until ready to use.

2 Make cake mix according to package directions. Fill prepared teacups 3/4 full of cake mix and place on cookie sheets.

3 Bake and let cool before frosting and decorating.

ainty Dragonflies

1 pound vanilla candy coating or vanilla almond bark (8-10 squares)

Food coloring, optional (do not use liquid; powder or paste works best with candy coating)

8 8-inch pretzel rods

16 large classic-shaped pretzel twists

Assorted decorating sugars or sprinkles

Makes 8 dragonflies

These are especially fun to make with friends— just try not to get in the cook's way.

1 Melt candy coating according to package directions. Remove from heat and pour into two or three small bowls.

2 Add food coloring to each bowl, if desired. Stir to blend color.

3 Place pretzel rods on a foil-lined cookie sheet sprayed with nonstick cooking spray about 3 inches apart from each other. These are the dragonflies' long bodies.

4 Carefully spoon the warm, melted candy coating over each pretzel rod to cover completely.

5 Dip each pretzel twist in the candy coating and place one on each side of the upper half of the pretzel rod. The pretzel twists should rest on top of the pretzel rod and just barely touch one another. This forms the dragonfly's wings.

6 Sprinkle each dragonfly pretzel with colored sugars or sprinkles.

7 Place cookie sheet in freezer for 5-10 minutes to allow candy coating to harden on pretzels.

8 Remove from freezer and carefully take each dragonfly off cookie sheet to serve.

Fruit Petal Punch

2 quarts raspberry-apple juice blend, chilled

2 liters sparkling water, chilled

1/2 cup rose petal syrup or grenadine syrup*

Ice cubes

2 pints fresh raspberries, strawberries, or blackberries

Edible, pesticide-free pink rose petals

1 Combine the juice and sparkling water in a large punch bowl.

2 Slowly stir in the syrup, tasting regularly until you reach your desired sweetness and fragrance.

3 Carefully stir in ice cubes and berries. Float flowers on top and ladle punch into cups. Top each cup of punch with a few edible rose petals.

 Fairy Godmother Tip: Try making homemade rose petal syrup—it's easy! Place 6 cups water, 2 cups sugar, and 2 cups pesticide-free rose petals in a large saucepan. Stir. Bring to boil for 10 minutes, remove from heat, cool, and store covered.

Rose petal syrup may be found in the international foods section of some supermarkets. Grenadine syrup is readily available in all supermarkets and may be substituted for the rose petal syrup but will not add a rose scent or taste to the punch.

Serves 10–12

Secret Garden Fairy Tea

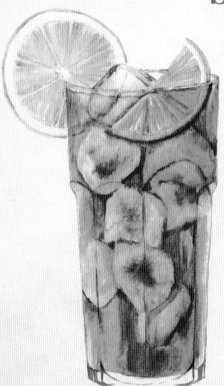

1 lemon, sliced

1 orange, sliced

1 cup strawberries

2 kiwis, peeled and thinly sliced

6 bags mango or peach tea

6 cups boiling water

2 cups white grape or white cranberry juice

1/2 cup honey or agave nectar

1 Freeze all fruits in a single layer on a baking sheet for 1 hour or up to 1 day.

2 In a heat-proof container, combine tea and boiling water. Steep 5 minutes, then remove tea bags and discard.

3 Stir in juice and honey or agave nectar. Transfer to a container with a lid. Chill for 4 hours or overnight.

4 To serve, combine frozen fruit with chilled ice tea.

Serves 10–12

Flowerpot Dessert

1 watermelon, sliced

12 6-inch wooden skewers

12 2-inch clay flowerpots and saucers, washed and dried

1 angel food or pound cake, cut into 2-inch cubes

1 quart ice cream or your favorite frozen confection, any flavor

Assorted decorating sprinkles

12 colorful straws cut to fit the length of the wooden skewers

Makes 12 flowerpots

No matter how much they beg, resist the urge to share your ice cream with your critter friends—even the talking ones. Birdseed and veggies are still best.

1 Line two cookie sheets with foil or parchment paper and set aside until ready to use.

2 To make fruit flowers, cut each watermelon slice into a flower shape with a 2- to 3-inch flower-shaped cookie cutter.

3 Insert the wooden skewer into the watermelon flower, starting at the bottom of the flower and moving it carefully up through the fruit in the center. Refrigerate flowers until ready to serve.

4 Place flowerpots in saucers and set on a cookie sheet. Put several cubes of cake into each clay pot, filling it halfway to the top. Press down the cake, making sure to cover the hole in the bottom of each pot. Fill each flowerpot with a scoop of your favorite ice cream or frozen confection. Garnish with sprinkles.

5 Insert a straw into the center of the ice cream in each flowerpot. Store in a freezer until ready to serve or store covered up to 8 hours.

6 When ready to serve, remove flowerpots from freezer and fruit flowers from refrigerator. Insert skewered flowers into the straws in each flowerpot and serve immediately.

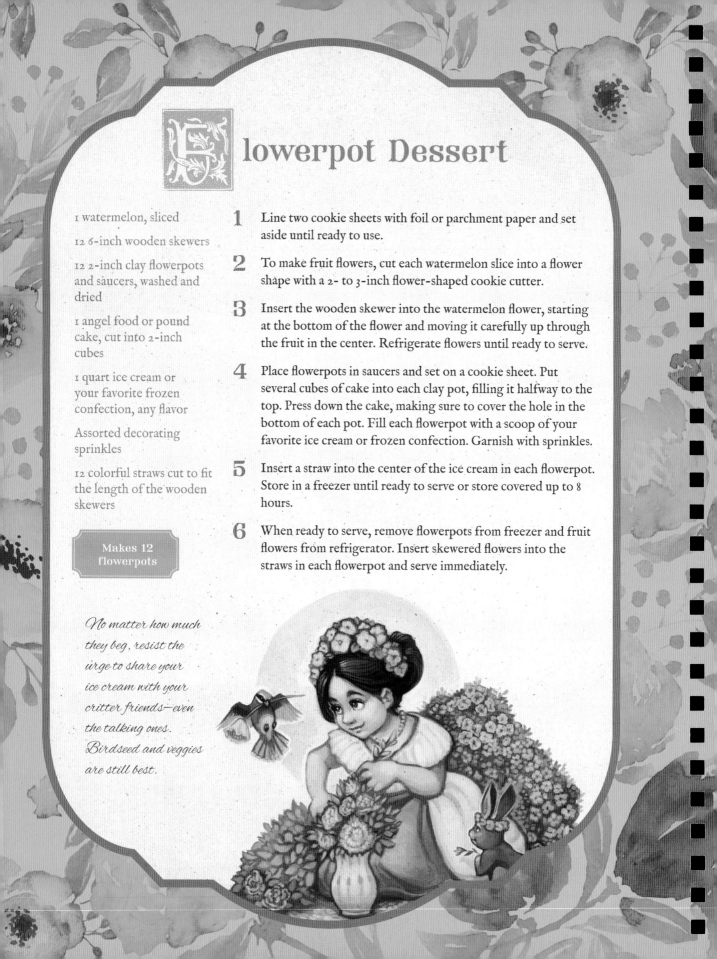

Flower Garden Quiche Muffins

1 17.3-ounce package refrigerated piecrust dough

2 eggs

1/2 cup chopped yellow bell pepper

1/4 teaspoon salt

1/8 teaspoon pepper

1/2 cup heavy cream or half-and-half

1/2 cup grated swiss or gruyère cheese

1 teaspoon flour

6-8 ripe black olives, halved

1 green bell pepper, cut into thin strips and shapes of various lengths

Makes 10–12 muffins

1 Preheat oven to 400 degrees. Generously spray a 12-cup muffin pan with nonstick cooking spray.

2 Dust piecrust dough with a little flour and cut out shapes with a 2- to 3-inch flower cookie cutter.

3 Place each cutout inside each muffin cup. Cover and freeze any leftover piecrust dough for later use.

4 Prick the bottom of each crust with the tines of a fork. Set aside until ready to fill.

5 In a medium-size mixing bowl, combine eggs, bell pepper, salt, pepper, cream or half-and-half, grated cheese, and flour. Pour mixture into pastry shells, filling each almost to the top.

6 Bake for 10-15 minutes or until slightly puffed and lightly browned. Remove from oven and cool 5 minutes on a wire rack before taking each quiche out of the muffin pan.

7 Move quiche cups to wire rack and press 1/2 black olive into the center of each to create the center of a flower.

8 To serve, put one quiche cup on each plate and use green pepper strips to create a stem and leaves.

Catch a Ladybug Cookies

Red paste food coloring

Vanilla frosting

24 vanilla or chocolate wafers

1/2 cup mini chocolate chips

Brown M&M's

Makes 24 cookies

1 Add several drops of food coloring into frosting. Mix well.

2 Frost each wafer to create ladybug shell.

3 Place 5-7 mini chocolate chips on each wafer to create ladybug spots. Place an M&M on the top edge of each cookie for the ladybug head.

DID YOU KNOW?

Ladybugs are also called ladybirds, barnabees, the Bishop-that-burneth, and bishy bishy barnabees.

A ROYAL BALL

Queen of Hearts Fruit Tarts

Croquembouche

Royal Court Lemonade

Petits Fours

Fancy Finger Sandwiches

Magical Meringues

Mon Petit Macarons

Her Majesty's Madeleines

Pretty as a Princess Napoleons

ueen of Hearts Fruit Tarts

SWEET PASTRY DOUGH:

2 1/2 cups all-purpose flour

3 tablespoons sugar

1 cup (2 sticks) unsalted butter, cut into small pieces

2 large egg yolks

1/4 cup ice water

PASTRY FILLING:

4 large egg yolks

1/2 cup sugar

1/4 cup cornstarch

1/4 teaspoon kosher salt

1 1/2 cups whole milk

1 teaspoon pure vanilla extract

4 tablespoons (1/2 stick) unsalted butter, cut into small pieces

GARNISH:

Assorted fresh seasonal fruits

Makes 8 tarts

Fairy Godmother Tip: In a hurry? Try these shortcuts: substitute refrigerated piecrust dough for the sweet pastry dough and substitute a rich, thick lemon or vanilla yogurt like Noosa for the pastry filling. Easy peasy.

SWEET PASTRY DOUGH:

1 In the bowl of a food processor, combine flour and sugar. Add butter and process until mixture resembles coarse meal.

2 In a small bowl, lightly beat egg yolks. Add ice water.

3 With the food processor running, add the egg-water mixture in a slow, steady stream through the feed tube. Pulse until dough holds together without being wet or sticky. If dough is too dry, add more ice water, 1 tablespoon at a time.

4 Divide dough into two equal balls and flatten each into a flat disc. Wrap in plastic and place in the refrigerator to chill 1 hour or longer.

5 Remove dough from refrigerator and roll out about 1/4 inch thick on a lightly floured work surface.

6 Using individual tart pans as you would a cookie cutter, cut out the dough for each pan. Use your fingers to press edges and tear off excess dough. Lightly push the dough into each tart pan with your index finger.

7 Place tart shells on a baking sheet and chill uncovered in the refrigerator until firm, about 30 minutes.

8 Preheat oven to 375 degrees. Remove the tart shells from the fridge and prick the bottom of the dough all over with a fork.

9 Depending on the size of your tart shells, bake for 8-10 minutes or until light golden brown.

10 Remove from oven and cool in pans for 2-3 minutes before removing tart shells from tart pans.

PASTRY FILLING:

1 In a medium saucepan, whisk together the egg yolks, sugar, cornstarch, and salt.

2 Whisk in the milk. Cook over medium-high heat, whisking constantly, until the mixture has thickened to the consistency of creamy salad dressing, about 2-4 minutes.

3 Remove from heat and whisk in the vanilla, then the butter, a few pieces at a time until melted and smooth.

4 Pour mixture into a bowl. Place a piece of parchment or wax paper directly on the surface of the pastry filling and refrigerate until completely cool, at least 2 hours or up to 2 days.

TARTS:

1 Spoon pastry cream into each tart shell almost up to the top of the pastry crust. Top with assorted fruits. Serve immediately or store in the refrigerator uncovered up to 5 hours.

roquembouche

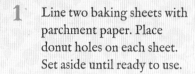

75-80 glazed donut holes

Vanilla candy coating

Sprinkles

1 18-inch Styrofoam cone, covered in parchment paper

Toothpicks

Fresh flowers or bows

Serves 12–14

1 Line two baking sheets with parchment paper. Place donut holes on each sheet. Set aside until ready to use.

2 Melt candy coating according to package directions. Drizzle candy coating over all of the donut holes and decorate with sprinkles. Place in the refrigerator for 15 minutes to chill.

3 Remove donut holes from the fridge. Insert toothpicks into the Styrofoam cone one row at a time, leaving about 1 inch of each toothpick extending out of the cone.

4 Insert donut holes on each toothpick. Continue until the cone is covered, filling open spaces with flowers or bows.

If you're going to enlist the help of woodland friends, be sure they've washed their paws!

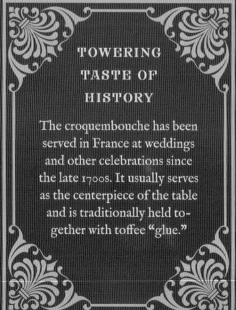

TOWERING TASTE OF HISTORY

The croquembouche has been served in France at weddings and other celebrations since the late 1700s. It usually serves as the centerpiece of the table and is traditionally held together with toffee "glue."

Perfect Petits Fours

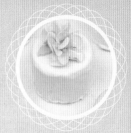

ICING:

6 cups powdered sugar

2 tablespoons light corn syrup

1/2 cup water

1 teaspoon no-color almond extract

Gel or paste food coloring (optional)

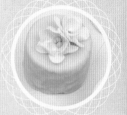

PETITS FOURS:

1 family-size pound cake loaf

TOPPINGS:

Sprinkles, fresh edible flowers, or store-bought sugar decorations

> **Makes about 16 petits fours**

ICING:

1 In a large saucepan on low heat, mix powdered sugar, corn syrup, water, and almond extract together until mixture is warm and looks smooth and creamy.

2 Remove saucepan from heat and cool for about 10 minutes in pan.

3 If using food coloring, divide icing equally between 2-3 small bowls and stir enough food coloring into each one until desired color is reached. Set aside.

PETITS FOURS:

1 Trim 1/4 inch of crust from the pound cake (top, bottom, and both ends). Cut cake into 1-inch-thick slices.

2 Using 1/2- to 1-inch cookie cutters of assorted shapes, cut 2-3 shapes from each slice of pound cake. Place cut-out cakes on a wire rack set over a foil-lined sheet pan.

3 Spoon icing over each cutout and decorate with assorted toppings. Allow to stand uncovered at room temperature for about 30 minutes or until dry.

4 Carefully lift cakes from wire rack using an offset spatula and transfer to a serving platter. Petits fours may be kept in an airtight container up to 3 days.

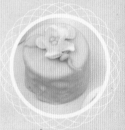

Royal Court Lemonade

1 pint strawberries, blueberries, or raspberries

2-3 sprigs mint, basil, rosemary, or lavender, removed from stems (leaves only)

8 cups water

1/4 cup agave, honey, or pure maple syrup (or more or less to taste)

10 lemons, sliced and squeezed (about 1 1/2 cups lemon juice)

Fresh sliced fruits and herbs (optional)

> **Serves 8-10**

1 Place berries and mint in a blender with 1 cup of water. Blend until smooth. Add agave or honey and blend again to mix.

2 Pour berry mixture into a large pitcher with lemon juice and remaining 7 cups of water. Stir to blend.

3 Chill for at least 1 hour before serving to enhance flavors. Add fresh sliced fruits and herbs to glass to serve, if desired.

GREAT FRUIT-AND-HERB COMBINATIONS TO TRY:

- Strawberries or blackberries + mint or basil
- Blueberries + lavender
- Raspberries + mint or lemon balm
- Peach + thyme

ancy Finger Sandwiches

4 slices hearty white bread, crusts removed

1 teaspoon dijon mustard

4 squares thinly sliced swiss or gruyère cheese

4 pieces deli ham or turkey, thinly sliced

1/2 cup red raspberry seedless jam

2 eggs

2 tablespoons whole or 2 percent milk

1/4 teaspoon salt

1 tablespoon butter

1/4 cup powdered sugar (for garnish)

Makes 6 finger sandwiches

1 Spread 2 slices of bread equally with mustard. Place 1 slice of cheese on each mustard-covered slice, followed by 2 slices of ham or turkey and the last piece of cheese. Spread a small amount of jam on the other 2 pieces of bread, then firmly press them, spread side down, to create 2 sandwiches.

2 Generously spray a heavy skillet with nonstick cooking spray and place over medium heat.

3 As the skillet heats, whisk the eggs, milk, and salt in a shallow bowl until foamy, like soap suds.

4 Place the butter in the center of the pan. Holding one sandwich together firmly, briefly submerge one side into the egg batter and then coat the other side. Repeat for the second sandwich.

5 Place the first sandwich in the pan and grill on the first side for about 3 minutes until golden brown. Flip it over with a spatula and grill on the second side for another 2-3 minutes. Remove pan from heat and transfer the sandwich from the pan to a plate.

6 Repeat for the second sandwich.

7 While sandwiches are cooling, heat remaining raspberry jam in a microwave-safe dish for 15-20 seconds until it liquefies. Remove from microwave and set aside.

8 Slice each sandwich into 3 small finger sandwiches, sprinkle with powdered sugar, and serve immediately with raspberry dipping sauce.

Magical Meringues

4 egg whites, room temperature

1/4 teaspoon cream of tartar

1 cup superfine sugar

Paste food coloring (optional)

Makes 18–24 meringues

1 Preheat oven to 250 degrees. Line two cookie sheets with foil.

2 In a large bowl, whip egg whites with an electric mixer until soft peaks form.

3 Add cream of tartar. Continue beating and very slowly add sugar, 1 tablespoon at a time.

4 Continue beating on high until glossy and stiff peaks form. Add optional food coloring and blend to incorporate color.

5 Drop well-rounded teaspoons, or use a pastry bag fitted with a star or round tip, onto prepared baking sheets.

6 Bake for 90 minutes. Turn off oven and leave the door closed for another hour to let cool and dry out.

7 Remove from oven and baking sheets and store in an airtight container until ready to serve.

MAGICAL MERINGUES

HER MAJESTY'S MADELEINES

er Majesty's Madeleines

Makes
1 dozen

2 eggs

1/3 cup granulated sugar

1/4 teaspoon sea salt

1 teaspoon vanilla extract

1/4 teaspoon almond extract

1/2 cup all-purpose flour, sifted

1 teaspoon grated lemon zest

4 tablespoons unsalted butter, melted and cooled

Powdered sugar for dusting

1 Preheat oven to 375 degrees.

2 Using a pastry brush, heavily brush softened butter over each of the 12 molds in a madeleine pan, carefully buttering every ridge. Dust the molds with flour, tilting the pan to coat the surfaces evenly. Turn the pan upside down and tap it gently to dislodge the excess flour.

3 In a large bowl, combine the eggs, granulated sugar, and salt. Using a handheld mixer on medium-high speed, beat vigorously until pale, thick, and fluffy, about 5 minutes.

4 Beat in the vanilla and almond extracts. Sprinkle the sifted flour over the egg mixture and stir or beat on low speed to incorporate.

5 Gently fold in the lemon zest and half of the melted butter until just blended. Fold in the remaining melted butter.

6 Divide the batter among the prepared molds, using a heaping tablespoon of batter for each mold. Bake the madeleines until the tops spring back when lightly touched, about 8-12 minutes.

7 Remove the pan from the oven and invert it over a wire rack, then tap it on the rack to release the madeleines.

8 Let the madeleines cool on the rack for 10 minutes. Using a fine mesh sieve, dust the tops with powdered sugar and serve.

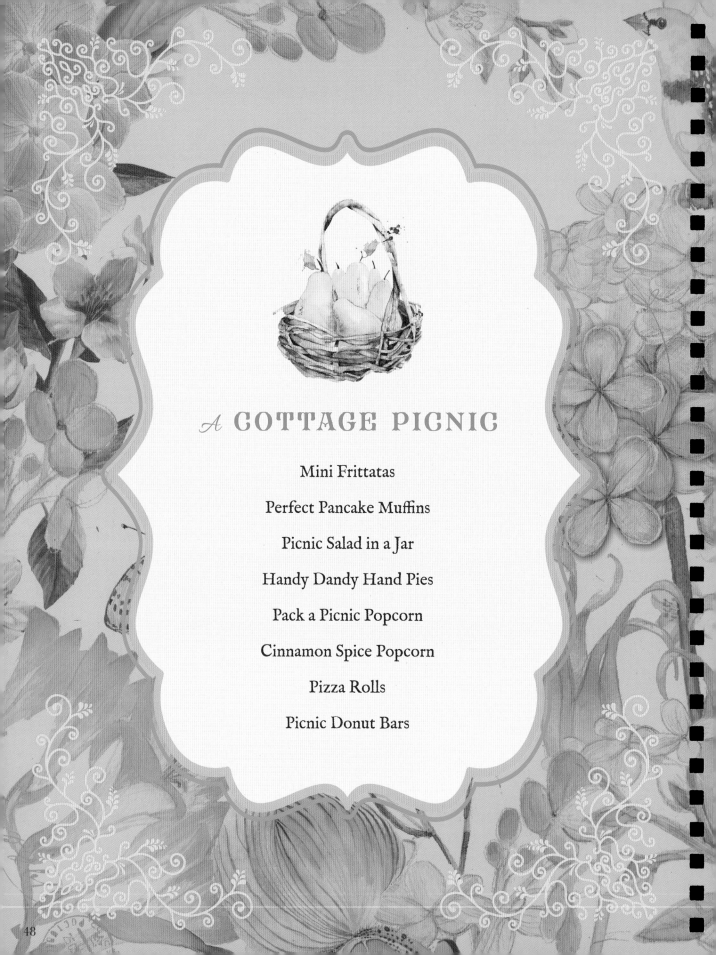

A COTTAGE PICNIC

Mini Frittatas

Perfect Pancake Muffins

Picnic Salad in a Jar

Handy Dandy Hand Pies

Pack a Picnic Popcorn

Cinnamon Spice Popcorn

Pizza Rolls

Picnic Donut Bars

ini Frittatas

8 large eggs

1/2 cup whole milk

1/2 teaspoon freshly ground black pepper

1/4 teaspoon salt

4 ounces thinly sliced ham, chopped

1/3 cup freshly grated Parmesan cheese

2 tablespoons chopped fresh Italian parsley leaves

1 Preheat oven to 375 degrees. Spray two 12-count mini muffin tins with nonstick cooking spray.

2 Whisk the eggs, milk, pepper, and salt in a large bowl, blending well. Stir in the ham, cheese, and parsley.

3 Fill prepared muffin cups almost to the top with the egg mixture and bake until the egg mixture puffs and is just set in the center, about 8-10 minutes.

4 Using a rubber spatula, loosen the frittatas from the muffin cups and slide the frittatas onto a platter. Serve immediately.

Makes 24 frittatas

Perfect Pancake Muffins

Makes 12 muffins

MUFFINS:

1/2 cup pancake mix

1/3 cup milk

1/4 cup pure maple syrup

ASSORTED TOPPINGS:

Chopped prosciutto, crumbled bacon, or cooked breakfast sausage

Fruits such as berries, bananas, or apples

Chopped nuts or seeds

1 Preheat oven to 350 degrees. Lightly coat 12 muffin cups with nonstick cooking spray and set aside until ready to use.

2 Combine pancake mix, milk, and syrup together until blended. Pour batter into prepared muffin pans, filling about 3/4 full. Garnish each muffin with your topping of choice.

3 Bake for 12-14 minutes or until golden and serve with maple syrup or dust with powdered sugar.

TROLL TOLL

Trolls can't resist muffins, so keep a few extras in your pocket in case you have to cross a bridge and forgot your fare.

Picnic Salad in a Jar

Makes 2 salads

1. Blend dressing ingredients in a food processor or blender. Split the dressing evenly between two mason jars.

2. Add corn on top of dressing. Add pepper and edamame.

3. Sprinkle on cheese, tomatoes, and olives and top with the zucchini. Cover and refrigerate for up to 2 days.

4. When ready to serve, shake the jar vigorously and dig in or pour onto a plate.

AVOCADO SPINACH DRESSING:

1/2 cup fresh packed spinach

1/2 ripe avocado

Juice of 1 lemon

2 tablespoons extra virgin olive oil

2 tablespoons Greek yogurt

1/2 teaspoon salt

1/4 teaspoon pepper

SALAD:

1/2 cup corn

1/2 cup chopped red bell pepper

1/2 cup shelled edamame

1/4 cup mozzarella cheese (optional)

1/2 cup cherry tomatoes

3-4 chopped green or kalamata olives (optional)

1 1/2 cups spiraled or thinly sliced zucchini

Fairy Godmother Tip: Create a salad bar with extra vegetables and toppings where you and your fellow princesses can layer your own picnic salads.

Pizza Rolls

1 can crescent rolls

1 package pepperoni

4 mozzarella cheese sticks

1 pinch oregano (optional)

1 pinch red pepper flakes

1 cup red sauce

1. Preheat oven to 325 degrees. Lay out crescent rolls on a baking sheet.

2. Combine oregano, if desired, red pepper flakes, and red sauce. Spread sauce on each roll.

3. Place 3-5 pepperonis on the wide end of each crescent roll. Place half of a cheese stick across the wide end of each crescent roll.

4. Roll each crescent roll up by starting at the wide end and rolling toward the pointy end.

5. Bake for about 15 minutes or until golden brown.

Makes 8 pizza rolls

Short, surly, and always hungry, dwarfs routinely ambush unwary picnickers to pilfer free food. Have a threatening tub of soapy water nearby to keep them at bay—the one thing dwarfs hate more than being hungry is the thought of being clean!

Picnic Donut Bars

Makes 10–12 bars

1/2 cup butter, room temperature

1 cup sugar

2 1/4 cups all-purpose flour

2 teaspoons baking powder

3/4 teaspoon baking soda

1/8 teaspoon sea salt

1/4 teaspoon freshly grated nutmeg

2 eggs

1 egg yolk

1 cup buttermilk

1 teaspoon vanilla

1/2 teaspoon almond extract

2 cups strawberries, chopped

2 cups powdered sugar

1/2 cup milk

Pink sprinkles

1. Preheat oven to 350 degrees. Coat an 8x10-inch pan with cooking spray and set aside until ready to use.

2. With a mixer or by hand, cream the butter and sugar together in a large bowl until well combined.

3. Whisk the flour, baking powder, baking soda, salt, and nutmeg in a separate bowl.

4. In a separate medium bowl, whisk together the eggs, egg yolk, buttermilk, vanilla, and almond extract.

5. Add the dry and wet ingredients to the butter mixture alternately and blend until just mixed.

6. Fold in the strawberries and place the batter into the prepared pan. Bake about 20-30 minutes or until golden brown. Cool completely and cut into squares.

7. While bars are cooling, make the glaze by whisking the powdered sugar and milk together to combine, adding more milk as necessary to form a runny glaze.

8. Place the bars on a wire rack, pour the glaze over the tops, and garnish with sprinkles. Let bars set completely before serving.

Pack a Picnic Popcorn

1 1-ounce envelope ranch dressing mix

2 teaspoons sweet paprika

1 teaspoon light brown sugar

2 86.8-gram bags gourmet microwave popcorn

Serves 10

1. Stir together ranch dressing mix, paprika, and brown sugar in a small bowl.

2. Prepare 1 bag of gourmet microwave popcorn according to package directions and pour into a large bowl. Sprinkle immediately with half of the ranch mixture, tossing to coat.

3. Prepare the second bag of popcorn according to package directions. Add to the bowl with the seasoned popcorn and toss with remaining ranch mixture. Store popcorn in an airtight container up to 2 days.

Popcorn also makes a hit at tournaments and jousting events. And if hours of watching knights pummel each other sounds terribly dull, at least you'll have something delicious to snack on.

Cinnamon Spice Popcorn

2 tablespoons butter

1 tablespoon honey

1 teaspoon ground cinnamon

1/4 teaspoon ground nutmeg

1/4 teaspoon powdered ginger

4-6 cups popped corn

1/2 cup of your favorite dried fruit, such as dried cranberries, raisins, etc.

1/2 cup sunflower seeds

Makes 4-6 cups popcorn

1. Heat butter and honey in a microwave-safe bowl. Stir in the cinnamon, nutmeg, and ginger.

2. Place popped corn, dried fruit, and seeds into a large bowl. Drizzle on spice blend and toss to coat.

A TASK FOR DRAGONS

Dragons make the best popcorn poppers, but only use one with adult supervision (and plenty of water nearby). And of course, be prepared to surrender at least half your popcorn afterwards.

andy Dandy Hand Pies

FILLING:

1 cup chopped cherries, strawberries, or blueberries

3 tablespoons brown sugar

2 teaspoons cornstarch

1/2 teaspoon orange zest

Pinch of salt

PIE SHELLS:

1 can piecrust dough

EGG WASH:

One egg mixed with 2 teaspoons of water

Makes 4 pies

1   Preheat oven to 375 degrees. Line a baking sheet with parchment paper and set aside until ready to use.

2   In a bowl, mix the chopped berries with the brown sugar, cornstarch, orange zest, and salt.

3   On a flour-dusted surface, roll and cut the piecrust dough into small 4-inch circles.

4   Spoon 1 tablespoon of filling onto one circle of dough. Place another dough circle on top of the filling and crimp it down with a fork until the edges are sealed. Repeat this until all the dough is used up.

5   Cut an X on top of each unbaked pie. Brush each pie top with egg wash.

6   Bake for 20 minutes and allow the pies to cool 10 minutes before serving.

53

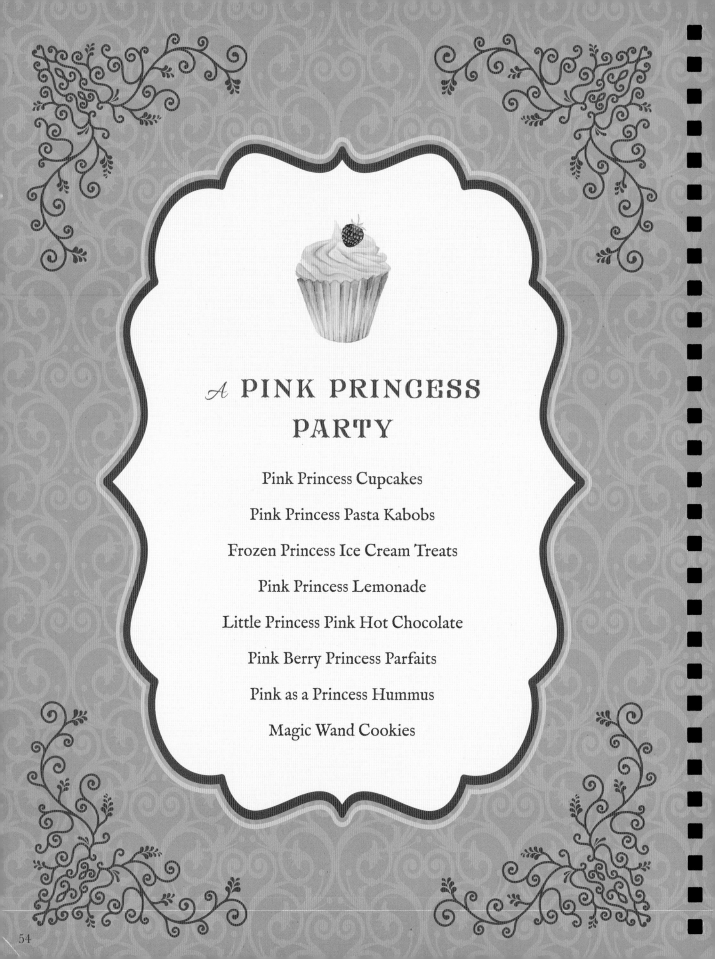

A PINK PRINCESS PARTY

Pink Princess Cupcakes

Pink Princess Pasta Kabobs

Frozen Princess Ice Cream Treats

Pink Princess Lemonade

Little Princess Pink Hot Chocolate

Pink Berry Princess Parfaits

Pink as a Princess Hummus

Magic Wand Cookies

Pink Princess Cupcakes

1 1/4 cups unsalted butter, room temperature

1/2 cup superfine granulated sugar

6 large eggs, room temperature

2 teaspoons vanilla extract

2 teaspoons strawberry extract

1/2 teaspoon almond extract

3 1/2 cups self-rising flour

1/2 teaspoon salt

1/2 cup finely chopped fresh strawberries (about 8-10 strawberries)

Pink fondant

Luster dust

Vanilla frosting

Pink or white Sixlets

Disco dust

1 Preheat oven to 325 degrees. Lightly spray the inside of a cupcake pan with nonstick cooking spray. Set aside until ready to use.

2 In a large bowl, cream together butter and sugar with a hand mixer until light and fluffy.

3 Beat in eggs one at a time, mixing well after each egg. Stir in vanilla, strawberry, and almond extracts.

4 In a separate medium mixing bowl, whisk together self-rising flour and salt, then stir into the butter-and-egg mixture. Fold in chopped strawberries.

5 Divide batter evenly between cupcake pan cups and bake for 20-25 minutes.

6 Carefully remove cupcakes from oven and place on a cooling rack for 5 minutes. Remove cupcakes from cupcake pan and place each one on the rack to cool for 30 minutes.

7 Cut 24 1- to 2-inch crowns out of fondant using a cookie cutter. Using a dry paintbrush, coat crowns with luster dust. Set aside until ready to use.

8 Frost cupcakes with vanilla frosting and place one fondant crown on top of each cupcake. Garnish the outer edge of each cupcake with Sixlets and sprinkle with disco dust.

...cess Ice Cream Treats

...okie sheet with foil or parchment paper and set aside until ready

...g bowl, combine powdered sugar, 2 tablespoons milk or half-... and vanilla. Mix and add 1 extra tablespoon of milk or half-and-... ...ssary to create a smooth icing. Stir in a small amount of pink ...ng, mixing well.

...ing to one side of each donut and place on prepared cookie

...th sprinkles and candies and place all frosted donuts uncovered ...in the freezer for at least 1 hour.

1 quart vanilla ice cream or raspberry sorbet

1 can whipped topping

5 Remove donuts from freezer, place one scoop of ice cream into the hole of each donut, and top with a decorative squirt of whipped topping. Return to freezer uncovered at least 1 hour or until ready to serve. Treats may be made up to 8 hours in advance and stored covered after completely frozen.

Makes 12 treats

Pink Princess Pasta Kabobs

Makes 12 kabobs

12 6-inch wooden skewers

1 9-ounce package cheese tortellini, cooked al dente, rinsed and slightly cooled

36 seedless green grapes

24 strawberries (stems removed)

Pesticide-free edible pink flowers, for garnish

Fairy Godmother Tip: Pink, of course, is the only color to wear to a Pink Princess party. Orange has become fashionable these days, but really, darling, no one should show up looking like a kumquat.

1 Line a cookie sheet with foil and set aside until ready to use.

2 Carefully place cheese tortellini, strawberries, and grapes on each skewer.

3 To finish, secure one edible flower through the stem end on each kabob and place completed kabobs on the prepared cookie sheet. Serve immediately or cover and store in refrigerator for up to 3 hours. Remove from refrigerator and let stand at room temperature one hour before serving.

Pink Princess Lemonade

FRUIT ICE CUBES:

24 maraschino cherries

6 thin slices of lemon, quartered

1 liter distilled or filtered water

LEMONADE:

2 liters strawberry sparking flavored water, chilled

1/2 cup grenadine syrup

Juice of 8-10 lemons

1 cup sugar, or more or less to taste

Serves 10–12

ICE CUBES:

1 Place 1 cherry and 1/4 lemon slice into each of the 24 ice cube tray sections.

2 Add distilled water equally into each section, about 3/4 full. Freeze at least 4 hours or until cubes are frozen solid.

LEMONADE:

3 In a punch bowl, combine chilled sparkling flavored water, grenadine syrup, lemon juice, and sugar. Stir well with a whisk to blend.

4 Remove ice cubes from freezer and add to punch bowl. Serve immediately.

 Fairy Godmother Tip: To show off pretty fruits in ice cubes for a party punch, use distilled or filtered water to make crystal-clear ice cubes. Tap water, my dear, contains chemicals which cause water to become cloudy and white when frozen.

ittle Princess Pink Hot Chocolate

Serves 10–12

10-12 large marshmallows

1 teaspoon cornstarch

8 cups vanilla soy milk

2 cups white chocolate chips

2 teaspoons vanilla extract

1/4 cup grenadine syrup or maraschino cherry juice

Pink sprinkles

1 Combine marshmallows and cornstarch in a large resealable plastic bag. Shake to coat marshmallows. (This will keep them from sticking to the pastry cutter.)

2 Remove marshmallows from bag and press each marshmallow with your hand to flatten. Use a 1/2-inch pastry cutter to cut the marshmallows into assorted shapes. Set aside until ready to use.

3 Heat milk over low heat until simmering. Add white chocolate chips and stir constantly over low heat until melted and combined with milk. Remove from heat and stir in vanilla extract and grenadine syrup or maraschino cherry juice.

4 Garnish with marshmallow cutouts and pink sprinkles and serve immediately. Hot chocolate may be covered and stored at room temperature for up to 3 hours. Reheat over low heat, garnish, and serve.

Pink Berry Princess Parfaits

1 cup vanilla candy coating

2 tablespoons honey or maple syrup

Mini pink heart sprinkles

1 1/2 cups strawberry yogurt

1 cup strawberries

1 cup raspberries

1 cup whipped cream or whipped topping

Makes 8 parfaits

1. Melt candy coating in the microwave in 30-second intervals, stir, and heat until the coating is smooth and melted. Be careful not to overheat and burn the coating. Place the candy coating into a piping bag or a resealable plastic bag with a small corner snipped off.

2. With a pencil, draw star shapes on parchment paper and turn over the paper so that the pencil does not transfer to the melted chocolate. Follow the template to pipe out 8 star shapes onto parchment or wax paper. Allow to cool and harden in the fridge about 10-15 minutes or until ready to use.

3. Place 8 parfait glasses upside down into a small dish filled with the honey. Make sure the rim of the glass is coated with honey. Immediately dip the glass rim into a small dish filled with the mini heart sprinkles.

4. Carefully spoon a small amount of the strawberry yogurt into each glass, then add strawberries, raspberries, and whipped cream, alternating layers. Garnish with a candy coating star.

agic Wand Cookies

1/2 cup (1 stick) butter, room temperature

3/4 cup granulated sugar

1 egg

1 teaspoon vanilla

Pink paste food coloring

2 cups flour

1/2 teaspoon baking soda

1/4 teaspoon salt

Assorted candy or craft sticks

Assorted small candies and sprinkles

Makes 12–15 cookies

1. Preheat oven to 375 degrees. Line two cookie sheets with parchment paper or foil. Spray lightly with nonstick cooking spray and set aside until ready to use.

2. Cream butter in a large mixing bowl; add sugar, beating until light and fluffy. Add egg, vanilla, and pink paste food coloring, mixing well.

3. Add flour, baking soda, and salt, blending well. Dough will be very stiff.

4. Roll dough on parchment paper that has been lightly dusted with powdered sugar. Roll dough into 1/4- to 1/2-inch thickness and cut out with a 2-inch star cookie cutter.

5. Place cookies 2 inches apart on prepared cookie sheets and press candy sticks on each one at the bottom of the star. Take a little extra cookie dough and adhere to exposed candy stick to cover completely. Flatten slightly.

6. Bake for 8-10 minutes or until lightly browned. Remove cookies from oven and cool on cookie sheet for 5 minutes. Move cookies to wire racks to completely cool another 15 minutes before decorating with candies and sprinkles.

Pink as a Princess Hummus

1 medium beet

1 large garlic clove, unpeeled

1 15-ounce can white beans, rinsed and drained

Juice of 1/2 lemon

1/4 cup olive oil

1 tsp salt

Makes 4 cups

1 Preheat oven to 400 degrees.

2 Wash beet well; place with garlic clove on a sheet of foil. Bring up sides of foil and fold to make a packet, leaving room for heat to circulate around the beet and garlic.

3 Bake for 45 minutes or until beet is tender when poked with a knife. Open packet and allow to cool before handling.

4 Remove skin off of the garlic and the beet.

5 Combine the garlic and beet with all the remaining ingredients in a food processor and puree until smooth.

6 Serve with veggies, pita chips, or corn chips.

ROYAL ROOTS

Beets are filled with many helpful nutrients like beta-carotene and folic acid. And in a pinch, they can even be used for magical transport (see page 88), though your carriage can end up looking more like a battering ram. Be judicious in your choice of vehicular veggies.

59

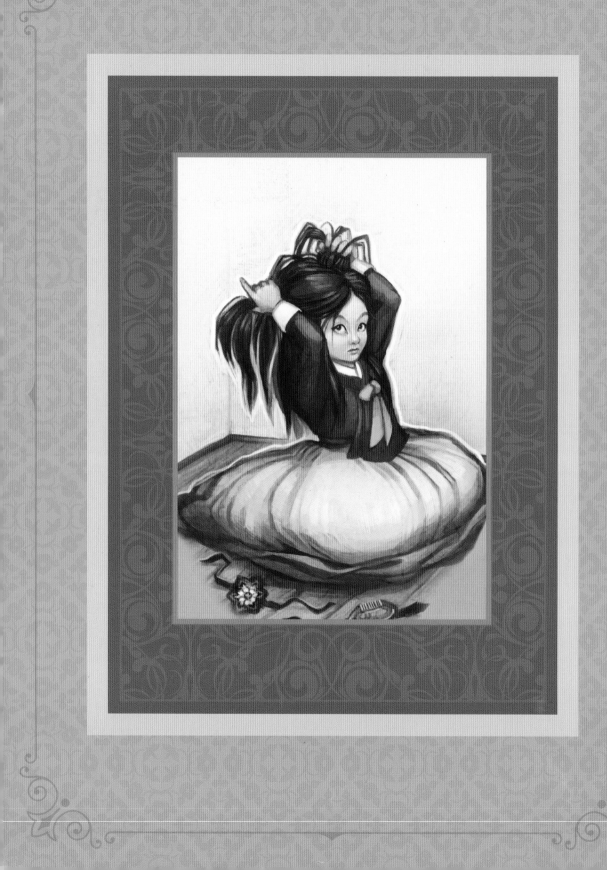

SECTION THREE

Princess Practices

Proper Place Settings

Every princess worth her salt should be able to set a proper table. Luckily, it's easy to learn. Remember: place settings are about more than just choosing the right fork for your salad (though that's part of it); using the proper placement when setting a table ensures that all your royal guests feel welcome and at ease with a familiar setup. (Plus, your banquet will be so beautiful!)

Place Settings Diagram

SETTGIN KEY

A Butter Knife	F Napkin	K Soup Bowl
B Bread Plate	G Salad Fork	L Dinner Knife
C Dessert Spoon	H Dinner Fork	M Salad Knife
D Dessert Fork	I Dinner Plate	N Dinner Spoon
E Water Goblet	J Salad Plate	O Soup Spoon

TABLE MANNERS
Fit *for a* Princess

You don't need to extend your pinky finger to be a classy, well-mannered princess, but here are a few tips that every princess should keep in mind while eating at a royal banquet.

PRINCESSES ALWAYS:

A Wait to eat until everyone is seated

B Say "please" and "thank you"

C Keep a napkin on their lap

D Try everything on their plate (with one notable exception: see the *Poison Apple Exception* below)

E Ask politely for others to pass the food

PRINCESSES NEVER:

A Reach over other guests for trays of food

B Lick their fingers (at least not at a ball—maybe at a BBQ . . .)

C Talk with food in their mouths

D Stick food (or utensils) up their nose

E Stand on their chair or on the table

POISON APPLE
EXCEPTION

If you find yourself presented with a poison apple (see page 111), all etiquette rules should be tossed out the window. You might want to toss out the witch, too.

Fairy Godmother Tip: Table manners might seem unimportant, but it's the polite thing to do for everyone else around you. And there's not much I can do for you if you act like a hippo, dearie.

Courtly Manners

hen meeting new people at court, princesses should always smile and say hello. Be sure to curtsy (see THE CURTSY on page 69) and/or shake their hand. Make eye contact and listen when they speak. Courtesy is always in style!

BEING ANNOUNCED AT FOREIGN COURTS

When you visit another kingdom, the local herald will announce your arrival. Be sure to speak clearly when you tell him your name, and wait patiently until you are announced to enter the court.

 Fairy Godmother Tip:
Don't worry if the herald mispronounces your name, dearie. He has a tough job and a lot of names to remember!

Using Proper Titles of Address

hen addressing people of varying nobility, be sure to use the proper title:

KING/QUEEN:
"Your Majesty"

PRINCE/PRINCESS:
"Your Royal Highness"

LORD/LADY:
"Your Lordship"/"Your Ladyship"

DUKE/DUCHESS:
"Your Grace"

EARL (OR COUNT)/COUNTESS:
"My Lord"/"My Lady"

KNIGHT:
"Sir"

DAME:
"My Lady"

OTHER COURTIERS:
"Sir"/"Madam"

COURTLY KINDNESS

If you see someone sitting by themselves in the royal court, don't be afraid to introduce yourself and make a new friend.

♥

Always say "please," "thank you," and other kind words when addressing members of the court or your royal staff.

♥

From the richest courtier to the lowliest peasant, all people deserve your respect. Treat everyone with kindness and courtesy.

Make sure you treat the cook with particular kindness. Being in a hot kitchen all day is hard work, and he just might slip you a hand pie (see page 53).

THE ROYAL COURT & HOUSEHOLD

KING: *the male sovereign of the land; rules alongside the queen*

QUEEN: *the female sovereign of the land; rules alongside the king*

HERALD: *the loudest voice in the kingdom*

LADY-IN-WAITING: *servant of the queen or princess; a well-meaning busybody*

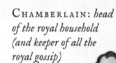 

CHAMBERLAIN: *head of the royal household (and keeper of all the royal gossip)*

JESTER: *a humorous entertainer of the court*

ROYAL TUTOR: *a strict teacher for the royal family; has an unusual obsession with Latin*

COURTIERS: *noble-men and noblewomen in sparkly outfits; can always be found cozying up to the king and queen*

ROYAL DOG WALKER: *an underrated but highly rewarding position*

PRINCESS: *beautiful female heir to the throne*

PAGE: *young servant, often tasked with delivering messages or apprenticed to a knight*

TRANSFORMED PRINCE: *typically in frog form; the spell can be broken with true love's kiss or a very friendly handshake*

KNIGHT: *an individual of great valor and courage; typically clad in chainmail*

ROYAL QUARTET: *musicians for the balls and other courtly soirees; not above improvisation*

ROYAL CHEF: *head of the kitchen and the mastermind behind every royal feast*

EVIL SORCERER: *grumpy wizard with a wand in his hand and a chip on his shoulder; rarely invited to royal events*

ROYAL TAILOR: *responsible for designing, sewing, and fitting gowns and other courtly apparel; has an impeccable sense of style*

GIFT-BESTOWING FAIRIES: *goodhearted, but not very bright; perfect guests at any party because they ALWAYS give a gift*

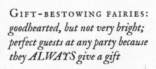

ROYAL PHYSICIAN: *highly skilled in medicine; rarely uses leeches*

FALCONER: *tends to the royal birds of prey; trains them to hunt, deliver messages, and yodel*

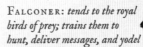

Princess Decorum

Fairy Godmother Tip: Despite the mechanics, the most important thing to remember is that a smile and a wave from a princess can brighten someone's day. Never pass up that opportunity, darling!

THE WAVE

o, we're not talking about the move spectators do in the stands at jousting tournaments. Whether from horseback on an outing or from your carriage in a parade, your wave will let your subjects know that they have a princess who cares about them—a princess they can be proud of.

ELEMENTS *OF A* PRINCESS WAVE

 THE SMILE: You might be surprised that the first vital element of a perfect wave has nothing to do with your hands. Instead, it is all about the expression on your face. As you wave, your smile should be kind, friendly, and genuine. Make eye contact. Let your subjects know that you are just as happy to see them as they are to see you.

 THE ANGLE: Even though there may be hundreds of people flocking to see you, be sure your wave is directed at someone in particular. If there are crowds on either side of you, be sure to give both sides some attention. Even if you can't wave to every person, your subjects will be able to sense your sincerity.

 THE MOTION: With the elbow raised to chest height, move your hand back and forth with a small flourish in the wrist. Be careful not to fan your hand too hard (you'll be worn out before the parade begins!), and don't let your wrist get too floppy.

Curtsy originally comes from the word courtesy, referring to proper bearing or manners in the court. An outward curtsy is a courteous gesture toward others.

STEP 1:

If you are wearing a long-skirted ball gown, hold it out to the sides so it doesn't get in the way or crumple on the floor.

STEP 2:

Cross your right foot behind your left foot. Be sure to plant your toe firmly on the ground behind you for stability.

THE CURTSY

 ssential for any princess's repertoire, the curtsy is a simple yet elegant way to show good manners. A curtsy is a sign of respect to other members of the court or even to your dance partner.

STEP 3:

Bending at the knees (NOT the waist), slowly and evenly lower your body. Slightly lower your head as you descend.

STEP 4:

Smoothly rise and bring your right foot back to its original position.

ANKLE CROSSING

 hen sitting, especially in a formal setting, it is best to cross your legs at the ankles, tucking one foot gently behind the other. Sure, it might be tempting to spread your legs out, put your feet up on a table, or cross your legs at the knee, but each of these positions has a clear downside:

A With your legs spread out, it is much harder to keep yourself covered (especially while wearing a skirt), and you'll be tempted to slouch, which is murder on the back and neck (see PROPER POSTURE below).

B Putting your feet up is just fine when you are back in your bedchamber reading a book by the fire, but when out on official princess business, it is far more polite to keep your shoes off the furniture.

C Crossing your legs at the knees, though not inappropriate, can make your leg fall asleep, and no one likes to feel the pinpricks as you try to stand on a sleepy leg!

Proper Posture

 ood posture isn't just about looking taller or keeping the royal choir director happy. Did you know that having good posture can increase your blood flow, prevent achy muscles, improve your confidence, and make you a happier, healthier person?[1] So take a stand for health and confidence with great posture.

Three Exercises for Princess-Perfect Posture

ou can always balance a book on your head (make sure it's not too heavy!), but here are a few other techniques to try.

THE STRAW

This is a technique many dancers use to improve balance and posture.

1   Stand with your feet shoulder width apart. Imagine there is a straw running through your body, from the bottoms of your feet out the top of your head.

2   Starting at the center (your core), pretend the straw is being stretched outward. Imagine your legs, torso, and neck getting longer. (If it helps, form your hands into fists. Keep one directly in front of your belly while slowing raising the other toward your face as if you are stretching the straw.) Make sure your shoulders stay down and your chin stays level with the floor.

3   If you feel balanced, rise onto your tippy toes and slowly lower yourself back down. Keep your body long, breathe, and try not to wobble.

²www.trainonline.com/ standing-wall-angels-exercise

THE WALL ANGEL²

This exercise will strengthen (and straighten) your back to help improve your posture.

1   Stand with your back, shoulders, and head touching a wall. Move your feet about a foot out from the wall, and bend your knees slightly.

2   Imagine there is a string from behind your belly button to the wall, and pull the string back. (This uses your abdominal muscles.) Make sure there's no space between the wall and your lower back.

3   Raise your arms so your elbows are even with your shoulders (about a 90-degree angle), and touch your elbows and the backs of your hands to the wall.

4   Inhale and slowly raise your hands higher above your head, keeping them against the wall. Raise as far as you can and hold.

5   Exhale and release, bringing the hands back down until the elbows are even with the shoulders again. Repeat twice, and remember to breathe.

THE SHOULDER CIRCLE

You can do this exercise while sitting or standing to develop good posture.

1   Draw your shoulders up toward your ears and allow them to drop. Repeat twice. On the third time, keep your shoulders raised.

2   In a rounded motion, settle your shoulders back and down, opening up your chest. Adjust to a comfortable position without letting your shoulders drop forward.

3   If your chin is jutting out, gently push it back to keep your neck and spine aligned.

Drawing & Painting

ll truly refined princesses must master the art of, well, art. While drawing and painting are best learned by practice, there are some tips and tricks you should keep in mind as you begin your lessons:

- Find inspiration for your art in the world around you. (Even commonplace things can be beautiful.)

- Everyone makes mistakes—that's why pencils have erasers!

- Take your time; it's not a race.

- Look at other works of art and learn from different artists' styles. (They say imitation is the highest form of flattery.)

- Draw what you love. (If you know it well, an object, person, or place will be easier to visualize and re-create.)

- Practice, practice, practice!

A NOTE ON ART CRITICS:

There are many people who will want to critique your artwork (and other aspects of your life, for that matter). Keep in mind that helpful criticism provides objective, specific feedback and suggests ways you can improve; this is very different from criticism meant to hurt or discourage you. You don't need that kind of negativity, so ignore it and keep drawing. And beware: sometimes we are our own worst critic. No matter what, don't give up! If drawing is something you enjoy, keep practicing, and you'll see improvement in no time!

or practice, use this guide to draw a royal castle. Practice keeping the proportions correct by following the pattern of the boxes, then color in your masterpiece. (You can also ask the Queen or King to copy this page for you so you can practice again and again.)

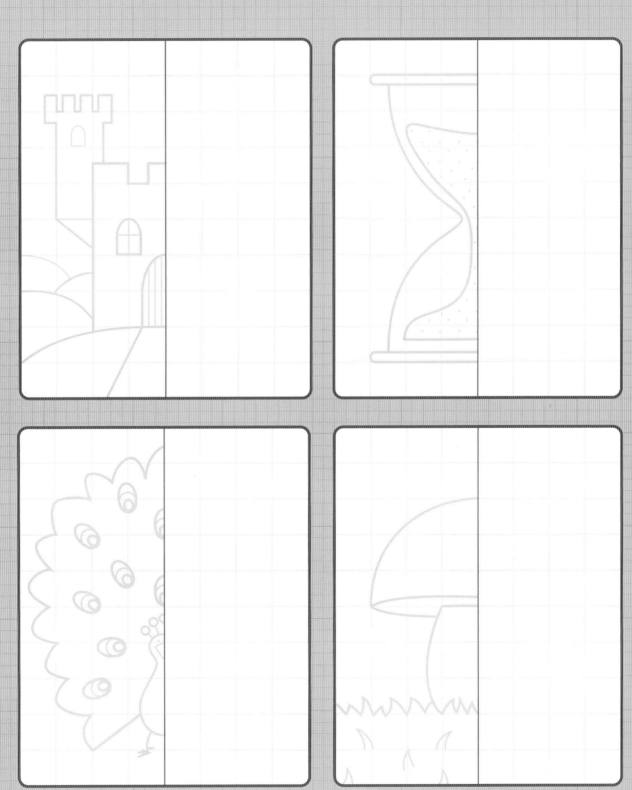

Music

Music is so much more than do-re-mi. It is a powerful, universal language that every princess should endeavor to learn. The study of music will teach you patience and discipline, and it will also open your eyes (and ears) to the beauty of this enchanting art form. From the simplest melody to the most complicated concerto, your music can make the world a better place.

MUSICAL TERMINOLOGY

- **CRESCENDO**: gradually louder
- **DECRESCENDO** (also called "diminuendo"): gradually softer
- **STACCATO**: quick and detached; choppy
- **LEGATO**: smooth and connected
- **PIANO**: quiet
- **FORTE**: loud
- **MELODY**: the main tune of a song
- **HARMONY**: additional notes that support or complement the melody
- **A CAPELLA**: without musical accompaniment

Notation Basics

Repeat Sign

Staff

Treble Clef Sign

Whole Note (4 counts)　Half Note (2 counts)　Quarter Note (1 count)　Eighth Note (1/2 count)　Quarter Rest (1 count)　Eighth Rest (1/2 count)

Penmanship

Whether you are writing a letter or signing a royal decree, your handwriting should reflect your royal station. It should be easy to read and, if possible, beautiful to look at. But that doesn't mean that every princess writes the same way. On the contrary, each princess has unique handwriting that reflects her signature style (pardon the pun), and all styles are equally beautiful.

CALLIGRAPHY

For artistically inclined princesses, *calligraphy* (decorative lettering done with a pen or paintbrush) takes good handwriting to the next level. With practice, even your words can become works of art! Give it a try:

By order of the Princess

By order of the Princess

By order of the Princess

By order of the Princess

By order of the Princess

By order of the Princess

Foreign Languages

our royal duties may take you to faraway lands, and you will surely meet with dignitaries and ambassadors from many different kingdoms, so it is helpful to know some basic greetings in the major world languages.

LANGUAGE	GREETING	PRONUNCIATION
English	Hello	hell-O
Chinese (Mandarin)	Ni hao	NEE-how
Spanish	Hola	OH-la
French	Bonjour	bohn-ZHOOR
Japanese	Kon-nichiwa	kohn-nee-tchee-wah
German	Guten tag	gootahn taag
Arabic	Ahlan	ah-LAHN
Italian	Ciao	chow
Russian	Zdravstvuyte	ZDRA-stvooy-tyeh
Hebrew	Shalom	sha-LOME
Hindi	Namaste	nah-mah-STAY
Swahili	Jambo	JAHM-bo

Riddling with a Dragon

Nearly every princess encounters a dragon at least once in the course of her reign, so it's best to be prepared. Dragons are wise, wily beasts, but luckily, they are easily distracted. You see, they can never resist a riddle. Test your wits on the riddles below. If you can you solve these, you'll be ready to face any dragon! (And you might just want to keep a few of these handy . . .)

HANDY RIDDLES

'Tis true I have both face and hands,
And move before your eyes,
Yet when I go, my body stands,
And when I stand, I lie.

(Answer: A clock.)

What force and strength cannot get through
I with a gentle touch can do;
And many in the streets would stand
Were I not, as a friend, at hand.

(Answer: A key.)

What has seven windows but only three that close?

(Answer: A face.)

It walks on four legs in the morning, two legs at noon, and three legs in the evening. What is it?

(Answer: A person growing older.)

Who walks and walks and carries his house with him?

(Answer: A turtle.)

What is that which has been tomorrow and will be yesterday?

(Answer: Today.)

What always runs but never walks,
Often murmurs, never talks,
Has a bed but never sleeps,
Has a mouth but never eats?

(Answer: A river.)

Alive without breath,
As cold as death,
Clad in mail never clinking,
Never thirsty, ever drinking.
What am I?

(Answer: A fish.)

Horseback Riding

hen choosing a horse, there are many breeds and colors to consider. You might decide on a horse whose mane complements your hair or your eyes. On the other hand, you can never tell a horse's temperament from its beautiful coat, so choose wisely. Your horse can become your dear friend and trusted companion—and whether roan or chestnut, they're such good listeners!

MADAME LINGUA'S ROYAL LEXICON

unicorn
[ˈyü-nə-kȯrn]

The magical cousin to the horse, unicorns are best known for their dazzlingly white coats and the single signature horn protruding majestically from their foreheads. Though they are usually too proud to admit it, unicorns will do almost anything for a ripe, juicy apple.

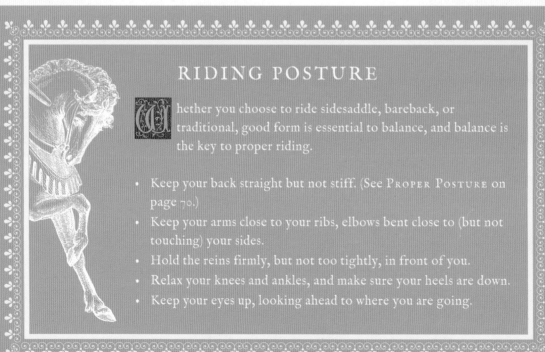

RIDING POSTURE

hether you choose to ride sidesaddle, bareback, or traditional, good form is essential to balance, and balance is the key to proper riding.

- Keep your back straight but not stiff. (See PROPER POSTURE on page 70.)
- Keep your arms close to your ribs, elbows bent close to (but not touching) your sides.
- Hold the reins firmly, but not too tightly, in front of you.
- Relax your knees and ankles, and make sure your heels are down.
- Keep your eyes up, looking ahead to where you are going.

Bay

Gray

White

Chestnut

Black

Dun

Buckskin

Palomino

Perlino

Cremello

Roan

Pinto

 ## TYPES OF GAITS

A horse's *gait* describes the way and speed at which it moves. There are four natural gaits, though if you are preparing for a royal parade, you can train your horse to move in other ways, as well.

- WALK: The slowest gait, the walk involves four separate steps: left hind leg, left front leg, right hind leg, right front leg. Then the pattern is repeated. Let your horse walk for a relaxing ride around the palace grounds. It is normal to feel a gentle side-to-side motion as your horse walks.

- TROT: Faster than a walk, a trot consists of two steps, with opposite legs moving in unison: left hind leg with right front leg, then right hind leg with left front leg, and so on. Coax your horse into a trot when you need to politely avoid tedious royal suitors. Be warned: a trot can be bumpy!

- CANTER: Even faster than a trot, the canter consists of three steps, with one hind leg propelling the horse forward onto the opposite front leg and the other hind leg before moving the final front leg. When you listen to a horse cantering, you will hear a distinct *clomp-clomp-clomp*. A canter is comfortable for both the horse and rider, so use when on a long journey to another kingdom.

- GALLOP: The gallop is the fastest gait and moves through four steps: each hind leg and then each front leg. The horse is momentarily suspended in the air—all four feet off the ground—before the step repeats. Use a gallop when you are running late for a royal appointment or need to escape from a troll.

HORSE VS. CARRIAGE

hile horseback riding provides more excitement and exercise, there are times when riding in a carriage is a better option. Either mode of transportation is perfectly appropriate for a princess.

CHOOSE A CARRIAGE:

- when you are in the middle of a good book and can't put it down to hold the reins.
- when your lady-in-waiting spent hours styling your hair and you don't want to ruin her work.
- when your skirt is too large to be draped over a saddle.

CHOOSE A HORSE:

- when you need a little more freedom.
- when you want to travel quickly.
- when you tour your kingdom in disguise.
- when you are battling a dragon or other large beast.
- when you want some fresh air.

Archery

ourtiers and commoners alike enjoy a good tournament. Whether archery, jousting, or fencing is the sport of choice, be sure to brush up on your skills and wow the crowd (even if you have to enter in disguise).

Fairy Godmother Tip: Be sure there aren't any mischievous pageboys wandering through the shooting range BEFORE you release the arrow, the poor dears.

Taking a Proper Archery Stance

1. Stand with your non-dominant shoulder facing the target and your feet comfortably apart (about shoulder width). Stand up straight, relax your shoulders, and don't lock your knees.

2. Pull an arrow from your quiver and nock it (or load it) on the bowstring.

3. Extend the bow out toward the target and smoothly draw the string back toward you, keeping your elbow high. Touch your hand to your chin to add stability.

4. Now you have the proper form, so aim, breathe, and release. Hold that position until you hear the arrow hit the target. Bull's-eye!

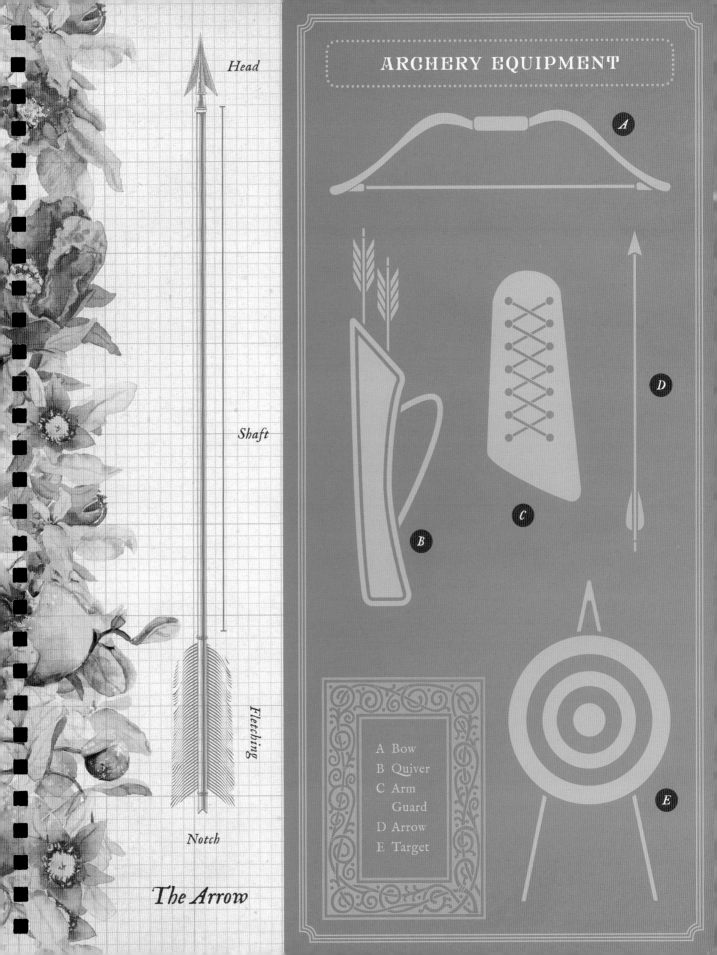

Head

Shaft

Fletching

Notch

The Arrow

ARCHERY EQUIPMENT

A

B

C

D

E

A Bow
B Quiver
C Arm
  Guard
D Arrow
E Target

Fencing and Swordsmanship

ll princesses should be well acquainted with the art of combat, especially with a sword. You never know when you'll need to defend yourself and your kingdom from danger—whether from a dragon, an invading army, or even a particularly persistent suitor.

TYPES OF SWORDS:

- Broadsword
- Cutlass
- Dagger
- Scimitar
- Gladius
- Rapier
- Longsword
- Saber
- Katana
- Foil

COMMON FENCING TERMS

- PARRY: a defensive maneuver to block an attack
- LUNGE: an offensive (attacking) move, pushing off from the back leg to thrust your weapon toward an opponent
- EN GARDE: a French term meaning "on guard"; advising your opponent to be ready for an attack
- FEINT: a pretend attack, meant to distract your opponent from your true aim
- RIPOSTE: an attack made immediately after blocking an opponent's blow

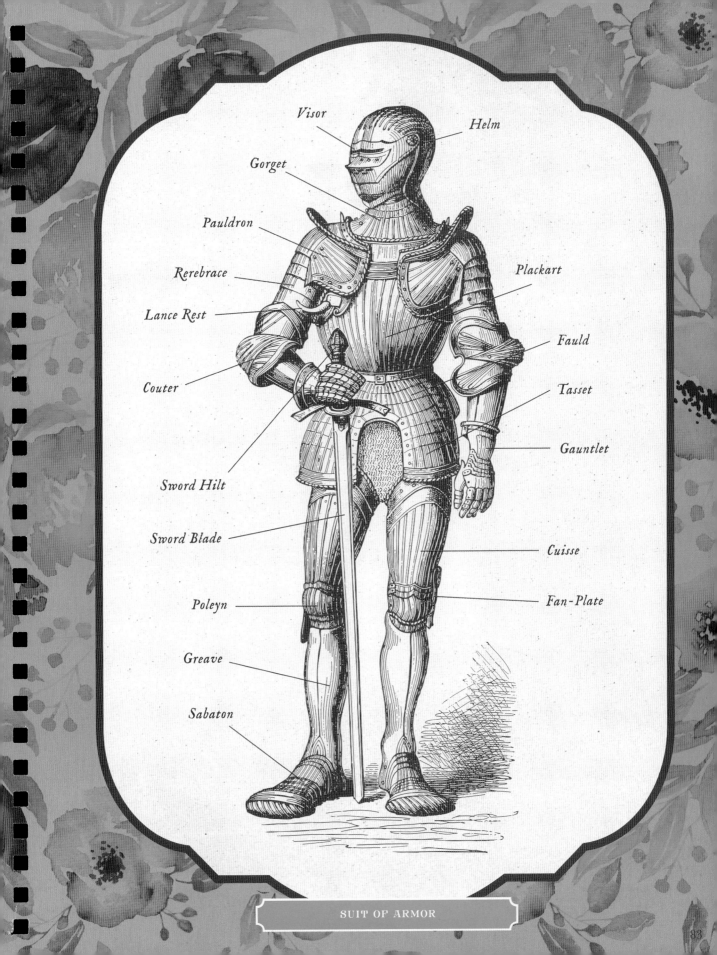

Visor

Helm

Gorget

Pauldron

Plackart

Rerebrace

Lance Rest

Fauld

Tasset

Couter

Gauntlet

Sword Hilt

Sword Blade

Cuisse

Fan-Plate

Poleyn

Greave

Sabaton

SUIT OF ARMOR

Dealing with Enchantments

There's always someone who wants to put a spell on the princess—it's part of the job description. But that doesn't mean you can't be prepared and avoid falling into the classic DID (damsel-in-distress) traps. Armed with knowledge, you'll be able to avoid or break any spell long before you ever need true love's kiss.

Always be suspicious of strange food and drink—especially the kind that specifically tells you to eat it.

MADAME LINGUA'S ROYAL LEXICON

true love's kiss

[troo luhvz kis]

A powerful anti-charm and universal cure, true love's kiss can break nearly any spell. It is unclear why so many sorcerers and witches choose to include such a simple remedy in their otherwise complicated plots, but we're not complaining.

ENCHANTMENT SOURCES TO AVOID

UNTENDED SPELLBOOKS
Books seem innocent enough, but never, EVER read something aloud in a language you can't understand.

BAD-TEMPERED WIZARDS
Wizards are almost always grumpy and *are* always looking for an excuse to curse the kingdom (mostly, that means cursing you).

DRAGONS
Dragons possess significantly more magic than most people realize. Their most powerful charm is their deep, soothing voice, which though a delightful addition to the royal chorus, is also unfortunately deadly.

JEALOUS STEPMOTHERS
Most stepmothers are kind and loving. It's the ones plotting to poison your apples and steal your throne that you'll want to watch out for.

Enchantment	Description	Remedy
SLEEPING SPELL	Sometimes called the "Sleeping Death"; a princess under a sleeping spell is nearly impossible to wake; may cause snoring and halitosis (100-year morning breath can be deadly)	True love's kiss is the go-to remedy, but a very loud alarm clock will also do the trick.
TRANSFORMATION	Like the classic frog prince, princess is turned into an animal or hideous beast; spell attempts to hide a princess's beauty (and true identity) from others	Moonlight, water from an enchanted pond, and time are common remedies. (Remember: true beauty/ kindness/goodness cannot be hidden by outward appearances.)
LOSS OF VOICE/ SIGHT/HEARING	Takes away a necessary sense or faculty; often the result of a shady business deal in which a princess trades attribute (voice, etc.) for chance at love	Fulfill the contract, or better yet, NEVER make deals with witches!
TRANCE	Similar to sleepwalking, a princess typically has no recollection of anything she did while under a trance; spell may be triggered by music, a magic word, or even a snap of the fingers	Wear very thick earmuffs or sing a song you love as a distraction.
IMPRISONMENT	Room, tower, or other location cursed to keep princess from leaving a specified area; involves magic locks, walls, doors, and windows	Always keep a few extra hairpins in your 'do for picking locks; if that fails, it never hurts to sing at the top of your lungs until someone (helpful birds, a handsome prince, your fairy godmother, etc.) hears you.

COMMON ENCHANTMENTS AND WHAT TO DO

A Guide to Woodland Creatures

Deer

Squirrels

Birds

Unicorn

Magpies

Centaur

Dragon

Wolves

hen it comes to woodland creatures—magical, talking, or otherwise—some are as friendly as they are furry, while others are best avoided at all costs. Remember: all creatures large and small, warts and all, deserve your kindness.

GNOMES

BADGER

HAG

PHOENIX

WILL-O'-THE-WISP

DWARFS

FAIRIES

SWAN

FOX

Transportation

rom flying carpets to tamed dragons, princesses have a wide range of transportation options to pick from. Here are three of the most popular.

ENCHANTED COACH

Usually made from a pumpkin and the occasional eggplant, enchanted coaches are the accepted way to arrive in style. Always check the expiration date on the enchantment!

MAGIC CARPET

Not as stylish as the coach but infinitely faster, magic carpets have been around as long as genies have been pestering princesses (in other words, forever).

HORSEBACK RIDING

Fun and freeing, horseback riding is a favorite of the more adventuresome princesses. Still, it's best not to wander off alone— and don't forget your poncho!

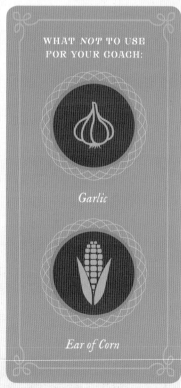

WHAT *NOT* TO USE FOR YOUR COACH:

Garlic

Ear of Corn

Fairy Godmothers

Whether you need a quick getaway from the ball or a wardrobe makeover, your fairy godmother has your back. Fairy godmothers (or FGMs, as they are referred to by members of the magical community) are known for their impeccable timing and catchy songs, but be sure to check the expiration date/time on their spells. Many a princess has found herself trapped in an oversized gourd after leaving the ball too late and missing her curfew.

WATCH THE CLOCK!

When dealing with your fairy godmother, you might find a small pocketwatch to be extremely helpful. Certain times of day are especially important to keep in mind:

12 AM (MIDNIGHT): Expiration time for most spells.

4 PM (TEA TIME): The one thing FGMs love more than helping princesses like you is a hot, buttered crumpet, so don't bother calling until later.

9 PM (BEDTIME): If you need help getting ready for the ball, be sure to call your FGM before she retires for the evening. FGMs simply don't materialize in nightcaps.

 f you want to be a true princess, there are some characteristics you must work on. Some characteristics are easy to see, like brown eyes or long hair. Some characteristics are not seen on the outside; instead, they are things a person does or feels. They are deep within a princess's heart. Many of these princess characteristics will be easy for you; some may be hard. Sometimes we make mistakes and have to try again. Just remember: you can get better at anything when you practice.

In this section, you will learn about seven important princess characteristics, read a story about another princess who is working on being her best, too, and find a PRINCESS CHALLENGE to help you practice how to be a true princess.

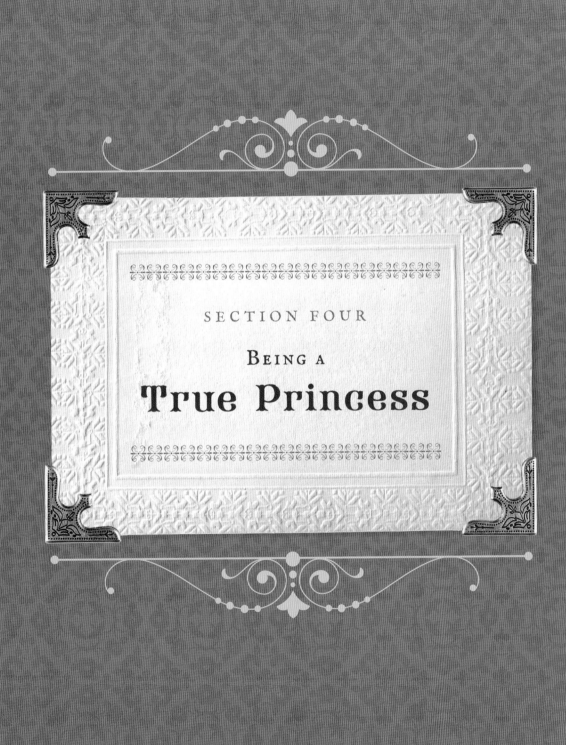

SECTION FOUR

BEING A

True Princess

Kindness

A real princess must be kind. Kindness means being friendly and considerate to others—whether they are princesses or your little brother. Being kind is pretty simple once you think about it. Just ask yourself what would make others happy. What would make your friend, mom, sister, or even someone you just barely met happy? Do the simple things like saying hello, smiling, listening, picking up something that fell, helping with a job, or sharing kind words or a note. True kindness is what counts. People love to be around princesses who are truly kind. And when a princess is truly kind, she is also truly happy!

KINDNESS IN ACTION

THE LITTLE PRINCESS

BY FRANCES HODGSON BURNETT

The story of *The Little Princess* tells of a kind, intelligent little girl who has lived all her life in India with her father. When Sara turns eight, her father sends her to England to go to school. Sara has all the finest dresses and dolls. Though she is not a "real" princess, she looks, acts, and even imagines herself to *be* a princess. She is kind to the youngest of the girls at school and makes friends quickly with others who need a friend.

One day in the middle of Sara's birthday party, tragedy strikes. Miss Minchin, who runs the school, informs Sara that her father is dead and she has nothing. Sara is told she may stay at the school as a servant and must put on her plainest black dress and live in the attic with the scullery maid. Though she is very sad and no longer looks like a princess, Sara decides she will still act like a true princess. She will be polite and treat others with kindness even when she is tired, cold, and hungry. Here is how the author, Frances Hodgson Burnett, tells of Sara sharing with a little girl who has even less than she.

or several days, it had rained continuous-ly; the streets were chilly and sloppy and full of dreary, cold mist; there was mud everywhere—sticky London mud—and over everything the pall of drizzle and fog. Of course, there were several long and tire-some errands to be done—there always were on days like this—and Sara was sent out again and again, until her shabby clothes were damp through. The absurd old feath-ers on her forlorn hat were more draggled and absurd than ever, and her downtrod-den shoes were so wet that they could not hold any more water. Added to this, she had been deprived of her dinner, because Miss Minchin had chosen to punish her. She was so cold and hungry and tired that her face began to have a pinched look, and now and then some kind-hearted person passing her in the street glanced at her with sudden sympathy. But she did not know that. She hurried on, trying to make her mind think of something else. It was really very neces-sary. Her way of doing it was to "pretend" and "suppose" with all the strength that was left in her. But really, this time it was hard-er than she had ever found it, and once or twice, she thought it almost made her more cold and hungry instead of less so. But she persevered obstinately, and as the muddy

water squelched through her broken shoes and the wind seemed trying to drag her thin jacket from her, she talked to herself as she walked, though she did not speak aloud or even move her lips.

Suppose I had dry clothes on, she thought. *Suppose I had good shoes and a long, thick coat and merino stockings and a whole umbrella. And suppose, suppose—just when I was near a baker's where they sold hot buns, I should find sixpence—which belonged to nobody. Suppose if I did, I should go into the shop and buy six of the hottest buns and eat them all without stopping.*

Some very odd things happen in this world sometimes.

It certainly was an odd thing that hap-pened to Sara. She had to cross the street just when she was saying this to herself. The mud was dreadful—she almost had to wade. She

picked her way as carefully as she could, but she could not save herself much; only, in picking her way, she had to look down at her feet and the mud, and in looking down—just as she reached the pavement—she saw something shining in the gutter. It was actually a piece of silver—a tiny piece trodden upon by many feet but still with spirit enough left to shine a little. Not quite a sixpence, but the next thing to it—a fourpenny piece.

In one second, it was in her cold little red-and-blue hand.

"Oh," she gasped, "it is true! It is true!"

And then, if you will believe me, she looked straight at the shop directly facing her. And it was a baker's shop, and a cheerful, stout, motherly woman with rosy cheeks was putting into the window a tray of delicious newly baked hot buns, fresh from the oven—large, plump, shiny buns, with currants in them.

It almost made Sara feel faint for a few

seconds—the shock, and the sight of the buns, and the delightful odors of warm bread floating up through the baker's cellar window.

She knew she need not hesitate to use the little piece of money. It had evidently been lying in the mud for some time, and its owner was completely lost in the stream of passing people who crowded and jostled each other all day long.

"But I'll go and ask the baker woman if she has lost anything," she said to herself, rather faintly. So she crossed the pavement and put her wet foot on the step. As she did so, she saw something that made her stop.

It was a little figure more forlorn even than herself—a little figure which was not much more than a bundle of rags, from which small, bare, red, muddy feet peeped out, only because the rags with which their owner was trying to cover them were not long enough. Above the rags appeared a shock head of tangled hair and a dirty face with big, hollow, hungry eyes.

Sara knew they were hungry eyes the moment she saw them, and she felt a sudden sympathy.

"This," she said to herself, with a little sigh, "is one of the populace—and she is hungrier than I am."

The child—this "one of the populace"—stared up at Sara and shuffled herself aside a little, so as to give her room to pass. She was used to being made to give room to everybody. She knew that if a policeman chanced to see her, he would tell her to "move on."

Sara clutched her little fourpenny piece and hesitated for a few seconds. Then she spoke to her.

"Are you hungry?" she asked.

The child shuffled herself and her rags a little more.

"Ain't I jist?" she said in a hoarse voice. "Jist ain't I?"

"Haven't you had any dinner?" said Sara.

"No dinner," more hoarsely still and with more shuffling. "Nor yet no bre'fast—nor yet no supper. No nothin'."

"Since when?" asked Sara.

"Dunno. Never got nothin' today—nowhere. I've axed an' axed."

Just to look at her made Sara more hungry and faint. But those queer little thoughts were at work in her brain, and she was talking to herself, though she was sick at heart.

If I'm a princess, she was saying, *if I'm a princess, when they were poor and driven from their thrones, they always shared with the populace if they met one poorer and hungrier than themselves. They always shared. Buns are a penny each. If it had been sixpence, I could have eaten six. It won't be enough for either of us. But it will be better than nothing.*

"Wait a minute," she said to the beggar child.

She went into the shop. It was warm and smelled deliciously. The woman was just going to put some more hot buns into the window.

"If you please," said Sara, "have you lost fourpence—a silver fourpence?" And she held the forlorn little piece of money out to her.

The woman looked at it and then at her—at her intense little face and draggled, once-fine clothes.

"Bless us, no," she answered. "Did you find it?"

"Yes," said Sara. "In the gutter."

"Keep it, then," said the woman. "It may have been there for a week, and goodness knows who lost it. You could never find out."

"I know that," said Sara, "but I thought I would ask you."

"Not many would," said the woman, looking puzzled and interested and good natured all at once.

"Do you want to buy something?" she added, as she saw Sara glance at the buns.

"Four buns, if you please," said Sara. "Those at a penny each."

The woman went to the window and put some in a paper bag.

Sara noticed that she put in six.

"I said four, if you please," she explained. "I have only fourpence."

"I'll throw in two for makeweight," said the woman with her good-natured look. "I dare say you can eat them sometime. Aren't you hungry?"

A mist rose before Sara's eyes.

"Yes," she answered. "I am very hungry, and I am much obliged to you for your kindness; and"—she was going to add—"there is a child outside who is hungrier than I am." But just at that moment, two or three customers came in at once, and each one seemed in a hurry, so she could only thank the woman again and go out.

The beggar girl was still huddled up in the corner of the step. She looked frightful in her wet and dirty rags. She was staring straight before her with a stupid look of suffering, and Sara saw her suddenly draw the back of her roughened black hand across her eyes to rub away the tears which seemed to have surprised her by forcing their way from under her lids. She was muttering to herself.

Sara opened the paper bag and took out one of the hot buns, which had already warmed her own cold hands a little.

"See," she said, putting the bun in the ragged lap, "this is nice and hot. Eat it, and you will not feel so hungry."

The child started and stared up at her, as if such sudden, amazing good luck almost frightened her; then she snatched up the bun and began to cram it into her mouth with great wolfish bites.

"Oh, my! Oh, my!" Sara heard her say hoarsely, in wild delight. "Oh, my!"

Sara took out three more buns and put them down.

The sound in the hoarse, ravenous voice was awful.

"She is hungrier than I am," she said to herself. "She's starving." But her hand trembled when she put down the fourth bun. "I'm not starving," she said—and she put down the fifth.

The little ravening London savage was still snatching and devouring when she turned away. She was too ravenous to give any thanks, even if she had ever been taught politeness, which she had not. She was only a poor little wild animal.

"Good-bye," said Sara.

When she reached the other side of the street, she looked back. The child had a bun in each hand and had stopped in the middle of a bite to watch her. Sara gave her a little nod, and the child, after another stare—a curious, lingering stare—jerked her shaggy head in response, and until Sara was out of sight, she did not take another bite or even finish the one she had begun.

At that moment, the baker-woman looked out of her shop window.

"Well, I never!" she exclaimed. "If that young'un hasn't given her buns to a beggar child! It wasn't because she didn't want them, either. Well, well, she looked hungry enough. I'd give something to know what she did it for."

. . . Sara found some comfort in her remaining bun. At all events, it was very hot, and it was better than nothing. As she walked along, she broke off small pieces and ate them slowly to make them last longer.

"Suppose it was a magic bun," she said, "and a bite was as much as a whole dinner. I should be overeating myself if I went on like this." ♣

e'll stop here for now, but if you read the rest of the story, you will meet the baker woman and the little hungry child again. See what wonderful surprise happens because Sarah showed kindness. Read the rest of the story at www.readcentral.com/book/Frances-Hodgson-Burnett/Read-A-Little-Princess-Online.

KINDNESS CHALLENGE

 Since all princesses are a little different, pick one or two of these ideas to practice kindness.

- Write a secret note for your mom or dad. Tell about a special memory you have or say thank you for something your mom or dad does for you. Decorate your note with lace or stickers and place it on their pillow.
- Do a smile experiment. Smile at as many people as you can during the day, and count how many people smile back.
- Sometimes it is hardest to be kind to someone who is not always kind to you. Think of someone who is harder for you to get along with or someone you don't know very well, and do one kind thing for that person. It could be as simple as smiling and saying hello to a new child at school or playing a game with your brother or sharing cookies with a neighbor. When you are kind, others are likely to be kind too.

Courage

 It is not only knights and princes who need courage. It is a girl thing, too. Courage is doing something hard even though you may be afraid. Sometimes we need courage because something is difficult at first, like riding a bike. Sometimes we need courage to go to the doctor. Sometimes we need courage to say hello to someone new. Sometimes we need courage to slay the dragon. Princesses run into all kinds of tricky situations. A true princess must do her best to have courage.

BEAUTY AND THE BEAST

RETELLING BASED ON THE STORY BY
MADAME PRINCE DE BEAUMONT

ave you ever been afraid of monsters? Everyone is afraid of monsters at one time or another. Well, in this story, a princess agrees to go and live with a very scary monster in order to save her father. This princess is not just full of courage; she also has great love and kindness in her heart. And as a princess allows that kindness and love to grow, more and more people, and maybe even a beast, can feel that love.

here was once a very rich merchant who had three sons and three daughters. He saw to it that his children received the best education and took great joy in his little ones. His sons were handsome and his daughters beautiful, especially his youngest.

Everyone admired this youngest child, and she came to be called Beauty. While Beauty spent much of her time reading good books, her sisters enjoyed parties and balls.

All at once, the merchant lost his whole fortune, except a small country house. He told his children, with tears in his eyes, they must go there and work for their living. While the two older sisters complained,

Beauty was determined to help her father and be happy. When they settled in their country house, the merchant and his three sons worked to become fine farmers. Beauty rose early in the morning, determined to help make a good life in the country. When her chores were done, she read and played on her harpsichord and did indeed find joy in her new life. Unfortunately, Beauty's sisters did little more than wallow in misery and mock Beauty because she chose to be happy.

One day, news came that a ship had safely returned carrying goods that belonged to the good father. There was hope that perhaps they would have riches again. As the father set out to check on his wares, Beauty's sisters begged for new dresses and ribbons. Her father asked what Beauty would like from town. She asked for a single rose, as no roses were found in the country.

The good father went to claim his goods, but he was refused. So, with no hope of gaining back his wealth, he left town to return to his children.

As he traveled home, he began to think of his children and what joy it would be to return to them, though he carried no new dresses or ribbons. As he rode, he entered a large forest. Soon, rain began to fall, and then it grew colder and began to snow. The wind howled, and twice he fell from his horse. He was concerned that he would be lost in the storm, cold and hungry, and then he heard the howling of wolves all around him. He saw through the trees a light coming through the storm. He followed the light and soon came to a castle, but no one greeted him at the gate. He put his horse in a stable that was already full of sweet grain. He then entered the main hall, but there was no one within the great castle either. He

found a fire and warmed himself and then ate of the food that was laid out on the table. As he began to feel full and warm, he said, "I hope the master of the house or his servant will forgive me for entering uninvited. I am sure someone will soon arrive." But the night grew late, and no one came, so he wandered around the castle until he found a fine bed chamber and fell fast asleep.

It was late morning when the good merchant awoke. He discovered fresh clean clothes waiting for him and dressed. When he looked out the window expecting to see snow, he was quite surprised to see a beautiful garden full of flowers. He ate the breakfast he found waiting for him, giving thanks to whoever, or whatever, had provided such wonderful chocolate and eggs to a lost traveler. Then he ventured into the garden.

As he walked beneath an arbor of roses, he thought of Beauty's wish and plucked a rose from the vines. Suddenly, he heard a great noise and saw a most frightful beast charging toward him.

The beast growled, "You are very ungrateful. I have saved your life, and, in return, you steal my roses, which I value beyond anything. For this, you shall die."

The merchant fell to his knees. "My Lord, please forgive me; I did not know these roses were so precious to you. I was only trying to bring one fine rose to my daughter who has not looked upon a rose for over a year."

"I am no Lord," replied the monster. "I am a Beast. I care nothing for your life, but I will forgive you if you bring to me one of your daughters. She must be willing to take your place. If none of your daughters are willing, you must promise to return yourself." Thinking that he would at least have the chance to see his children before he returned to the Beast—and his own death—the merchant made an oath that he would return. The beast gave him a chest full of treasures. And with that, he sent the merchant on his way.

As he rode, the merchant comforted himself knowing that the treasures would provide for his children, and he would soon look upon their faces.

When his children saw him, they ran to greet him, but he burst into tears. He handed down the lovely rose to Beauty and told his children all about the strange castle and the terrible Beast. Beauty insisted that she return in her father's place, glad to give her life to save her beloved father. The father refused her kind offer. "You are young, my dear, and must live your life. I am old and shall go and accept my fate."

"I shall then at least go with you, father, that you will not suffer with no one to comfort you. If you try to stop me, I will only follow you. I cannot bear to let you return to that Beast alone," insisted Beauty.

They soon set off to the Beast again. The horse knew the way and took them straight to the castle. They arrived as darkness fell and found the castle full of light and warmth

and food just as before. They warmed themselves by the fire and ate, though the merchant had little appetite. As soon as they finished eating and put their forks down, they heard the most horrible noise—a roar echoing through the castle filled their ears.

They turned and saw the Beast. He asked Beauty, "Have you come willingly?"

Though she could only manage a whisper, Beauty quickly answered, "Yes."

The Beast offered, "I can see that you are kind and full of courage." To the merchant, he pronounced, "You may sleep in my castle tonight. Go your way in the morning. Never return here again."

And with that, the Beast turned and left.

The merchant instructed Beauty to bid him farewell early in the morning and return home to her brothers and sisters. He told her of the chest filled with treasures that would provide for her and her siblings.

The good father and loving daughter retired and fell asleep as soon as they lay down. And soon Beauty began to have the most wonderful dream. A fine lady appeared to her and spoke of her goodness and courage. The fine lady told Beauty she would be rewarded for giving her life for her father. When Beauty awoke, she told her father of the dream and refused to leave, so the merchant had no choice but to bid her farewell and return home. Though he did take comfort in Beauty's dream, he still wept as he rode back to his country home.

Beauty, too, shed tears as she thought of never being able to see her family or her home again. But she determined she may as well explore the castle while she still had breath. She supposed she would again see the Beast at dinner time and, perhaps, this may be her last day on earth.

As she wandered, she came across a door

with BEAUTY'S APARTMENT inscribed in it. She was quite surprised and entered in to find a fine library, a harpsichord, and eloquent living quarters. She marveled, "Surely this would not be provided for me if I were to only be here for a day and then meet my death." She took courage in this thought and opened a simple book from the reading table. Within it, she saw beautiful gold letters and read:

Welcome, Beauty, banish fear,
You are queen and mistress here.
Speak your wishes, speak your will,
Swift obedience meets them still.

She sighed, "My only wish is to see my poor father." As soon as she uttered the words, she glanced at a silver looking glass, and an image came into focus. She saw her father sadly greeting her brothers and sisters. Soon, the image faded. But Beauty was comforted to know that he was safely home.

The day passed quickly, and supper time drew near. As she sat down at the great table which was laid with delectable dishes, she heard the Beast approaching. She took a slow breath and tried to calm her heart and breath. The Beast entered the room and simply asked, "May I sit with you?"

"If that is your desire, Beast," Beauty stammered.

"Do you find me ugly?" he asked.

"I find you quite frightful," she honestly replied.

They talked a little, and Beauty enjoyed her fine supper. When it was time to go to bed for the evening, the Beast, instead of eating Beauty, asked, "Would you be willing to become my wife?"

Beauty was quite surprised. She glanced down at her hands and whispered, "No, I am sorry." ❧

he tale goes on, of course, and Beauty and the Beast fall in love and the enchantment is broken. They live, as many princesses and princes do—happily ever after. The author, Madame Prince de Beaumont, says that they are able to be happy because their love was founded on virtue. And it all began with Beauty's courage.

STORY QUESTIONS:

1 Why do you think Beauty had such kindness and was able to enjoy her new life in the country? Do you think that being able to be happy in the country helped her be happy even when she thought she might be eaten by the Beast?

2 What would you have done if you were Beauty?

3 "Do not give up; beginning is always the hardest." How does this quote go along with *Beauty and the Beast*?

♛ COURAGE CHALLENGE

- Think of a time when you have needed to have courage. How did you do? Write about it in your journal.
- Make yourself courage signs and put them in your room where you will be reminded to be courageous. Use some fun-colored paper and gel pens. Here are some ideas for simple sayings: *Take courage, have courage, and be kind* (Cinderella), *It takes courage to grow up and become who you truly are* (E.E. Cummings), *Courage is found in unlikely places* (J.R.R. Tolkien).

Gratitude

ratitude is showing appreciation for the kindness of others. It is doing simple things like saying "please" and "thank you." The wonderful thing about gratitude is that it actually makes a person happy. Scientists have done many studies to prove this. When a true princess shows gratitude, she actually feels happy. And guess what? That means that people around her feel happy, too. Gratitude and happiness are contagious!

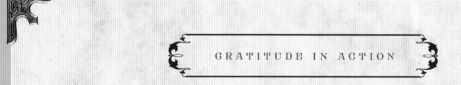

GRATITUDE IN ACTION

A GREAT GIFT

BY MICHELE ROBBINS

t seems that princes and princesses are always trying to find someone to love. This is the story of a prince who seems to always get himself into trouble as he searches for someone to love.

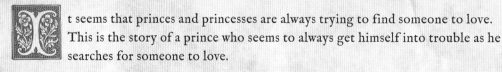

I n the faraway lands where sand becomes high mountains as far as you can see, there once lived a prince who had two problems. First, he always seemed to have misfortunes in his travels. Anytime he went away from home, he would lose his camel, or get robbed, or lose his way. His second problem was that, though he had searched far and wide (having many troubles along the way), he could not find a princess to love.

This prince came up with a plan: since he was always getting into mishaps, he decided that he would give a great gift to anyone who helped him with his troubles. But this gift would be hidden within another gift, a fine horse. Whoever could discover the greater gift would be wise indeed, and with this wisdom, this person would surely be able to help him find a princess to love.

First, the prince set out to the sea and boarded a boat in the hopes of finding his princess. Unfortunately, a great storm came up, and the boat was dashed to pieces by the waves. A kind merchant's daughter helped him grab onto a wooden board and float back to land. To thank the girl, the prince gave her a horse as dark as the stormy sea. Under the saddle of the horse, the prince hid three precious black opals. He never saw the girl again. But he heard that she became rich and married a great lord.

Next, the prince set out to cross the desert, hoping to find his princess in the cities to the east. Unfortunately, he only found himself captured by robbers. A lovely maiden slipped a knife into his napkin at dinner time, and the prince was able to cut himself free later that night. He gave the maiden a horse the color of the sands, so she could ride into the desert unseen. Hidden in the horse's tail were four pieces of gold. He never saw the maiden again, but he heard that she had ridden through the desert escaping the thieves and was able to find wealth and marry a rich merchant.

The prince did not give up. He set out on a journey to the mountains in the north, still hoping to find his princess. Unfortunately, by the time he reached the mountains, his food and water were gone, and he thought he would surely die. He could go no farther, so he lay down to rest beside a rock. Then he heard a sound he had not heard in months: someone was singing a beautiful melody. A girl dressed in simple clothing offered him fresh milk from her pouch and some nuts and fruit from her basket. She led him to her father's tent where he recovered from his journey. The girl had saved his life, and so he gave her a horse the color of creamy milk. Hidden in the braid of the horse's mane were five shimmering diamonds. The prince thanked the girl and her father for their help and then set off for home.

Upon reaching his home, he determined that his search must come to a close. He settled into life at his castle and tried to be happy. One day, before the sun even began to light the sky, the prince went on a walk

up the gentle hill by his castle. He observed a maiden leading a milky-white horse across the sand. She entered the castle gate just as the sun rose above the hill. The prince soon followed. When he entered the great hall, the girl from the mountain was waiting for him. In her hand, she held five shimmering diamonds. She asked the prince if he had lost them in the horse's mane. "No," he replied. "I placed them there in hopes that you might find them. They are yours."

The girl immediately sank to ground and gave thanks to the prince and to her God. "These diamonds will save my father's land, but I could not use them until I knew they were a gift. I have traveled all this way to ask you where they came from."

"You may use them to help your father at once," replied the prince, "but there is something more. I hid the jewels hoping that the one who found them would be wise enough to help me find a princess to love. I think I have found her. Your kindness and service saved me when I had lost hope at the mountain. You were observant and wise in finding the diamonds that had been so intricately braided into the horse's mane. You were honest and full of gratitude as you came to find me and inquire who the diamonds belonged to. Will you be my princess?"

The princess was very surprised by his request, but she had grown fond of him on the mountain. She happily agreed to love the prince forever. One diamond was used to save her father's land. He did indeed say thank you.

The prince and princess were soon married, and the four remaining diamonds were made into beautiful pendants for the princess and, in time, their three children. And they all lived happily . . . and gratefully . . . ever after. ⚓

STORY QUESTIONS:

1 Do you think the prince's plan was a good way to find a princess? Why or why not?

2 What do you think happened to the black opals and the gold?

3 Why does the girl from the mountain find the prince and thank him?

4 What would you have done if you had found the hidden jewels?

GRATITUDE CHALLENGE

- Think of something that a friend or family member has done for you. It could be something really big, like redecorating your room, or it could very simple, like giving you a hug each day when you come home from school. Write this person a special thank-you letter. Decorate with some gratitude swirls on the outside.
- Count how many times you can say "thank you" in one day. Remember that each time you show gratitude, you get a little happy lift, too.
- Do something secret for someone else without expecting any thanks. Perhaps you could make your mom's bed or sneak a yummy cookie into your friend's lunch box.

Honesty

he word *honesty* comes from a word that every princess must know: honor. In olden times, kings, queens, princes, and princesses were called *Your Honor*. "Yes, Your Honor" is a phrase used when talking to royalty. Honor means you are true, you can be trusted, and you are fair. A true princess must be honest. Honesty means doing what you say you will do and always speaking the truth. When you are honest, people can trust you and they will want to be with you. A princess must be honest and true no matter the circumstances. When a princess speaks, she must speak the truth. If a princess makes a promise, she must keep her promise.

HONESTY CHALLENGE

hoose a challenge that will help you be honest.

- Write down one promise to yourself and keep it. Here are some ideas: *I will be kind to my little sister; I will share my favorite toy, I will do a helpful job with my dad.*
- Follow your family rules even when no one is watching you.
- If you make a mistake, admit it and do your best to fix it.

105

Intelligence

A true princess must be intelligent. Do not let yourself be fooled by all the pink and fluff and sparkles. A princess is much more than what you see. A true princess must have a strong and active mind (just think about how the miller's daughter outwitted Rumpelstiltskin!). She must learn and think and be ready to act for herself. She mustn't let her brain turn to pink bubble gum and think Prince Charming will just happen along and save the day. Life is amazing, and being smart sure helps you navigate challenges and enjoy the beauties along the way.

INTELLIGENCE IN ACTION

THE PAPER BAG PRINCESS

A SUMMARY OF THE STORY
BY ROBERT MUNSCH

Of course, you are thinking: *Why would a princess choose a paper bag to wear anywhere?* Well, there are times when a person (or princess) may have some pretty challenging days, and she just must make do and solve her problems! She must be clever and quick, and, by all means, she must at least wear *something*. This is just what Princess Elizabeth does in Robert Munsch's rather funny tale. Here is the gist of his story:

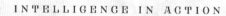

Princess Elizabeth lives in a great castle and has all the beautiful princess things, like dresses and a crown and even a prince. His name is Ronald, and they are going to be married. Then things get difficult. A dragon comes along and burns up all of Elizabeth's princess things and steals her prince. Now, Princess Elizabeth could sit down and cry or run into town to buy new dresses, or she could even run away from all the trouble. But Princess Elizabeth is smart and courageous! She quickly looks for something—anything—to put on. A paper bag is all that is left, so it will have to do. She must hurry off to defeat the terrible dragon and save her prince. Since Elizabeth is very smart, she is aware that dragons are strong, dangerous, and can burn your entire wardrobe. She knows she must defeat him with her brains.

When she gets to the dragon's lair, she can see Prince Ronald behind a barred window. She knocks on the door and asks, "Is it true that you are the smartest and fiercest dragon in the whole world?"

The dragon answers, "Yes."

Elizabeth challenges him, "Is it true that you can burn up ten forests with your fiery breath?"

"Oh, yes," answers the dragon.

He then burns up fifty forests. Elizabeth is impressed. He burns up a hundred more forests; again, Elizabeth is impressed. But when the dragon tries to breathe out flames again, he has none left—only a little puff of smoke.

Next, Elizabeth asks, "Dragon, is it true that you can fly around the world in just ten seconds?"

"Why, yes," says the dragon, and then he flies around the world two times. Unfortunately (for the dragon), he is so tired that he flops on the ground and falls asleep.

With the dragon defeated, she turns to free her prince. Unfortunately (for the prince), he finds Elizabeth to be a mess. He does not appreciate her paper bag dress or messy hair or smoky smell. Can you believe he tells her to come back "when she is dressed like a real princess"?

That is no way to treat a princess who just defeated the fiercest dragon in the whole world and saved your life! So then Princess Elizabeth does one more really smart thing. She tells Prince Ronald that he "may look like a real prince, but he is a bum."

After all this dragon business, guess what? They do not get married, and Princess Elizabeth skips off happily into the sunset. ♣

And let's suppose that that day, Princess Elizabeth rebuilds her castle and goes shopping for a new princess dress. She probably goes and reads a book on how to fix crowns and then fixes her own crown and makes it even more sparkly than it was before. I hope she saves some of her singed hair and that paper bag to remind her that she was smart and courageous. She solved a big problem and saved her village and a silly prince. And she did it all in a simple paper bag.

If you go find Robert Munsch's book *The Paper Bag Princess* at your library, you will see how scary that dragon is and get a look at Princess Elizabeth in that fabulous paper bag dress. Perhaps you should think about it for your Halloween costume next year.

1 What would you do if you were Princess Elizabeth and a dragon burned down your castle?

2 Can you think of another question you could ask the dragon to trick him into getting so tired that he couldn't move?

3 If Prince Ronald was a prince with a kind heart who really loved Elizabeth, what would he have said when she rescued him?

♛ INTELLIGENCE CHALLENGE

- Pick something new to learn about. Here are some ideas: *How does a light bulb work? What do children in Japan like to read? What is your grandmother's favorite food, and how does she cook it? How do you plant and grow a pumpkin?* (could come in handy if you need a carriage). There are so many things to choose—good luck!

- Did you know that most challenges you will have in life are really just about getting along with other people (a few of these people may seem like dragons, but mostly you will be figuring out how to solve problems with real people)? Next time you have a challenge, don't give up or yell or pout; use your brain and work to solve it.

- Work really hard in school. Read lots of good books (some may not have princesses in them), and get smarter and smarter each day!

Remember: you are much more than what you wear. You have an awesome brain. Learn, try new things, and be smart!

Sensitivity

You have heard of the five senses: sight, hearing, taste, touch, and smell. Well, there is a sixth sense that you don't learn about in science class. This sense is your heart sense. It is being sensitive to the feelings and needs of other people. You can use your other five senses to help you notice that someone is cold or sad or lonely, but you have to use your heart sense to do something to help that person feel warmth or happiness or friendship. Being sensitive means you see what others need and you want to help. A true princess must be sensitive.

THE REAL PRINCESS

BY HANS CHRISTIAN ANDERSEN

 his story is also known as *The Princess and the Pea*. It is a special princess who can sense a pea through twenty mattresses, but remember, it is an even more special princess who can sense a need and help another human being who is right next to her or perhaps even across the world.

 here was once a prince, and he wanted a princess, but then she must be a *real* princess. He traveled right round the world to find one, but there was always something wrong. There were plenty of princesses, but whether they were real princesses, he had great difficulty in discovering; there was always something which was not quite right about them. So, at last, he had to come home again, and he was very sad because he wanted a real princess so badly.

One evening, there was a terrible storm; it thundered and lightened and the rain poured down in torrents; indeed, it was a fearful night.

In the middle of the storm, somebody knocked at the town gate, and the old king himself went to open it.

It was a princess who stood outside, but she was in a terrible state from the rain and the storm. The water streamed out of her hair and her clothes; it ran in at the top of her shoes and out at the heel; but she said that she was a real princess.

Well, we shall soon see if that is true, thought the old Queen, but she said nothing. She went into the bedroom, took all the bed-clothes off, and laid a pea on the bedstead;

109

then she took twenty mattresses and piled them on the top of the pea and then twenty feather beds on the top of the mattresses. This was where the princess was to sleep that night. In the morning, they asked her how she had slept.

"Oh, terribly badly!" said the princess. "I have hardly closed my eyes the whole night! Heaven knows what was in the bed. I seemed to be lying upon some hard thing, and my whole body is black and blue this morning. It is terrible!"

They saw at once that she must be a real princess since she had felt the pea through twenty mattresses and twenty feather beds. Nobody but a real princess could have such a delicate skin.

So the prince took her to be his wife, for now he was sure that he had found a real princess, and the pea was put into the museum, where it may still be seen, if no one has stolen it.

Now *this* is a true story. ⚓

STORY QUESTIONS:

1 What do you think a *real* princess is like?

2 Do you think anyone could feel a pea through all those mattresses?

3 What princess test would you use to find a *real* princess?

SENSITIVITY CHALLENGE

Pick one or two of these ideas to practice being sensitive.

- Really look around you at school, at church, or at home and find someone who you could help to feel happy.
- Try putting a small rock under your pillow and see if you can get a good night's sleep.
- Do one thing to help your friend have a great day.
- Learn about children in another country who are in need. Talk with your parents about ways to help someone in need. See what you can do to make a difference for good!
- Get to know someone new. When you know about another person's likes, dislikes, and challenges, you can be not only a real princess but also a real friend.

Friendship

ou may have heard the saying: "To have a friend, you must be a friend." A friend can be someone who is much like you, or a friend could be very different. A friend may look different or live in a faraway place. The most important thing to understand about friendship is that a true friend is someone who listens, cheers, accepts, and loves another person for who she or he is. A friend is someone who makes you smile and laugh and loves you even when you make a mistake. A real princess must be a true friend.

FRIENDSHIP IN ACTION

SNOW-WHITE AND THE SEVEN DWARFS

ABRIDGED FROM THE BROTHERS GRIMM

 veryone needs a friend. Friends save us from loneliness and teach us new things, and sometimes a friend (or a bunch of rather short friends) can save your life. In *Snow-White and the Seven Dwarfs*, Snow-White is saved from the wicked queen by seven friends who are very different from her. See how Snow-White loves them for their kindness and always remembers their friendship.

 nce upon a time in midwinter, when the snowflakes were falling like feathers from heaven, a queen sat sewing at her window, which had a frame of black ebony wood. As she sewed, she looked up at the snow and pricked her finger with her needle.

Three drops of blood fell into the snow. The red on the white looked so beautiful that she thought to herself, "If only I had a child as white as snow, as red as blood, and as black as the wood in this frame."

Soon afterward she had a little daughter who was as white as snow, as red as blood, and as black haired as ebony wood, and therefore they called her Little Snow-White. And as soon as the child was born, the queen died.

A year later, the king took for himself another wife. She was a beautiful woman, but she was proud and arrogant, and she could not stand it if anyone might surpass her in beauty. She had a magic mirror. Every morning, she stood before it, looked at herself, and said:

Mirror, mirror, on the wall,
Who in this land is fairest of all?

To this, the mirror answered:

You, my queen, are fairest of all.

Then she was satisfied, for she knew that the mirror spoke the truth.

Snow-White grew up and became ever more beautiful. When she was seven years old, she was as beautiful as the light of day, even more beautiful than the queen herself.

One day, when the queen asked her mirror:

Mirror, mirror, on the wall,
Who in this land is fairest of all?

It answered:

You, my queen, are fair; it is true.
But Snow-White is a thousand times fairer than you.

The queen took fright and turned yellow and green with envy. From that hour on, whenever she looked at Snow-White, her heart turned over inside her body. The envy and pride grew ever greater, like a weed in her heart, until she had no peace day and night.

Then she summoned a huntsman and said to him, "Take Snow-White out into the woods. I never want to see her again. Kill her, and as proof that she is dead, bring her

magic mirror

[*ma-jik mir-ər*]

Magic mirrors will tell you the truth to any question you ask. This can be very useful, but be warned that grumpy mirrors (especially those woken up after midnight) do take pleasure in fibbing a little. If confronted with such a mirror, it's best to ask only questions with a "Yes" or "No" answer. Even the grumpiest mirror can't lie *that* way.

lungs and her liver back to me."

The huntsman obeyed and took Snow-White into the woods. He took out his hunting knife and was about to stab it into her innocent heart when she began to cry, saying, "Oh, dear huntsman, let me live. I will run into the wild woods and never come back."

Because she was so beautiful, the huntsman took pity on her, and he said, "Run away, you poor child."

Just then, a young boar came running by. The huntsman killed it, cut out its lungs and liver, and took them back to the queen as proof of Snow-White's death.

The poor child was now all alone in the great forest, and she was so afraid that she began to run. She ran over sharp stones and through thorns. She ran as far as her feet could carry her, and just as evening was about to fall, she saw a little house and went inside in order to rest.

Inside the house, everything was small but so neat and clean that no one could say otherwise. There was a little table with a white tablecloth and seven little plates, and each plate had a spoon, and there were seven knives and forks and seven mugs as well. Against the wall, there were seven little beds, all standing in a row.

Because she was so hungry and thirsty, Snow-White ate a few vegetables and a little bread from each little plate, and from each mug she drank a drop of wine. Afterward, because she was so tired, she lay down on a bed and fell asleep.

After dark, the masters of the house returned home. They were the seven dwarfs who picked and dug for ore in the mountains. They lit their seven candles, and as soon as it was light in their house, they saw that someone had been there, for not everything was in the same order as they had left it.

Then the seventh one, looking at his bed, found Snow-White lying there asleep. The seven dwarfs all came running up, and they cried out with amazement. They fetched their seven candles and shone the light on Snow-White. "Oh, good heaven! Oh, good heaven!" they cried. "This child is so beautiful!" They were so happy that they did not wake her up but let her continue to sleep.

The next morning, Snow-White woke up, and when she saw the seven dwarfs, she was frightened. But they were friendly and asked, "What is your name?"

"My name is Snow-White," she answered.

"How did you find your way to our house?" the dwarfs asked further.

Then she told them that her stepmother had tried to kill her, that the huntsman had spared her life, and that she had run the entire day, finally coming to their house.

The dwarfs said, "If you will keep house for us, then you can stay with us, and you shall have everything that you want."

"Yes," said Snow-White, "with all my heart."

So she kept house for them. Every morning, they went into the mountains looking for ore and gold, and in the evening, when they came back home, their meal was ready. During the day, the girl was alone.

The good dwarfs warned her, saying, "Be careful about your stepmother. She will soon know that you are here. Do not let anyone in."

Now the queen, believing that she had eaten Snow-White's lungs and liver, could think only that she was again the first and the most beautiful woman of all. She stepped before her mirror and said:

Mirror, mirror, on the wall,
Who in this land is fairest of all?

It answered:

You, my queen, are fair; it is true.
But Snow-White, beyond the mountains
With the seven dwarfs,
Is still a thousand times fairer than you.

This startled the queen, for she knew that the mirror did not lie and that Snow-White was still alive. Then she thought and thought again how she could kill Snow-White. Coloring her face, the queen disguised herself as an old peddler woman. In this disguise, she went across the seven mountains to the house of the seven dwarfs. Knocking on the door, she called out, "Beautiful wares for sale, for sale!"

Snow-White peered out the window and said, "Good day, dear woman; what do you have for sale?"

"Good wares, beautiful wares," she answered. "Bodice laces in all colors." And she took out one that was braided from colorful silk. "Would you like this one?"

I can let that honest woman in, thought Snow-White, then un-bolted the door and bought the pretty bodice lace.

"Child," said the old woman, "how you look! Come, let me lace you up properly."

The unsuspecting Snow-White stood before her and let her do up the new lace, but the old woman pulled so quickly and so hard that Snow-White could not breathe.

"You used to be the most beautiful one," said the old woman, and hurried away.

Not long afterward, in the evening time, the seven dwarfs came home. How terrified they were when they saw their dear Snow-White lying on the ground, not moving at all, as though she were dead. They lifted her up, and, seeing that she was too tightly laced, they cut the lace in two. Then she began to breathe a bit, and little by little, she came back to life.

When the dwarfs heard what had happened, they said, "The old peddler woman was no one else but the godless queen. Take care and let no one in when we are not with you."

When the wicked woman returned home, she went to her mirror and asked:

Mirror, mirror, on the wall,
Who in this land is fairest of all?

The mirror answered once again:

You, my queen, are fair; it is true.
But Snow-White, beyond the mountains
With the seven dwarfs,

wicked sorceress
[ˈwi-kəd ˈsòr-sə-rəs]

Typically beautiful but often known to disguise themselves as ugly old hags, wicked sorceresses seem determined to make life miserable for princesses. They are overly obsessed with appearances and are likely to cast powerful spells over anyone who gets in their way.

Is still a thousand times fairer than you.

When the queen heard that, all her blood ran to her heart because she knew that Snow-White had come back to life. "This time," she said, "I shall think of something that will destroy you."

Then she made a poisoned comb and she disguised herself, taking the form of a different old woman. Thus she went across the seven mountains to the seven dwarfs, knocked on the door, and called out, "Good wares for sale, for sale!"

Snow-White looked out and said, "Go on your way. I am not allowed to let anyone in."

"You surely may take a look," said the old woman, pulling out the poisoned comb and holding it up. The child liked it so much that she let herself be deceived, and she opened the door. Then the old woman said, "Now let me comb your hair properly."

She had barely stuck the comb into Snow-White's hair when the poison took effect, and the girl fell down, unconscious.

"You specimen of beauty," said the wicked woman. "Now you are finished." And she walked away.

Fortunately, it was almost evening, and the seven dwarfs came home. When they saw Snow-White lying on the ground as if she were dead, they immediately suspected her stepmother. They examined her and found the poisoned comb. They had scarcely pulled it out when Snow-White came to herself again and told them what had happened. Once again, they warned her to be on guard and not to open the door for anyone.

Back at home, the queen stepped before her mirror and said:

Mirror, mirror, on the wall,
Who in this land is fairest of all?

The mirror answered:

You, my queen, are fair; it is true.
But Snow-White, beyond the mountains
With the seven dwarfs,
Is still a thousand times fairer than you.

When the queen heard the mirror saying this, she shook and trembled with anger. "Snow-White shall die," she shouted, "if it costs me my life!"

Then she went into her most secret room and she made a poisoned apple. From the outside, it was beautiful, white with red cheeks, and anyone who saw it would want it. But anyone who might eat a little piece of it would die. Then, coloring her face, she disguised herself as a peasant woman and thus went across the seven mountains to the seven dwarfs. She knocked on the door.

Snow-White stuck her head out the window and said, "I am not allowed to let anyone in. The dwarfs have forbidden me to do so."

"That is all right with me," answered the peasant woman. "I'll easily get rid of my apples. Here, I'll give you one of them."

"No," said Snow-White, "I cannot accept anything."

"Are you afraid of poison?" asked the old woman. "Look, I'll cut the apple in two. You eat the red half, and I shall eat the white half."

Now the apple had been so artfully made that only the red half was poisoned. Snow-White longed for the beautiful apple, and when she saw that the peasant woman was eating part of it, she could no longer resist, and she stuck her hand out and took the poisoned half. She barely had a bite in her mouth when she fell to the ground, dead.

The queen looked at her with a gruesome stare, laughed loudly, and said, "White as snow, red as blood, black as ebony wood! This time, the dwarfs cannot awaken you."

Back at home, she asked her mirror:

Mirror, mirror, on the wall,
Who in this land is fairest of all?

It finally answered:

You, my queen, are fairest of all.

See Poison Apple Exemption on page 63

Then her envious heart was at rest—as well as an envious heart can be at rest.

When the dwarfs came home that evening, they found Snow-White lying on the ground. She was not breathing at all. She was dead. They lifted her up and looked for something poisonous. They undid her laces. They combed her hair. They washed her with water and wine. But nothing helped. They laid her on a bier, and all seven sat next to her and mourned for her and cried for three days. They were going to bury her, but she still looked as fresh as a living person and still had her beautiful red cheeks.

They said, "We cannot bury her in the black earth," and they had a glass coffin made. They laid her inside and with golden letters wrote on it her name and that she was a princess. Then they put the coffin outside on a mountain, and one of them always stayed with it and watched over her. The animals, too, came and mourned for Snow-White.

Snow-White lay there in the coffin a long, long time, and she did not decay but looked like she was asleep, for she was still as white as snow, as red as blood, and as black haired as ebony wood.

Now it came to pass that a prince entered these woods and happened onto the dwarfs' house. He saw the coffin on the mountain with beautiful Snow-White in it.

Then he said to the dwarfs, "Let me have the coffin. I will give you anything you want for it."

But the dwarfs answered, "We will not sell it for all the gold in the world."

Then he said, "Then give it to me, for I cannot live without being able to see Snow-White. I will honor her and respect her as my most cherished one."

As he thus spoke, the good dwarfs felt pity for him and gave him the coffin. The prince had his servants carry it away on their shoulders. But then it happened that one of them stumbled on some brush, and this dislodged from Snow-White's throat the piece of poisoned apple. She opened her eyes and was alive again.

"Good heavens, where am I?" she cried out.

The prince said joyfully, "You are with me." He told her what had happened and then said, "I love you more than anything else in the world. Come with me to my father's castle and become my wife." Snow-White loved him, and she went with him. Their wedding was planned with great splendor and majesty. Snow-White invited her dearest friends, the seven dwarfs who had saved her life three and four times over. And they all rejoiced together.

Now do you wish to know what happened to Snow-White's wicked stepmother? She, too, was invited to the wedding. After putting on her beautiful clothes, she stepped before her mirror and said:

Mirror, mirror, on the wall,
Who in this land is fairest of all?

The mirror answered:

You, my queen, are fair; it is true.
But the young queen is a thousand times fairer
than you.

The wicked woman uttered a curse, and she became so frightened that she did not know what to do. At first, she did not want to go to the wedding, but she found no peace. She had to go and see the young queen. When she arrived, she recognized Snow-White. The evil queen was so full of envy and anger that she couldn't move but fell down dead. ❧

1 The dwarfs tried to warn Snow-White not to talk to or let any strangers in the house. Why do you think she didn't listen? How many times did the evil stepmother trick Snow-White?

2 Sometimes our friends or family warn us of dangers, just like the dwarfs tried to warn Snow-White. Have you ever been warned but failed listen to your friends or gotten tricked anyway?

3 Who are your best friends (don't forget that those in your family can be some of your best friends, too!)? How do your friends show they are true friends?

4 What do you do to help your friends?

5 Fairytales and fables were told hundreds of years ago as a way to teach lessons to children. What lessons are taught in this four-hundred-year-old story? Do you think children today need to learn these lessons, too?

♕ FRIENDSHIP CHALLENGE

- Pick one thing you could do to be a better friend. Here are a few ideas: listen when your friend tells you something, cheer up your friend if he or she feels sad, or help your friend make good choices.
- Don't get tricked like Snow-White. Teachers, parents, leaders, and friends often warn us of things we shouldn't do. There are lots of things that can bring us down or hurt us. Alcohol, cigarettes, and drugs can be just as dangerous as that poisonous apple. Gossip (saying mean things about others), bad manners, and inappropriate words (swears) can make us rail and curse like that evil stepmother. Listen to your true friends and stay away from these kinds of dangers.
- If you are with a group of friends and you notice someone all alone, invite that person to join in the fun. Remember: there were seven dwarfs, and there is always room for one more friend!
- Make a friendship banner. Get a piece of paper, and in your best, most fancy writing, make a list of three to five promises you would make to your friends. Here are a few ideas for the promises: *I will always speak the kindest words. I will try my best to forgive. I will love my friend with all my heart.* After you write your promises, decorate your banner with lace and jewels and hang it in your room.

Inner Beauty

hether hundreds of years ago or in this very day, there has been much focus on what people look like on the outside. Princesses and common folk alike often worry too much about what dress they should wear to the ball. The most important kind of beauty, however, is something that you may not see at first glance. It is the kind that comes only from the inside. Inner beauty, unlike curly hair or long eyelashes, is not something you are born with. You must work hard to develop this characteristic. Inner beauty is like taking all the other characteristics and carefully mixing them together in your heart and your actions to create something truly wonderful, something truly royal. Inner beauty grows as a princess or young lady is kind, intelligent, honest, grateful, friendly, courageous, sensitive to others, and forgiving. Now you have learned all about these characteristics from princesses in these stories—except for forgiveness. Be sure to look for how Cinderella has great inner beauty, even enough to forgive.

INNER BEAUTY IN ACTION

CINDERELLA

OR, *THE LITTLE GLASS SLIPPER* (ABRIDGED)

BY CHARLES PERRAULT

here are many, many versions of Cinderella that have been told for hundreds of years in many countries. Some involve magic birds or trees. Others tell of girls who must live with cows before meeting their prince. But all these stories have magic, some kind of shoe or slipper, and, most importantly, a kind and courageous girl who is not thought to be royal become just that—a true princess.

nce there was a gentleman who had a young daughter of unparalleled goodness and sweetness of temper just like her mother, who was the best creature in the world. When the mother became very ill and died, this gentleman married, for his second wife, the proudest and haughtiest woman that was ever seen. She had two daughters of her own, who were, indeed, exactly like her

in all things.

No sooner were the ceremonies of the wedding over but the stepmother began to show her true colors. She could not bear the good qualities of this pretty girl, because they made her own daughters appear the more odious. She employed her in the meanest work of the house. The young girl had to scour the dishes and floors and clean madam's and the misses' bed chambers. She slept on a wretched straw bed while her sisters slept in fine rooms on the softest of beds and where they had looking glasses so large that they could see themselves from head to foot.

The poor girl bore it all patiently. When she had done her work, she used to go to the chimney corner and sit down there in the cinders and ashes, which caused her to be called Cinderseat. Only the younger sister, who was not so rude as the older one, called

her Cinderella. However, Cinderella, notwithstanding her rags, was a hundred times more beautiful than her sisters.

It happened that the king's son gave a ball and invited all persons of fashion to it. Our young misses were also invited. They were delighted and wonderfully busy in selecting the gowns, petticoats, and hair dressing that would best become them. This was a new difficulty for Cinderella, for it was she who ironed her sisters' linen and pleated their ruffles. They talked all day long of nothing but how they should be dressed.

"For my part," said the eldest, "I will wear my red velvet suit with French trimming."

"And I," said the youngest, "shall wear my gold-flowered cloak and my diamond stomacher."

They consulted Cinderella in all these matters, for her advice was always good. Indeed, she even offered her services to fix their hair, which they very willingly accepted. As she was doing this, they said to her, "Cinderella, would you not like to go to the ball?"

"Alas!" said she. "You only tease me; it is not for such as I am to go to the ball."

"You are quite right," they replied. "It would make the people laugh to see a Cinderseat at a ball."

Anyone but Cinderella would have fixed their hair awry, but she was very good and dressed them perfectly well. At last, the happy day came. They went to court, and Cinderella followed them with her eyes as long as she could. When she lost sight of them, she started to cry.

Her godmother, who saw her all in tears, asked her what was the matter.

"I wish I could. I wish I could." She was not able to speak the rest, being interrupted by her tears and sobbing.

This godmother of hers, who was a fairy, said to her, "You wish that you could go to the ball; is it not so?"

"Yes," cried Cinderella, with a great sigh.

"Well," said her godmother, "be a good girl, and I will see that you shall go. Now run into the garden and bring me a pumpkin."

Cinderella went immediately to gather the finest she could get. Her godmother scooped out all the inside of it, leaving nothing but the rind. Then she struck the pumpkin with her wand, and it was instantly turned into a fine gold coach.

She then went to look into a mousetrap where she found six mice and ordered Cinderella to lift up the trapdoor. She gave the mice a little tap with her wand, and with that, the mice were turned into fine horses of a beautiful mouse-colored dapple gray.

Being at a loss for a coachman, Cinderella said, "I will go and see if there is a rat in the rat trap that we can turn into a coachman."

"You are right," replied her godmother. "Go and look."

Cinderella brought the trap to her, and in it, there were three huge rats. The fairy chose the one which had the largest beard, touched him with her wand, and turned him into a jolly coachman.

After that, she said to her, "Go again into the garden, and you will find six lizards behind the watering pot. Bring them to me."

She had no sooner done so but her godmother turned them into six footmen who skipped up immediately behind the coach. The fairy then said to Cinderella, "Well, you see here a coach fit to take a princess to the ball. Are you not pleased with it?"

"Oh, yes," she cried, "but must I go in these rags?"

Her godmother then touched her with her wand, and, at the same instant, her clothes turned into cloth of gold and silver, all beset with jewels. This done, she gave her a pair of glass slippers, the prettiest in the whole world. Being thus decked out, she got up into her coach, but her godmother,

See What Not to Use for Your Coach on page 88

above all things, commanded her not to stay past midnight, telling her that if she stayed one moment longer, the coach would be a pumpkin again, her horses mice, her coachman a rat, her footmen lizards, and her clothes just as they were before.

She promised her godmother to leave the ball before midnight, and then she drove away, scarcely able to contain herself for joy. The king's son, who was told that a great princess, whom nobody knew, had arrived, ran out to receive her. He gave her his hand as she alighted from the coach and led her into the hall. There was immediately a profound silence. Everyone stopped dancing and the violins ceased to play, so entranced was everyone with the beauty of the unknown maiden.

The king himself, old as he was, could not help watching her and telling the queen softly that it was a long time since he had seen so lovely a creature.

The king's son led her to the most honorable seat and afterwards took her out to dance with him. She danced so very gracefully that they all more and more admired her.

She went and sat down by her sisters, showing them a thousand civilities and sharing the oranges and citrons which the prince had presented her with. In all this, they did not recognize her. While Cinderella was thus amusing her sisters, she heard the clock strike eleven and three-quarters, whereupon she immediately made a curtsy to the company and hurried away as fast as she could.

Arriving home, she ran to seek out her godmother, and, after having thanked her, she said she wished she might go to the ball the next day, as the king's son had invited her.

As she was eagerly telling her godmother everything that had happened at the ball, her two sisters knocked at the door, which Cinderella ran to and opened.

"You stayed such a long time!" she cried, rubbing her eyes and stretching as if she had been sleeping.

"If you had been at the ball," said one of her sisters, "you would not have been tired. The finest princess was there, the most beautiful that mortal eyes have ever seen. She showed us a thousand civilities and gave us oranges and citrons."

Cinderella asked them the name of that princess, but they told her they did not know it and that the king's son would give all the world to know who she was. At this, Cinderella, smiling, replied, "She must, then, be very beautiful indeed; how happy you have been! Oh, that I could see her."

The next day, the two sisters were at the ball, and so was Cinderella, but dressed even more magnificently than before. The king's son was always by her. All this was so far from being tiresome to her, and, indeed, she quite forgot what her godmother had told her. She thought that it was no later than eleven when she counted the clock striking twelve. She jumped up and fled, as nimble as a deer. The prince followed but could not overtake her. In her hurry, she left behind one of her glass slippers, which the prince picked up most carefully. She reached home, quite out of breath, wearing her old rags and having nothing left of all her finery but one of the little glass slippers, the mate to the one that she had dropped.

The guards at the palace gate were asked if they had not seen a princess go out. They replied that they had seen nobody leave but a young girl dressed only in rags.

When the two sisters returned from the ball, Cinderella asked them if they had been well entertained and if the fine lady had been there.

They told her yes, but that she hurried away immediately when it struck twelve and with so much haste that she dropped one of her little glass slippers, the prettiest in the world. The king's son picked it up. And just as he had done nothing but look at her all the time at the ball, when she left, he gazed only upon the slipper. Certainly he was very much in love with the beautiful person who owned the glass slipper.

What they said was very true, for a few days later, the king's son had it proclaimed, by sound of trumpet, that he would marry the girl whose foot this slipper would just fit. They began to try it on the princesses, then the duchesses and all the court, but in vain. It was brought to the two sisters, who did all they possibly could to force their foot into the slipper, but they did not succeed.

Cinderella, who saw all this and knew that it was her slipper, said to them, "Let me see if it will not fit me."

Her sisters burst out laughing and began to banter with her. The gentleman who was sent to try the slipper looked earnestly at Cinderella and said that it was only just that she should try as well, for he had orders to let everyone try.

He had Cinderella sit down, and, putting the slipper to her foot, he found that it fit her as if it had been made of wax. Her two sisters were greatly astonished but then even more so when Cinderella pulled out of her pocket the other slipper and put it on her other foot. Then in came her godmother and touched her wand to Cinderella's clothes, making them richer and more magnificent than any of those she had worn before.

And now her two sisters found her to be that fine, beautiful lady whom they had seen at the ball. They threw themselves at her feet to beg pardon for treating her so badly. Cinderella took them up and, as she embraced them, said that she forgave them with all her heart and wanted them always to love her.

She was taken to the young prince. He thought she was more charming than ever and, a few days after, married her. Cinderella, who was no less good than beautiful, gave her two sisters a home in the palace and, that very same day, matched them with two great lords of the court. ♣

♛ INNER BEAUTY CHALLENGE

- Think of someone you love to be with. Find a friend or parent to talk about this person's characteristics with. Is this person older, younger, kind, grouchy, or friendly? Do you think this person has inner beauty? Why do you like to be with him or her?

- Design your own ball gown, but instead of decorating with laces and sparkles, decorate with characteristics you want to have. Use colored pens and pencils to write words about the kind of princess and person you want to be. You could even write a story on the gown.

- Forgiveness is an important part of inner beauty. Think about someone you may be frustrated with or who hurt your feelings. Make up your mind to forgive. If you can, make something nice for that person, like a note or a cookie, or just give them a hug. You will feel wonderful!

- Pick one part of inner beauty and make a goal to practice it every day. Write down your goal and tape it on your mirror or beside your bed. You can add smiley faces on days you really do well.

y Princess Goals

 eady to become a True Princess? Setting goals can help you. First, choose one of the characteristics in this chapter you'd like to improve (it's best to work on one thing at a time). Write that in the space for "Characteristic." Then write down one thing you're going to do differently to be more like that kind of princess. You might start by doing one of the Princess Challenges, or maybe you can think of a way you'll act differently at school or at home. Keep track of each of the things you're doing, how you feel, and watch as you become a True Princess!

Characteristic: _____

What I'm going to do: _____

How I felt: _____

_____

Characteristic: _____

What I'm going to do: _____

How I felt: _____

_____

Characteristic: _____

What I'm going to do: _____

How I felt: _____

_____

Characteristic: _____

What I'm going to do: _____

How I felt: _____

_____

Characteristic: _____

What I'm going to do: _____

How I felt: _____

_____

Characteristic: _____

What I'm going to do: _____

How I felt: _____

_____

All princesses need a break from the pressures of palace life now and then. These games are the perfect way to unwind and spend time with your subjects or with other princesses. And remember: princesses NEVER cheat!

SECTION FIVE

Activities & Games

Forget the royal tailor and design your own beautiful ball gown.

PREPARATION

Photocopy the dolls and dresses onto stiff paper (like cardstock). Cut out the pieces, color and decorate the dresses, and let the royal fashion show begin!

DECORATION MATERIAL IDEAS

- Markers
- Colored Pencils
- Glitter
- Sequins

- Rhinestones
- Glitter Gel Pens
- Puff Paint
- Metallic Marker

- Fabric or Old Wallpaper
- Dried Flowers
- Lace
- Ribbon

our Highness, May I?

Never underestimate how far royal manners can take you.

PREPARATION

Choose one princess to be "Your Highness." Mark off a play field approximately 20 feet long. "Your Highness" stands at one end, and the other princesses stand at the other.

HOW TO PLAY

1 Princesses stand in a row at one end of the play field and take turns asking for permission to move toward "Your Highness" in creative ways.

2 Each princess begins by calling out, "Your Highness, may I . . . ?" and fills in the blank with the number of steps she'd like to take. Princesses should be creative as they ask to move toward "Your Highness." For example, a princess might ask, "Your Highness, may I take three Ball Gown Twirls?" and then proceed to twirl three times, with dress in hand, toward "Your Highness." (See Examples for more ideas for creative movements.)

3 "Your Highness" responds to each request in one of two ways:

   1) "Yes, you may."

   2) "No, you may not. But you may take . . ." (She then inserts the number/type of steps that the princess may take.)

4 The first princess to touch "Your Highness's" hand and curtsy wins!

EXAMPLES

- Ball Gown Twirls
- Glass Slipper Skips
- Fencing Lunges
- Bunny Hops

- Giant Steps
- Dainty Steps
- Fairy Flutters
- Royal Somersaults

Don't Eat the Poison Apple!

Beware: not all apples (or old hags, for that matter) are as innocent as they appear.

PREPARATION

For this game, fill a tub or basin with at least 6 inches of water. Float a red apple in the water for each princess in the game plus at least one green "poison" apple.

HOW TO PLAY

1   Have the princesses form a single-file line in front of the basin. Blindfold each princess for her turn and ask her to pull one apple from the basin. If she draws a red apple without touching the green one, she is safe. If she picks or touches the "poison" apple, she must move to the side, lie down, and pretend to sleep. She is "out."

2   Return all the apples to the basin and repeat the process, again blindfolding the princesses who picked the red apples in the first round. Princesses continue to draw apples from the basin until all but one has drawn a "poison" apple. The last princess still "awake" wins.

Who's Got the Pea?

Can a delicate princess sense the location of the pea?

PREPARATION

Use a pea or other small object (like a button, pearl, or ring) as a game piece. Choose one princess to be "It." Have all the other princesses form a circle around her, facing inward.

HOW TO PLAY

1   All the princesses in the circle put their hands behind their backs. The princess who is "It" hands the pea to one of the other princesses in the circle and then closes her eyes. The princesses in the circle begin to pass the pea around behind their backs while chanting, "One, two, three; who's got the pea?" three times.

2   After the chant, the princess who is "It" can open her eyes. She must guess which princess now has the pea behind her back. Once she guesses correctly, the princess who had the pea is "It" and the chanting and passing begins again.

reak the Spell

*A wicked sorcerer's spell has made the princesses
fall into a deep sleep. Can you break the spell?*

PREPARATION

Clear a space where all the princesses in the game can lie down comfortably. Choose one
princess to be "It." Have all the princesses lie down on their backs and pretend to sleep.

HOW TO PLAY

1   The princess who is "It" must try to break the spell and awaken the sleeping princesses,
    but she cannot touch them. The only way to break the spell is to make the other
    princesses laugh. The princess who is "It" can tell jokes or stories or make funny noises
    to try to get the other princesses to giggle. When a princess laughs, she stands and joins
    the first princess, and they work together to break the spell for the others. Play continues
    until only one princess remains under the spell. The last princess left "asleep" wins. She is
    "It" in the next round of the game.

rincess, Princess, Queen

By the power vested in me, I crown thee Queen of the game!

PREPARATION

Clear a space for all the princesses to sit in a circle with room to run around
the edges. Choose one princess to be "It" and hold the royal scepter.

HOW TO PLAY

1   With all the princesses sitting in a circle, the princess who is "It" goes
    around the circle, tapping each princess lightly on the shoulder with
    the scepter and dubbing her either "Princess" or "Queen." If she says
    "Princess," the princess stays seated. If she says "Queen," the newly
    crowned queen must jump up and try to catch the princess who is "It"
    before she can run around the circle and take her spot on the floor. If
    the princess who is "It" gets caught, she is sent to the "dungeon" (or
    the middle of the circle). Either way, the queen is now "It" and takes the
    scepter around the circle to crown a new queen.

> **CAUTION:**
>
> Be sure that the object
> used as a scepter is not
> sharp on either end, as
> the princesses will be
> running with it. A trimmed
> pool noodle or other soft
> object would be best.
> For younger princesses,
> it might be advisable
> to use their hands (and
> imaginations) rather than
> using a scepter.

Blind Man's Bluff

This classic game has always been a royal favorite!

PREPARATION

Mark out a playing field that is large and free of obstacles. Choose one princess to be "It." Secure a blindfold over her eyes and make sure she can't see.

HOW TO PLAY

1   Once the princess who is "It" is blindfolded, ask her to count to 20. As she counts, have the other princesses spread out and stand somewhere in the playing field. Once the countdown ends, the other princesses cannot move. The blindfolded princess then walks about trying to find the others. When she tags a princess, she must try to guess who she has caught. If she guesses wrong, she must continue to search for other princesses and the unidentified princess can move to a new spot. If she guesses correctly, the princess she tagged is now "It."

Her Majesty Commands

All princesses must practice giving—and obeying—royal commands.

PREPARATION

Choose one princess to be "Her Majesty" and have her sit on a specially decorated "throne."

HOW TO PLAY

1   "Her Majesty" asks the other princesses to perform certain tasks. She begins these royal decrees by saying, in her most regal voice, "Her Majesty commands you to . . ." and then proceeds to make a specific request (e.g., "spin around" or "touch your toes" or "clap your hands"). If she issues a command without saying "Her Majesty commands" first, the other princesses should NOT obey; instead, they should freeze. Any princess who follows that command is out. The last princess still following commands wins and is now "Her Majesty."

Kiss the Frog

The prince has been turned into a frog, and only a kiss from a princess can break the spell!

PREPARATION

Copy and enlarge the image of the frog prince to the right. (You may wish to laminate it.) Hang the frog picture on a wall at a comfortable height for the princesses playing the game. Also make several copies of the lips and cut them out. Be sure there are enough for each princess to have her own pair of lips. Place double-sided tape or mounting putty on the back of each pair of lips.

HOW TO PLAY

1   Have the princesses form a single-file line facing the frog. Blindfold each princess on her turn, spin her around three times, and ask her to stick the lips to the frog. The princess who "plants a kiss" closest to the frog's mouth wins.

 Fairy Godmother Tip: For younger princesses, you may choose to point them in the right direction or forego the spinning altogether. Goodness knows I don't like it, and I'm a fairy!

Princess Tales

The best stories begin with "Once upon a time . . ."

PREPARATION

Have the princesses sit in a circle. Have a timer or a watch with a second hand ready to keep track of time. Ask the princesses to come up with three items that they want to include in the story. These items can be enchanted (see below) or commonplace—anything from a wooden spoon to a unicorn.

HOW TO PLAY

1 Ask one princess to begin telling a story: "Once upon a time . . ." The story can be about anything, but it must, at some point, include all three items. Use a timer to make sure that the first princess is telling the story for only 20 seconds. When 20 seconds are up, the next princess must begin the story from where the first princess left off—even midsentence. Repeat until all the princesses have had a chance to tell part of the story AND all three items have been mentioned. When the tale begins to wrap up, be sure the last princess ends with "And they lived happily ever after. The end."

MADAME LINGUA'S ROYAL LEXICON

enchanted objects
[*in-ˈchant-ed* \ ˈäb-jĭkts]

Everyday objects with a life of their own are standard fare for a princess. From mirrors to teacups to cakes that bake themselves, there's no telling what inanimate objects you may encounter. When dealing with enchanted objects, it is wise to question the origin of the enchantment before making contact.

Frozen at the Ball

Don't be caught dancing without music—awkward!

PREPARATION

If the ballroom is occupied, clear a space for the princesses to twirl in safety. Prepare music that can easily be stopped and started again, and be sure the music is loud enough for all the princesses to hear.

HOW TO PLAY

1   Ask the princesses to practice their best dance moves for the ball while the music is playing. When the music stops, all princesses must freeze. If a princess moves after the music stops, she is "out" and must move to the side. The last princess standing on the dance floor wins.

VARIATION

Ask the princesses to dance with a partner. If a pair is caught moving after the music stops, they can perform a trick (like a dip, twirl, or choreographed move) and continue playing.

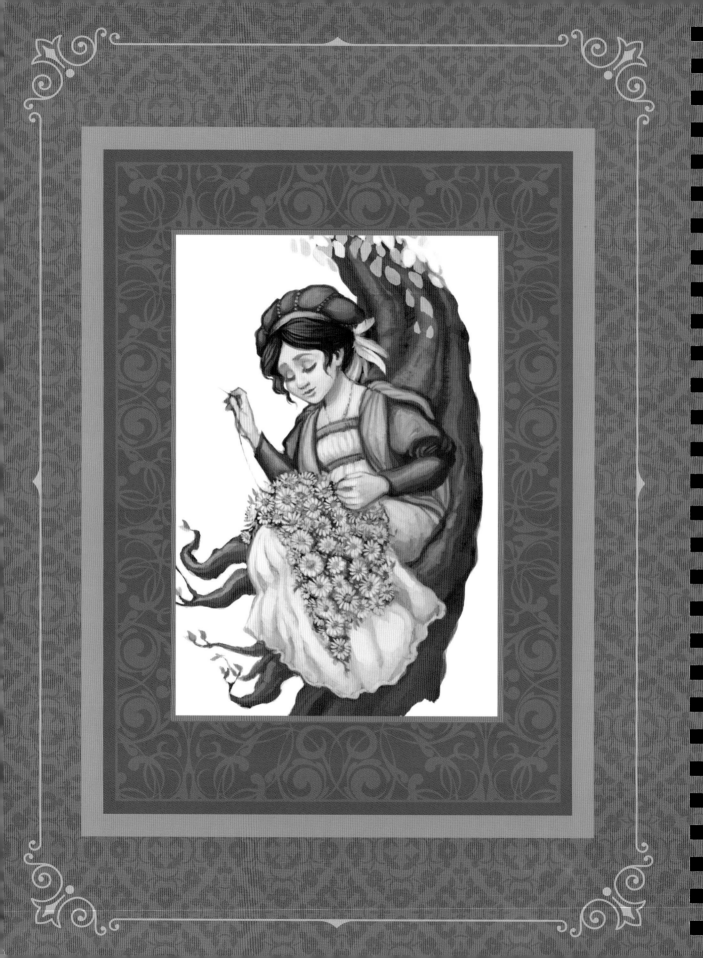

SECTION SIX

Things to Make

ake Your Own Tiara

BEADED TIARA

3 pink pipe cleaners

Assorted beads in assorted sizes (approximately 70 beads per tiara)

1 headband

1 bottle tacky glue

Assorted larger jewels for decorating

1. Thread beads onto each of the pipe cleaners, leaving about 2 inches of exposed pipe cleaner at each end. Bend each beaded pipe cleaner into an arched shape.

2. Position one of the beaded arches so it sticks up from the middle of the headband. Wrap each end of the exposed pipe cleaner around the headband and twist in place. Apply a small amount of glue to secure the pipe cleaner to the headband.

3. Wrap the other two pipe cleaners around the headband on either side of the central arch. Secure with glue.

4. To hide the pipe cleaners in the front of the tiara and to enhance the overall appearance, secure the larger jewels to the front of the headband with glue.

 Fairy Godmother Tip: Tacky glue may be found in all craft stores and is kid safe to use. It dries quickly, dries clear, and adheres wonderfully to all fabrics and textures. It's just like magic—almost.

1 headband

Ribbon (silver or iridescent)

Hot glue gun and glue sticks

Pipe cleaners (silver or iridescent)

Decorations (gemstones, sequins, fake pearls, etc.)

CRYSTAL TIARA

1. Glue the end of the ribbon to one end of the headband. Wrap the ribbon one time around the headband and glue in place again. Continue wrapping and gluing until the headband is completely covered in ribbon.

2. Bend a pipe cleaner into an arched shape. There are many different shapes you could try—consider choosing one from the gallery to the left.

3. Glue each end of the bent pipe cleaner to the inside of the headband so that the pipe cleaner is curved and centered on the headband.

4. Cut a pipe cleaner in half and bend each piece into an arch.

5. Glue one arch on one side of the center pipe cleaner. Position it so that the edge of the central arch runs down the middle of the new arch. Then glue the other arch on the other side so the tiara is symmetrical. Add a bit of glue where any of the arches overlap each other so that everything is held together securely.

6. You now have the frame of a basic tiara. Continuing adding arches of different heights and sizes. You might put some in the middle, or you might put pairs of arches on either side. To make an intricate-looking tiara, add several pairs of overlapping arches until you're satisfied with the look. Be sure to glue everything securely together!

7. Decorate your tiara by gluing gemstones, sequins, and fake pearls.

Possible Arch Shapes

BEADED TIARA

CRYSTAL TIARA

Jubilee Headbands

Silk flowers in various sizes and colors

1 bottle tacky glue

1 1/2- to 2-inch knit headband

Scissors

1 Carefully remove the silk flowers from their stems. You can usually pluck them off the stem, but you might have to use scissors.

2 Remove the leaves from the stems and set them aside for later use.

3 Lay the headband flat. Position various flowers on the headband until you reach an arrangement you like.

4 Carefully glue each flower in place.

5 Glue various leaves around the flowers to fill in the gaps so none of the headband can be seen.

6 Allow to dry one hour. Before wearing, use scissors to trim any glue or stems that might be poking through the inside of the headband.

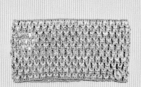

rystal Power Necklaces

1 1/2 yards pastel satin ribbon, 1/4 inch wide

3 different strands of pastel rock candy on strings

Fairy Godmother Tip: Rock candy strings may be found at traditional candy stores and online candy specialty stores. Get an extra one for your FGM, there's a good dear.

1 Cut the satin ribbon to the correct length to hang on a child's neck and create a large bow when tied.

2 Cut one color of rock candy into an approximate 3-inch-length strand. Cut the other 2 colors of rock candy strands into approximately 1 1/2- to 2-inch lengths.

3 Tie and double-knot the longest strand of rock candy in the center of the satin ribbon necklace by securing it with a small length of the remaining satin ribbon. Add the shorter strands of rock candy on either side of the longer strand, attaching them with the remaining pieces of satin ribbon and making sure to tie and double-knot each securely. Cut off excess ribbon.

4 Place the necklace loosely around the child's neck and tie together the two ends of satin ribbon to form a decorative bow at the nape of the neck. This adorable necklace won't last long with that sweet candy hanging from it!

parkling Scented Lotion

1/2 cup lotion or body cream

1/2 cup aloe vera gel

1 tablespoon colored craft glitter

4-5 drops fruit- or flower-scented fragrant oils, or a combination of both

1 Combine all ingredients in a small mixing bowl with a whisk.

2 Place in a clean jar with a lid and store up to two weeks.

3 To use, smooth onto arms and legs.

agic Bubble Wand

BUBBLES

1 cup water

3 tablespoons liquid dishwashing detergent

1 tablespoon glycerin

1/2 teaspoon sugar

WAND

Floral wire

Pliers to cut

Ribbon

Charms

TO MAKE THE BUBBLES:

1 Mix all ingredients together in a container with a lid. Small, wide-mouth mason jars work well.

2 Shake well and let set overnight before using.

 Fairy Godmother Tip: **If bubbles tend to be too heavy to float, add approximately 1 teaspoon more dishwashing liquid.**

TO MAKE THE WAND:

1 Cut a piece of wire approximately 14 inches long.

2 Carefully bend one end into a bubble wand shape about three inches wide. You might make it a star, or a heart, or a simple circle.

3 Trim the extra wire off, leaving about 4-5 inches for a handle.

4 Twist the handle inwards so it's round instead of sharp. Add ribbon and charms to decorate.

Possible Wand Shapes

HEART   STAR

CIRCLE   DIAMOND

nvitations to a Royal Ball

This craft uses a lot of specialty materials, but all of it can be found at your local craft store or online. The final results are beautiful and elegant!

Heavy cream paper (use vellum or a parchment type of paper for extra effect)

Heavy gold paper

Sequins (optional)

Ribbon

Tape

Sealing wax (your favorite color)

Monogram stamp in your initial(s)

Fairy Godmother Tip:
There are different types of sealing wax available, and they are each used a little differently. Some varieties include a wick that can be lit to melt and apply the wax without any other tools. Other varieties can be placed directly in a hot glue gun (this is the easiest way!). Be sure to read the manufacturer's directions.

1 Visit www.familius.com/the-everything-princess-book and download the invitation template. Print the template on a piece of cream, vellum, or parchment paper. Be sure to print off as many invitations as you'll need for your ball.

2 Cut out the invitations. They should measure about 5.75 inches by 5.75 inches when trimmed. Set aside.

3 Trim each piece of gold paper into a 8.5-inch-by-8.5-inch square.

4 Place each gold square gold-side down. For each square, carefully fold each corner up so all four corners meet together in the middle. Crease the edges down. Each gold square should now measure about 6 inches by 6 inches.

5 Unfold a gold square. In the middle, place one of the square invitations face up. Sprinkle the invitation with sequins (optional), and fold the gold corners back up so everything is packaged up.

6 Place a tiny piece of tape across where the four corners meet to hold everything shut. This will make it easy to tie the ribbon and apply the seal later on.

7 Cut a piece of ribbon about 12 inches long. Wrap the ribbon around the center of the back of the gold packet so that the ends of the ribbon meet up again on top of the four corners. Use a tiny piece of tape to attach the ribbon ends together.

8 Ask the king or queen to help make the wax seal. Follow the sealing wax manufacturer's directions to melt and drip a small pool of wax (about 1 inch wide) onto the center of the packet, right where the ribbon crosses over the four corners. You might need to gently spread the wax into a circle shape.

9 Wait a few seconds to allow the wax to slightly set up. Then gently press your monogram stamp into the center of the wax, wait 10 seconds, and carefully remove to reveal your initials. Allow wax to cool and harden completely.

10 Hire the fastest courier in the land to send out your glamorous invitations!

NIGHT TIME

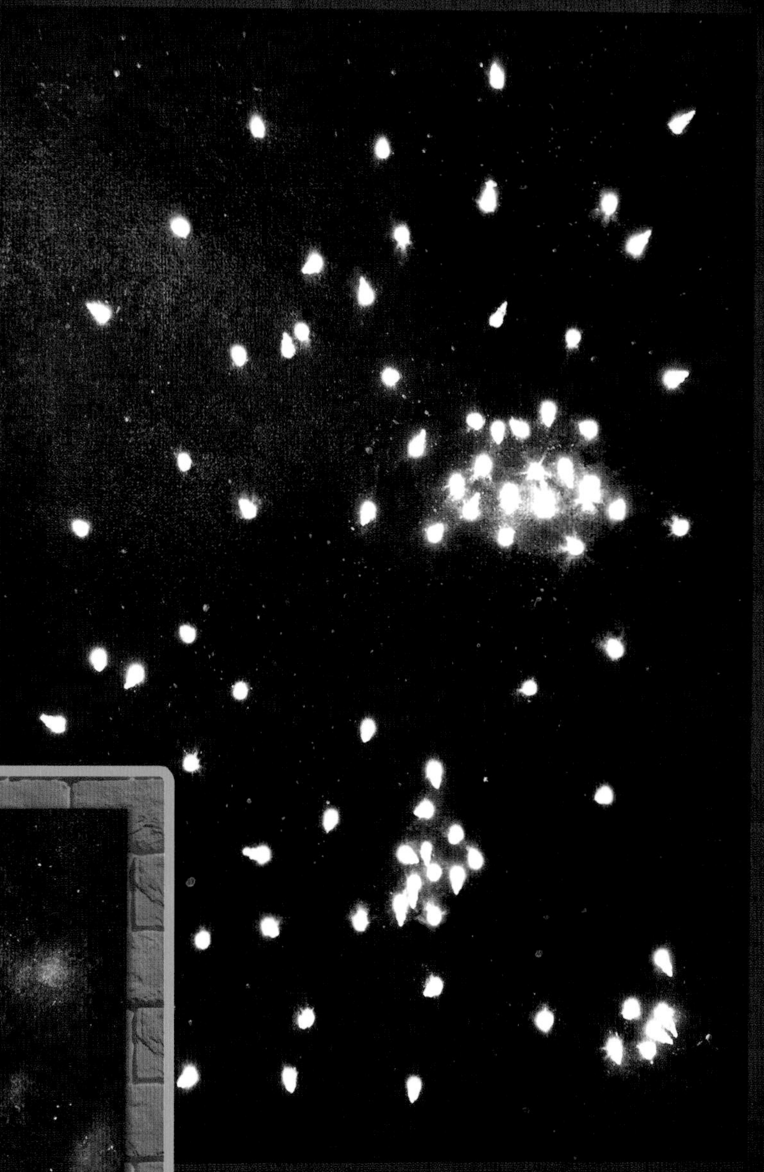

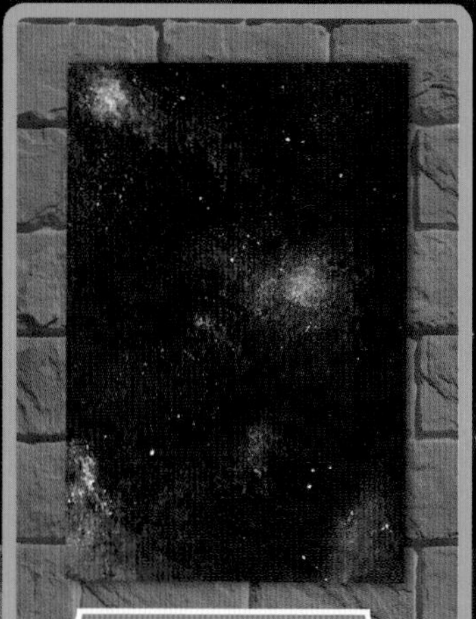

DAYTIME

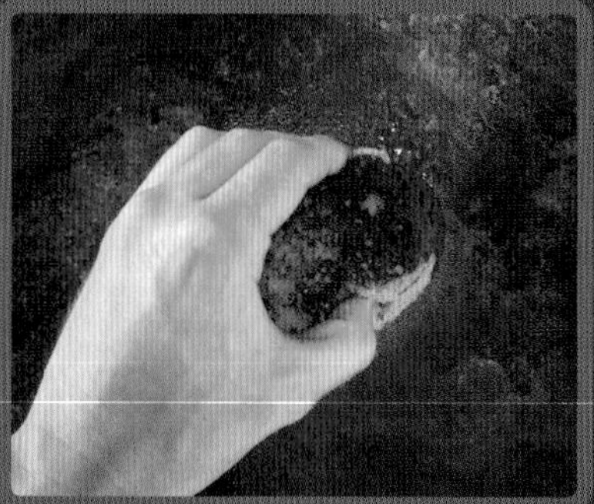

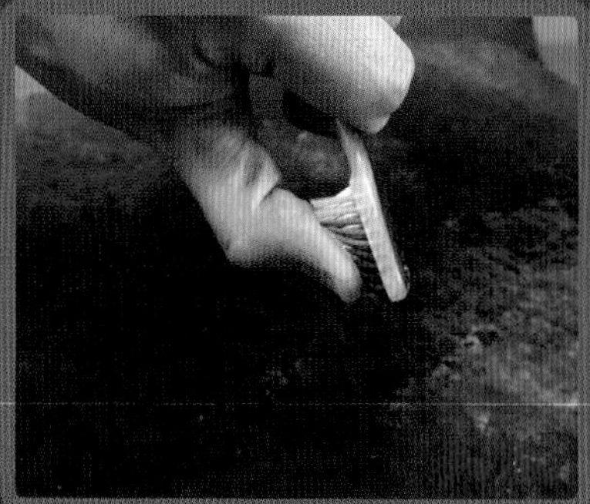

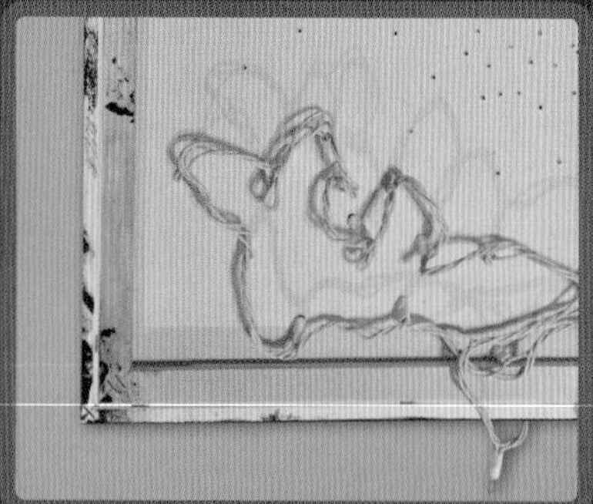

tarbright Nightlight

Turn a piece of artist's canvas into a shimmering nightscape nighlight.

18-inch-by-24-inch stretched canvas (be sure it's the kind that's stapled to a wood frame and not glued to cardboard)

Acrylic paint in black, purple, blue, and silver

Roller or large paintbrush

Paper plates

Sea sponge

Old toothbrush

Pencil

Awl or large nail

Strand of Christmas lights (100-count)

1. Paint the canvas (including the edges) black. You can use a large paintbrush; a small roller works great, too.

2. Put a pool of purple, blue, and black paint on a paper plate. Dip part of the sponge into one color of paint, then dip an adjacent part of the sponge into another color of paint. Gently tap the the sponge onto the canvas and watch as the colors mix and create beautiful night patterns.

3. Continue adding paint to the sponge and tapping out patterns onto the canvas. Alternate the colors you use and allow the paint to mix as you work.

4. When you're satisfied with the pattern you've created (you don't need to cover the whole canvas if you don't want to), allow to dry.

5. Put a small amount of silver paint on a paper plate. Dip the bristles of the toothbrush into the paint. Place your thumb on the bristles of the toothbrush, press down, and carefully hold the toothbrush over the canvas. Slowly slide your thumb off the bristles to allow the paint to flick off onto the canvas, creating tiny star specks. It's best to practice this effect a few times on a piece of paper before you do it on the canvas.

6. Speckle the entire canvas with silver stars. Allow to dry.

7. Turn the canvas over and mark a starry sky pattern on the back with a pencil. Count the dots to be sure there are 100 for each of the Christmas lights.

8. Use an awl or large nail to punch a hole where each dot is. Make each hole slightly smaller than the width of one of the lights.

9. Starting with the light farthest from the plug, press one bulb into the hole nearest the top of the canvas. The light should poke into the front of the canvas.

10. Add a bulb to each hole, working down from the top of the canvas towards the bottom. Once each hole has been filled, allow the cord and plug to extend past the bottom of the canvas.

11. Set your night sky on your dresser, plug it in, and enjoy your magical stars! Don't forget to make a wish.

rincess Silhouette

A side-profile photo of you (Note: the photo will be cut, so you might want to make a photocopy of it to use if you don't want the original to be ruined. You could also take a picture with a digital camera and print it out.)

Craft knife or scissors

Black paper

Pencil

Light-colored paper

Small picture frame

Glue

1. Using a craft knife or scissors, carefully cut the princess out of the photo (ask the king or queen for help).

2. Place the photo cutout on a piece of black paper and trace using a pencil.

3. Remove the photo piece and cut out the black silhouette.

4. Trim the light-colored paper so it fits your picture frame.

5. Carefully glue the black silhouette onto the center of the light-colored paper. If some of the pencil lines are showing on the black paper, you might want to glue that side down so they can't be seen.

6. Frame your silhouette and display proudly in your bedchamber.

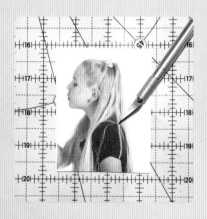

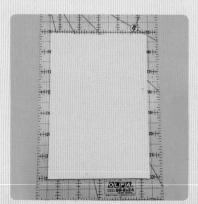
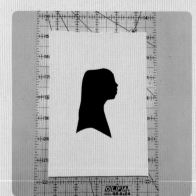

airytale Flip-Flops

1 pair of flip-flops

1/4 yard pink terry cloth fabric

1 bottle tacky glue

Assorted silk flowers, decorative buttons, bows, or scrapbook materials

FUZZY FLIP-FLOPS

1. Carefully disassemble each flip-flop by taking the toe portion completely out of the shoe. Lay each flip-flop on top of the terry cloth fabric and trace the outline of each shoe.

2. Cut out the 2 traced pieces of fabric. Place each piece on a flip-flop and mark where the holes for each toe portion will be. Cut a hole on each flip flop-shaped piece of fabric with a hole punch or snip a small hole with a pair of scissors.

3. Glue the foot portion of the fabric on each flip-flop with tacky glue. Let sit for 10 minutes to dry. Carefully slip the toe portion back in the hole of each flip-flop.

4. With the remaining fabric folded in half, cut a long strip lengthwise into a 1/2-inch width. Glue one end of the cut fabric to the toe portion of the strap and begin to wrap it around to completely cover one strap. Cut fabric and secure to flip-flop with glue. Cover the other strap of the flip-flop with fabric and cut and secure in the same way. Repeat for the second flip-flop.

5. Attach a decorative bauble, flower, or bow to the top center of each flip-flop strap and glue to secure. Allow to dry one hour prior to wearing.

1 1/2 yards of 1/4- to 1/2-inch-width grosgrain ribbon, solid, striped, or patterned

1 pair of flip-flops

1 bottle tacky glue

Purchased curly ribbon gift bows, 1 1/2-2 inches in diameter

2 buttons, rhinestones, or beads

 Fairy Godmother Tip: Craft and fabric stores provide a multitude of options for decorating flip-flops. Yarn, tulle, or satin ribbon may be substituted for grosgrain ribbon.

RIBBON FLIP-FLOPS

1. Cut a piece of grosgrain ribbon about 30 inches in length. Carefully glue the ribbon around the edge of one of the flip-flops. Trim the leftover ribbon and glue the edge in place. Repeat for the other flip-flop.

2. Cut a piece of grosgrain ribbon about 24 inches in lenth. Then cut the ribbon in half lengthwise so you have two long, skinny strips. Using one piece of ribbon for each flip-flop strap, wrap each side with grosgrain ribbon, cut to fit, and secure both ends with tacky glue.

3. Tie the curly ribbon bow onto the center top section of the flip-flop where the two straps join and secure with tacky glue. Additionally, decorate the center of the bow with a colorful button, rhinestone, or large, sparkly bead.

4. Repeat the same procedure on the other flip-flop. Allow to dry one hour prior to wearing.

FUZZY FLIP-FLOPS

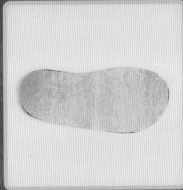

RIBBON FLIP-FLOPS

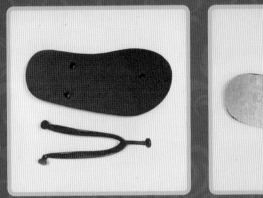
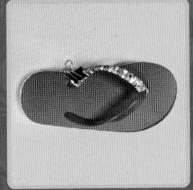

ewelry Box

Keep your valuables tucked away in this beautiful, bejeweled keepsake box.

Wooden keepsake box (available at any craft store)

Purple and pink acrylic paint (you can use different colors if you wish)

Metallic gold puff paint

Small golden letters (you can usually find stick-on kinds in the scrapbook section of your craft store)

Decorations (gems, glitter paint, metal embellishments, etc.)

Tacky glue

1 Paint the box purple and pink.

2 Glue the gold letters onto the top of the box. You might want to frame them in a metal embellishment.

3 Use the gold puff paint to decorate your box with gold swirls, lines, and dots. This will look like beautiful gold carvings.

4 Decorate the box with gems and glitter paint.

5 Allow to dry completely before hiding your princess treasures.

rincess Crowns

1 1/2-inch plastic headband

1 bottle tacky glue

1 roll each pink, blue, and sparkly blue tulle ribbon, 3 to 4 inches wide (or other colors of your choice)

Satin ribbon

1 Cut assorted colors of tulle into approximately 6- to 7-inch lengths.

2 Tie each piece in the middle in a double knot from one end of the headband to the other.

3 Trim each tied tulle knot to about 3 inches in length. Fluff out tulle bows.

4 In the center of the headband, tie an 18-inch length of tulle in a double knot to form a veil or ponytail. Tie on some 18-inch pieces of ribbon.

 Fairy Godmother Tip: Tulle by the roll is the suggested material choice, but tulle may also be purchased by the yard and cut into the appropriate width needed. 1/4–1/2 yard of each color of tulle will be ample to make 1 headband.

About the Creators

BARBARA BEERY

Barbara Beery, the bestselling author of *The Pink Princess Cookbook*, has appeared twice on the *Today Show* and the CBN with Pat Robertson. Beery's cooking school business has been featured in the *New York Times* and *Entrepreneur Magazine*, as well as dozens of other local and national publications. She has worked closely with Get Moving, Cookies for Kids' Cancer, Rachael Ray's Yum-o! Organization, and No Kids Hungry. She is the author of twelve books, which have sold more than 500,000 copies. She resides in Austin, Texas.

BROOKE JORDEN

Brooke earned a BA in English and editing from Brigham Young University. The author of *If It Fits, I Sits: The Ultimate Cat Quotebook* and coauthor of *The Ultimate Guide to Being a Superhero*, Brooke is also the managing editor at Familius. She and her husband live in Singapore with their daughter and cat.

MICHELE ROBBINS

Michele Lynne Robbins, the Mater Familius and Acquisitions Editor, has been the CEO of the Robbins Roost for twenty-two years, where she has homeschooled each of her nine children. When she is not running her domestic enterprise, she is found developing important book content, creating unique gifts, and loving the joys of family life and motherhood. She holds a BA in special education from Brigham Young University.

DAVID MILES

David Miles makes books for a living. He also reads books, writes books, sells books, shelves books, thinks about books, drives to books, sleeps to books, and cooks from books, but he doesn't eat books (which is fortunate). He has authored or illustrated ten books for children including *Book* and the *Let's Count* series. David graduated from Brigham Young University with a BS in, well, business management. He currently lives in California, where he enjoys trips to Yosemite and the central coast.

REBECCA SORGE

Rebecca Sorge loves telling stories and drawing pictures, so becoming an illustrator made perfect sense. She currently lives and works in Utah, creating art for children's books, magazines, posters, cards, and anything else people will let her draw on.

About Familius

Welcome to a place where moms and dads are celebrated, not compared. Where heart is at the center of our families, and family at the center of our homes. Where boo-boos are still kissed, cake beaters are still licked, and mistakes are still okay. Welcome to a place where books—and family—are beautiful. Familius: a book publisher dedicated to helping families be happy.

VISIT OUR WEBSITE: WWW.FAMILIUS.COM

Our website is a different kind of place. Get inspired, read articles, discover books, watch videos, connect with our family experts, download books and apps and audiobooks, and along the way, discover how values and happy family life go together.

JOIN OUR FAMILY

There are lots of ways to connect with us! Subscribe to our newsletters at www.familius.com to receive uplifting inspiration, a free ebook every month, and the first word on special discounts and Familius news.

GET BULK DISCOUNTS

If you feel a few friends and family might benefit from what you've read, let us know and we'll be happy to provide you with quantity discounts. Simply email us at orders@familius.com.

Website: www.familius.com
Facebook: www.facebook.com/paterfamilius
Twitter: @familiustalk, @paterfamiliusı
Pinterest: www.pinterest.com/familius

The greatest work you ever do will be within the walls of your own home.

LARGE PRINT

CRIME SCENE

PUZZLES

Let's get social!

 @Publications_International

 @PublicationsInternational

 @BrainGames.TM

www.pilbooks.com

INTRODUCTION

If you've marveled at the sharp minds, dogged investigative skills, and scientific advances that allow people to solve crimes, now it's your turn! In *Brain Games®: Large Print Crime Scene Puzzles*, you'll find an assortment of puzzles that will test your skills. Crime-scene themed puzzles will let you combine your love of puzzles with your love of crime stories. Plus we've included crime quizzes to test your investigative knowledge, memory puzzles to sharpen your visual memory, logic puzzles to enhance your reasoning skills, and more. If you're stuck, just turn to the answer key at the back for a hint.

"Seen at the Scene" puzzles ask you to spot small details of crime scenes, while "Overheard Information" puzzles test your memory. "Crack the Password" puzzles ask you to unscramble the criminal's passwords, while "Interception" puzzles push you to decode an intercepted message. With "Find the Witness" and "Motel Hideout" puzzles, you'll have to use your logical skills. Throughout the book, you'll solve puzzles themed around art thefts, bank robbery, and murder. You'll solve some puzzles with bursts of inspiration, while others will require hard work as you track down a chain of logic.

Are you ready to test alibis, solve crimes, and track down criminals? Just open the book to any page and start solving!

DETECTIVES

Complete the word search below to reveal a hidden message related to the puzzle's topic. Every word listed below is contained within the group of letters. Words can be found in a straight line horizontally, vertically, or diagonally. They may read either forward or backward. Once you find all the words, you can read the hidden message from the remaining letters, top to bottom, left to right.

BANACEK

BARETTA

BARNABY (Jones)

CANNON

DICK TRACY

FRIDAY (Sgt.)

HAMMER (Mike)

HARDY BOYS

HERCULE POIROT

JIM ROCKFORD

McGEE (Travis)

MILLER (Barney)

NANCY DREW

QUEEN (Ellery)

QUINCY

SPADE (Sam)

THE HARTS

THE SAINT

Leftover letters spell 2 of the most famous names in detective fiction, and the author who created them (6 words).

SHERLOCK HOLMES

DOCTOR WATSON   DOYLE

```
    S H E
    S T R A H E H T
  R L O B C E E D A P S
M I L L E R A F R I D A Y K
H B J I M R O C K F O R D
  A O L W E K U M T E N
  R E S E T B L S H E E
  N A N R T A E Y E G E
  D A D A D A N P O S C U O
  C B C H Y Q A O B A M Q T O
  Y R A C U C I Y I W
    M N I E R D N A
  T S M A N K O R T
  O N E N C O T A D
  R O Y Y N H L E
```

Answers on page 170.

PRIME SUSPECT

The police have drawn up a list of prime suspect descriptions for a recent bank robbery. However, due to a clerical error, although each item is in the correct column, only one entry in each column is correctly positioned. The following facts are true about the correct order.

1. Yellow is one row below medium and somewhere above mauve.
2. Thin is 2 rows above Spanish.
3. Hunched is 3 places below English.
4. White is somewhere above dark and 2 places above fat.
5. Italian is 2 places above purple.
6. Brown is one row below both yellow and African.
7. Cream is immediately below purple but 3 places below none.

Can you find the correct nationality, hair color, coat color, and build for each suspect?

	Nationality	Hair	Coat	Build
1	English	none	green	slim
2	Italian	white	yellow	thin
3	Spanish	red	mauve	fat
4	Mexican	gray	blue	round
5	African	brown	purple	medium
6	Chinese	dark	cream	hunched

6

Answers on page 170.

THE YELLOW-BRICK ROAD

The yellow-brick road splits into the blue- and red-brick roads, which lead respectively to the red city and the green city. In one of these cities, everyone tells the truth; in the other, everyone lies. You want to get to the city of truth. Two people are waiting at the fork in the road, one from each city. You can ask one person one question, and you ask this: "If I were to ask the other person which road leads to the city of truth, what would they tell me?" The person answers: "They would tell you to take the red road."

Which road should you take?

A. The red road.
B. The blue road.
C. It is impossible to say.

Answers on page 170.

IDENTITY PARADE

Oops! Four mugshots accidentally got sent through the shredder, and Officer Wallers is trying to straighten them out. Currently, only one facial feature in each row is in its correct place. Officer Wallers knows that:

1. C's nose is 1 place to the right of her mouth and 2 places to the right of D's hair.
2. C's eyes are 2 places to the left of her hair.
3. A's eyes are 1 place to the right of B's nose and 1 place to the right of D's mouth.

Can you find the correct hair, eyes, nose, and mouth for each person?

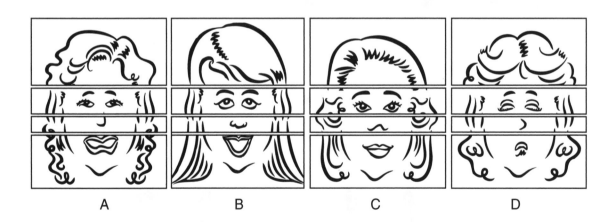

| A | B | C | D |

GAME BOARD PART I

Study this game board for one minute, particularly the shapes and their placement. After one minute, turn the page for a memory challenge.

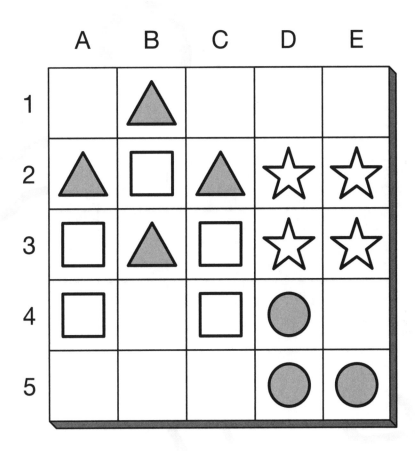

GAME BOARD PART 2

Do not read this until you've read the previous page!

Duplicate the board as seen on the previous page.

	A	B	C	D	E
1					
2					
3					
4					
5					

Answers on page 170.

CODE-DOKU

Solve this puzzle just as you would a sudoku. Use deductive logic to complete the grid so that each row, column, and 3 by 3 box contains the letters from the word POLICEMAN.

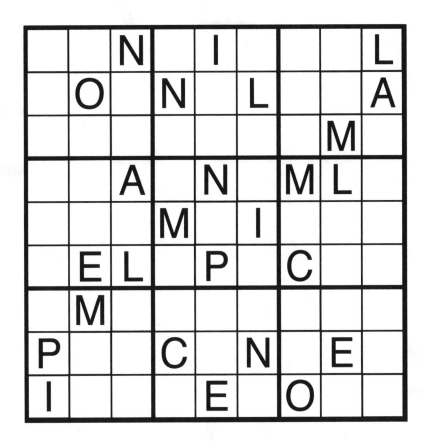

Answers on page 170.

MOTEL HIDEOUT

A thief hides out in one of the 45 motel rooms listed in the chart below. The motel's in-house detective received a sheet of four clues, signed "The Holiday Thief." Using these clues, the detective found the room number within 15 minutes—but by that time, the thief had fled. Can you find the thief's motel room quicker?

1. The number is not divisible by 4.
2. The first digit is as large or larger than the second digit.
3. The digits add up to 6.
4. The number is divisible by 6.

51	52	53	54	55	56	57	58	59
41	42	43	44	45	46	47	48	49
31	32	33	34	35	36	37	38	39
21	22	23	24	25	26	27	28	29
11	12	13	14	15	16	17	18	19

Answers on page 171.

BANK MAYHEM

A criminal mastermind who calls himself "Trixter" has hidden a stolen artifact in one of forty-five different safety deposit boxes at the local bank. Each box has a different number, and the miscreant has given the police a series of clues that will point to its hidden location. Using only these clues, find the one correct number—but be careful! Open the wrong box and the priceless artifact will be destroyed.

1. The first digit is either 1 or a prime number.
2. It is divisible by 7.
3. It is less than 60.
4. The sum of the digits is a multiple of 5.
5. The numbers multiplied together equals one of the digits.

82	84	86	88	90	92	94	96	98
64	66	68	70	72	74	76	78	80
46	48	50	52	54	56	58	60	62
28	30	32	34	36	38	40	42	44
10	12	14	16	18	20	22	24	26

13

Answers on page 171.

CRIMINALS

How many kinds of criminals can you find here? We count 8. To spell out a criminal, keep moving from one letter to the next in any direction—up, down, across, or diagonally. You may move in several different directions for each word. You can also use letters more than once—but not in the same word.

MOBBOO

TURERK

BLGGTC

RAGSIH

WINDEF

14

Answers on page 171.

HIGH FIVES

The High Fives school has made a list of its top 5 students and each student's subject of study and intended university. Unfortunately, someone has mixed up the details, and although each item is in the correct column, only one item in each column is correctly positioned. The following facts are true about the correct order:

1. Harvard is one place below Harris and one place above economics.
2. Physics is somewhere below Daisy.
3. Arnold is two places above Ink.
4. Philosophy is somewhere above Fate.
5. Yale is one place below physics and one place above Ellen.
6. Daisy is going to MIT.

Can you find the correct name, surname, subject, and university for each position?

	Name	Surname	Subject	University
1	Arnold	Fate	history	Princeton
2	Ben	Gopher	mathematics	Harvard
3	Cathy	Harris	physics	Yale
4	Daisy	Ink	economics	MIT
5	Ellen	Jelly	philosophy	Caltech

Answers on page 171.

EAVESDROPPING LOGIC

You overhear one woman accusing another of listening in on her private conversation with her boyfriend. You only hear a piece of the accused woman's response, which sounds like, "I'm sorry, nobody ould have heard you, but..."

Which of the following words would best fit in the place of "ould", assuming the woman was being genuinely apologetic?

A. "should"
B. "could"
C. "would"
D. All of the above would fit with this assumption

Answers on page 171.

FIND THE WITNESS

On Box Street, there are 5 adjacent houses that are identical to each other. You've been asked to visit Mr. Jones, but without any addresses on the doors you are not sure which house to approach. At the local coffee shop, you ask the waitress for help. She is able to provide the following information:

A. Mr. Jones has 2 neighbors.
B. The house in the middle is occupied by an elderly woman.
C. Mary lives between the elderly woman and a family of 3 children.
D. The 3 children live in House A.

Can you determine which is Mr. Jones's house?

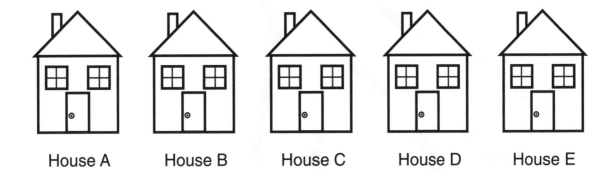

House A   House B   House C   House D   House E

Answers on page 171.

SHE'S A COP!

Find the answers in the grid in which police drama you would see the list of actresses. (Hint: this list is in alphabetical order of the TV show titles). Every word listed is contained within the group of letters. Words can be found in a straight line horizontally, vertically, or diagonally. They may be read either forward or backward.

Kathryn Morris as Lilly Rush

Marg Helgenberger as Catherine Willows

Mary McCormack as Mary Shannon

Mariska Hargitay as Olivia Benson

Vivica A. Fox as Nicole Scott

Angie Dickinson as Suzanne "Pepper" Anderson

Holly Hunter as Grace Hanadarko

Heather Locklear as Stacy Sheridan

Kyra Sedgwick as Brenda Leigh Johnson

Peggy Lipton as Julie Barnes

Poppy Montgomery as Samantha Spade

```
C T M D N R E L T O T I C E W
L S H P O L E J S D I O L I P
R A A G W M H S R C D A T W O
P C W T I O I S O A C H U I L
I O Q A O S V S U L O S E T I
S H L K N S N Q S U C C O S C
T H E I P D S I T I A E C O E
E R C I C D O A A R N G H U W
P S A P O E T R G L S G T T R
O E A M H R W G D P P W H M T
L H E C A O N O U E Q N E I H
I H W C D I L C M O R C I S O
T C E H V L T J H A N S A S U
I I I A I C O T E C N S V I S
A C S L N P L C W I T H O U W
```

19

Answers on page 172.

CHEMICAL REACTION

A certain chemical compound is formed by mixing 2 different chemicals. The first chemical is worth $90 per ounce; the second is worth $40 per ounce. The blend of chemicals is valued at $70 per ounce. How many ounces of the $90 chemical are needed to make 40 ounces of the blend?

A. 8
B. 16
C. 24
D. 30

Answers on page 172.

Study these illustrations for one minute then turn the page for a memory challenge.

Backache

Backboard

Backgammon

Backpack

Backflip

Backfire

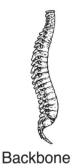

Backbone

BACK UP YOUR MEMORY PART 2

Do not read this until you've read the previous page!

How many of these did you see on the previous page?

BACKBOARD

BACK TEETH

BACKFIELD

BACKPACK

BACKSEAT

BACKSTITCH

BACKSTOP

BACK FLIP

BACKGAMMON

BACKGROUND

Answers on page 172.

FIND THE SUSPECT

The suspect was first seen at the top left corner of this maze. He visited each street corner exactly once, and ended back at the same corner on the map. Can you track his route?

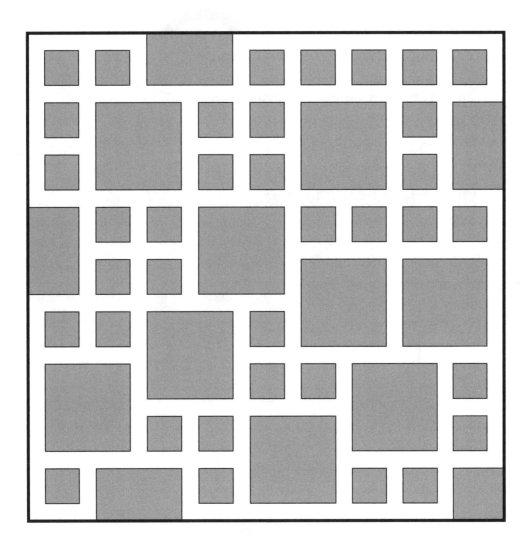

Answers on page 172.

BANK MAYHEM

A criminal mastermind who calls himself "Trixter" has hidden a stolen artifact in one of forty-five different safety deposit boxes at the local bank. Each box has a different number, and the miscreant has given the police a series of clues that will point to its hidden location. Using only these clues, find the one correct number—but be careful! Open the wrong box and the priceless artifact will be destroyed.

1. The sum of the digits is greater than 9.
2. The second digit is not prime.
3. It is greater than 60.
4. Both digits multiplied together equals the number immediately below it in the grid.

83	85	87	89	91	93	95	97	99
65	67	69	71	73	75	77	79	81
47	49	51	53	55	57	59	61	63
29	31	33	35	37	39	41	43	45
11	13	15	17	19	21	23	25	27

Answers on page 172.

EAVESDROPPING LOGIC

You overhear a boy and girl arguing. "I knew you knew all about it!" she shouts at him, "but you didn't know that I knew that, did you?" "Actually I did, I just didn't let on that I knew," he replies irritably. The girl is obviously shocked to hear this.

Presuming they are both expressing their honest opinions, which of the following is not true?

A. He didn't know that she knew that he knew that she knew all about it.
B. He knew that she knew that he knew all about it.
C. She didn't know that he knew that she knew that he knew all about it.
D. Two or more of the above.

Answers on page 172.

WORD TRIO

Fill in each empty box with a different letter so a trio of related words is formed.

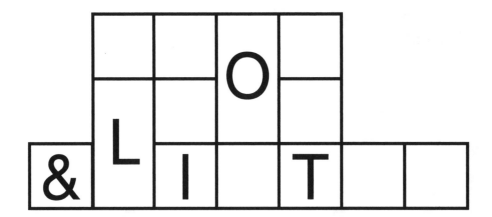

Answers on page 173.

SEQUENCE

Which 2 figures come next in the sequence?

♣ & ◀ Ω Π Ξ ✝ @ ♣ & ◀ Ω
Π Ξ ✝ @ ♣ & ◀ Ω Π Ξ ✝ @

A. Ω Π   B. ♣ &   C. ♣ ✝   D. ♣ &   E. & ♣

Answers on page 173.

RIDDLE

"Work this one out," said Alice to her work colleague. "I drive from my home to the office every morning. At the back of my house is a short, fairly narrow driveway approximately 300 yards long. I drive my car down this driveway in a westerly direction, yet when I stop the car at the end of the driveway it is facing east."

"Does the driveway go round in a circle?" asked her colleague.

"No," replied Alice, "it is absolutely straight."

What is the explanation?

Answers on page 173.

FAMOUS DETECTIVE SCRAMBLE

The left column contains the scrambled names of five famous fictional detectives. The right column contains the authors who created them. Unscramble the names and then match each detective to its creator!

Detectives:

1. HEMLOCK RESLOSH
2. SLAM SIMPER
3. D. AUSPICE UNTUG
4. FOOL NEWER
5. MONKEY ILLSHINE

Authors:

A. TEX TOURS
B. FORAGES NUT
C. AGHAST CHAIRTIE
D. ADAGE LONER LAP
E. ATRULY HONOR DANCE

29

Answers on page 173.

VISUALIZE THIS!

The detective is putting together the tools she needs. Can you determine the order of the 6 tools gathered from the information below?

The magnifying glass was one of the first three things gathered.

The notepad was not gathered immediately before or after the pencil, nor was it found last.

The fingerprint kit was found right before the flashlight.

The pencil was found third or fourth.

The magnifying glass was put in the kit, then three other items, and then the measuring tape.

The flashlight was found right before the measuring tape.

Answers on page 173.

TRAIN STATION TERRORS

"Trixter" is back at it again! This time he's hidden a stolen briefcase full of diamonds in one of forty-five different lockers at the train station. Each locker has a different number, and the miscreant has given the police a series of clues that will point to its hidden location. Can you find the diamonds?

1. It is odd.
2. It is divisible by 3.
3. The second digit is greater than 6.
4. The sum of the digits is less than 10.

11	12	13	14	15	16	17	18	19
21	22	23	24	25	26	27	28	29
31	32	33	34	35	36	37	38	39
41	42	43	44	45	46	47	48	49
51	52	53	54	55	56	57	58	59

Answers on page 173.

SEQUENCING

Can you complete the sequence below?

The detective is tracking down some stolen gems. She has found the pearls in the city of Edinburgh, the opals in the city of Oslo, and the garnets in the city of Athens. Where are the rubies most likely to be found?

A. Ulan Bator
B. Reykjavik
C. Yerevan
D. Bern

Answers on page 174.

Change just one letter on each line to go from the top word to the bottom word. Do not change the order of the letters. You must have a common English word at each step.

CLUES

_____

_____

_____

_____

_____

_____

TRIAL

33

CRIME RHYMES

Each clue leads to a 2-word answer that rhymes, such as BIG PIG or STABLE TABLE. The numbers in parentheses after the clue give the number of letters in each word. For example, "cookware taken from the oven (3, 3)" would be "hot pot."

1. Theft of a sushi ingredient (3, 5): _____

2. Fingerprint found at a cheese store robbery (4, 4): _____

3. Shoplifter from a butcher (4, 5): _____

4. Citrus-related robbery (4, 5): _____

5. Robber of drinks (8, 5): _____

6. Plans to steal boat (5, 4): _____

7. Thoughtful investigator (10, 9): _____

8. Foot impression found in the herbal garden (4, 5): _____

Answers on page 174.

CRIME CRYPTOGRAM

Cryptograms are messages in substitution code. Break the code to read the message. For example, THE SMART CAT might become FVO QWGDF JGF if **F** is substituted for **T**, **V** for **H**, **O** for **E**, and so on.

ZNK GIZUX'Y IUYZGX GIIAYKJ NOS UL G JGYZGXJRE IXOSK,

HAZ ZNK VUROIK XKLAYKJ ZU OTBKYZOMGZK. CNGZ JOJ NK JU?

NK YZURK ZNK YIKTK!

Answers on page 174.

COME TOGETHER

Set each of the tile sets into the empty spaces below to create 3 nine-letter words related to investigation. Each tile set is used only once.

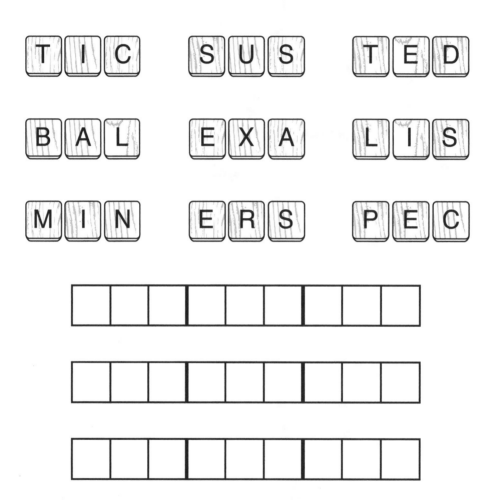

Answers on page 174.

MOTEL HIDEOUT

A thief hides out in one of the 45 motel rooms listed in the chart below. The motel's in-house detective received a sheet of four clues, signed "The Holiday Thief." Using these clues, the detective found the room number within 15 minutes—but by that time, the thief had fled. Can you find the thief's motel room quicker?

1. The sum of the digits is greater than 7.
2. The second digit is more than double the first digit.
3. The first digit is divisible by 2.
4. The second digit is divisible by 4.

51	52	53	54	55	56	57	58	59
41	42	43	44	45	46	47	48	49
31	32	33	34	35	36	37	38	39
21	22	23	24	25	26	27	28	29
11	12	13	14	15	16	17	18	19

Answers on page 174.

FIND THE WITNESS

On Box Street, there are 5 adjacent houses that are identical to each other. You've been asked to visit Mr. Linus, but without any addresses on the doors you are not sure which house to approach. At the local coffee shop, you ask the waitress for help. She is able to provide the following information:

A. Mr. Linus does not like dogs.
B. The dog living next door to Mr. Linus often tunnels under his other neighbor's fence to chase their cat.
C. There are no animals at House B.
D. House A owns a cat.
E. House C owns a cat.

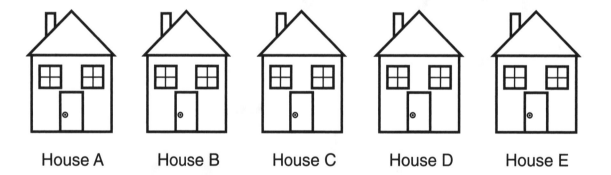

House A   House B   House C   House D   House E

Answers on page 175.

PLANTED EVIDENCE AT THE SCENE

Change just one letter on each line to go from the top word to the bottom word. Do not change the order of the letters. You must have a common English word at each step.

PLANT

_____

_____

_____

SCENE

Answers on page 175.

TREASURE HUNT

The treasure hunter visited eight cities, finding a clue in each one that led her to the treasure in the final city. Can you put the list of the eight cities she visited in order, using the information below?

She began in one of the two cities on the West coast.

The two cities in Texas were not visited sequentially.

Chicago was one of the first three cities visited, and was visited before either Texas city.

After visiting Dallas, she went to one other city before Boston, and neither were the first or final destination.

After going to Los Angeles, the treasure hunter visited two other cities before arriving in St. Louis.

Boston was visited immediately before Tallahassee.

Portland was visited after Austin, but not immediately, and sometime before Tallahassee.

Answers on page 175.

CRIME RHYMES

Each clue leads to a 2-word answer that rhymes, such as BIG PIG or STABLE TABLE. The numbers in parentheses after the clue give the number of letters in each word. For example, "cookware taken from the oven (3, 3)" would be "hot pot."

1. The case of the theft of the animal intestines was also called the case of the (6, 5): _____

2. A murder in December (8, 8): _____

3. The lawbreaker who sent hidden messages was the (10, 8): _____

4. To accuse a British "Sir" with a fancy title (6, 6): _____

5. A police inspector changes around assignments for the police under him (5, 4): _____

6. To take someone else's breakfast food (5, 7): _____

7. The smuggled dog was also called the (7, 6): _____

8. The incident of theft among the troupe of silent performers was called the (4, 5): _____

41

Answers on page 175.

BANK MAYHEM

A criminal mastermind who calls himself "Trixter" has hidden a stolen artifact in one of forty-five different safety deposit boxes at the local bank. Each box has a different number, and the miscreant has given the police a series of clues that will point to its hidden location. Using only these clues, find the one correct number—but be careful! Open the wrong box and the priceless artifact will be destroyed.

1. It is less than 90.
2. It is divisible by 2.
3. The first digit is greater than the second.
4. The square root of it is a whole number.

59	58	57	56	55	54	53	52	51
69	68	67	66	65	64	63	62	61
79	78	77	76	75	74	73	72	71
89	88	87	86	85	84	83	82	81
99	98	97	96	95	94	93	92	91

Answers on page 175.

CRACK THE PASSWORD

A detective has found a memory aid that the criminal left behind, a list of coded passwords. The detective knows that the criminal likes to scramble each password, then remove the same letter from each word. Can you figure out the missing letter and unscramble each word in this set to reveal the passwords?

SINE

PRIMERS

LEARN

MICAS

Answers on page 175.

HOMICIDE: LIFE ON THE STREETS

Every word listed is contained within the group of letters. Words can be found in a straight line horizontally, vertically, or diagonally. They may be read either forward or backward.

BALTIMORE	JUDGMENT
BAYLISS	JUSTICE
CAREER	LEWIS
CONFLICT	MUNCH
CRIME	PARTNERS
DETECTIVE	PEMBLETON
EVIDENCE	PHILOSOPHY
GIARDELLO	POLICE
INEQUALITY	RACE
INTERVIEW	SUSPECT

```
B E P T A H A H T S Y Y A Y B
Z K S E E V I T C E T E D H L
T L Q S M C Q U O M C C O P G
P C I S G B A H C Z E I W O N
A E I I H C L R C L P L I S G
R C A L D Z I E U N S O N O I
T E K Y F M B O T H U P T L A
N V U A E N S X P O S M E I R
E I V B M J O Q O G N I R H D
R D V V Y L H C G P B J V P E
S E C I T S U J J L E W I S L
I N E Q U A L I T Y V I E I L
U C B A L T I M O R E L W E O
O E X Y M W M T R O A V T E P
R E E R A C A J U D G M E N T
```

45

MOTEL HIDEOUT

A thief hides out in one of the 45 motel rooms listed in the chart below. The motel's in-house detective received a sheet of four clues, signed "The Logical Thief." Using these clues, the detective found the room number within 15 minutes—but by that time, the thief had fled. Can you find the thief's motel room quicker?

1. The sum of the digits is less than 6.
2. The first digit is not 4.
3. The second digit is not 2.
4. It is divisible by 2.

51	52	53	54	55	56	57	58	59
41	42	43	44	45	46	47	48	49
31	32	33	34	35	36	37	38	39
21	22	23	24	25	26	27	28	29
11	12	13	14	15	16	17	18	19

Answers on page 176.

OVERHEARD INFORMATION PART I

Read the story below, then turn the page and answer the questions.

The detective overheard the jewelry thief tell his accomplice about the different places where he stashed the loot. He said, "The sapphire is tucked in a running shoe in the spare closet. The diamond necklace is behind the mirror in the dining room. The ruby is at the bottom of the salt shaker. The emeralds are in a waterproof bag in the toilet tank."

OVERHEARD INFORMATION PART 2

(Do not read this until you have read the previous page!)

The investigator overheard the information about where the stolen loot was stored, but didn't have anywhere to write it down! Answer the questions below to help the investigator remember.

1. The sapphire is found in this location.

A. The toe of a slipper
B. The toe of a running shoe
C. The bottom of the salt shaker
D. In the refrigerator

2. What is found behind the mirror in the dining room?

A. The sapphire
B. The diamond ring
C. The diamond necklace
D. The emeralds

3. How many emeralds are there?

A. 1
B. 2
C. 3
D. We are not told.

4. What kind of gem is found in the salt shaker?

A. Sapphire
B. Diamond
C. Ruby
D. Emerald

Answers on page 176.

FINGERPRINT MATCH

There are 4 sets of fingerprints. Find each match.

A B C D

E F G H

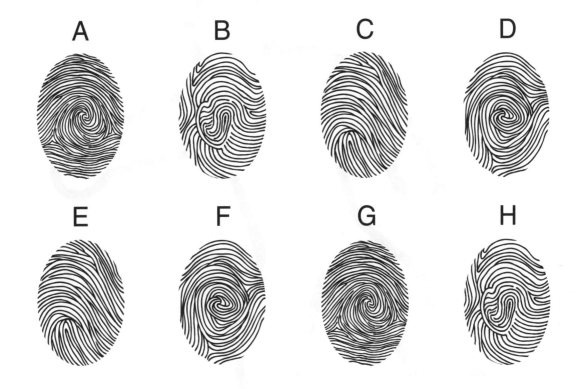

Answers on page 176.

TRAIN STATION TERRORS

"Trixter" is back at it again! This time he's hidden a stolen briefcase full of diamonds in one of forty-five different lockers at the train station. Each locker has a different number, and the miscreant has given the police a series of clues that will point to its hidden location. Can you find the diamonds?

1. It is not divisible by 3.
2. It is odd.
3. The sum of the digits is less than 10.
4. Both digits are greater than 2.
5. It isn't prime.

10	11	12	13	14	15	16	17	18
20	21	22	23	24	25	26	27	28
30	31	32	33	34	35	36	37	38
40	41	42	43	44	45	46	47	48
50	51	52	53	54	55	56	57	58

Answers on page 176.

CAN A CLUE SET YOU FREE?

Change just one letter on each line to go from the top word to the bottom word. Do not change the order of the letters. You must have a common English word at each step.

CLUE

‾‾‾‾‾‾

‾‾‾‾‾‾

‾‾‾‾‾‾

FREE

Answers on page 176.

CRIME RHYMES

Each clue leads to a 2-word answer that rhymes, such as BIG PIG or STABLE TABLE. The numbers in parentheses after the clue give the number of letters in each word. For example, "cookware taken from the oven (3, 3)" would be "hot pot."

1. Suspect swore he was getting fast food (3, 5): _____

2. Arsonist who hated musical instruments set this (4, 4): _____

3. Murder at the racetrack (12, 4): _____

4. Cantaloupe thief (5, 5): _____

5. Scoff at idea of using this poison (5, 7): _____

6. Provided poison (8, 7): _____

7. Noisy diamond heist (3, 6): _____

8. When the funeral home thought something might be going on (9, 9): _____

Answers on page 177.

MEALTIME CRIME

Cryptograms are messages in substitution code. Break the code to read the message. For example, THE SMART CAT might become FVO QWGDF JGF if **F** is substituted for **T**, **V** for **H**, **O** for **E**, and so on.

ZKDW GLG WKH KHDGOLQH UHDG IRU WKH EDNHUB WKHIW

WKDW WRRN SODFH GXULQJ WKH VROVWLFH LQ MXQH?

WKH VXPPHUWLPH NHB OLPH FULPH.

53

THE LAW

Every legal term listed is contained within the group of letters. Words can be found in a straight line horizontally, vertically, or diagonally. They may be read either forward or backward.

APPEAL	FINE
ARRAIGN	HEARING
CIVIL	JUDGE
COURT	JURY
DAMAGES	LAWYER
DISCOVERY	PLEA
DISMISS	RECORD
DOCUMENT	RULING
EVIDENCE	SENTENCE
FELONY	TRANSCRIPT

```
A E A Y B M V X H Q F W Y Z Y
T E U E V K S H D D P V V R S
R M L A V E A P P E A L U X S
U A G P G I H X T V W J A G I
O R A A J I D J R A E U N F M
C R M P B R U E A C Z D L E S
L A D O C U M E N T I G O L I
D I I A W T Q E S C V E Z O D
R G S E H F T S C Y E T T N E
R N C L D N V F R A S L Q Y V
E J O I E N D I I D R O C E R
Y A V S R E H N P R U L I N G
W O E U P P Q E T C Z I B Y J
A G R T F Y F N R U C I V I L
L L Y H O M F G N I R A E H S
```

Answers on page 177.

TREASURE HUNT

The treasure hunter visited eight cities, finding a clue in each one that led him to the treasure in the final city. Can you put the list of the eight cities he visited in order, using the information below?

1. The treasure hunter proceeded directly from Maryland to Wisconsin.

2. San Diego was one of the final four cities.

3. Oklahoma City was one of the first four cities.

4. The treasure hunter did not begin his search in Topeka, Milwaukee, or Boise.

5. The treasure hunter did not end his search in Charleston, Oklahoma City, or Baltimore.

6. After Milwaukee, he visited exactly two other cities before visiting Atlanta.

7. After Oklahoma City, he visited exactly two other cities before visiting San Diego.

8. South Carolina was visited immediately before Kansas.

9. The city whose name begins with a C was visited before the cities beginning with A or B.

10. The treasure hunter stopped in Idaho sometime after California but before Georgia.

Answers on page 177.

AKA

Match each criminal's name in the left column to his or her nickname in the right column.

1. Harry Hayward
2. Thomas Neill Cream
3. Stephen Richards
4. Elizabeth Bathory
5. Mary Frith
6. Monica Proietti

A. The Blood Countess
B. The Minneapolis Svengali
C. Machine Gun Molly
D. The Nebraska Fiend
E. Moll Cutpurse
F. The Lambeth Poisoner

Answers on page 177.

MOTEL HIDEOUT

A thief hides out in one of the 45 motel rooms listed in the chart below. The motel's in-house detective received a sheet of four clues, signed "The Logical Thief." Using these clues, the detective found the room number within 15 minutes—but by that time, the thief had fled. Can you find the thief's motel room more quickly?

1. The sum of the digits is either less than 5 or greater than 9.
2. If you multiply one of the digits by 2, you get the second digit.
3. If you spell out the number, it is more than 6 letters.
4. The number is not divisible by 7.

51	52	53	54	55	56	57	58	59
41	42	43	44	45	46	47	48	49
31	32	33	34	35	36	37	38	39
21	22	23	24	25	26	27	28	29
11	12	13	14	15	16	17	18	19

58

Answers on page 177.

FORGING MONEY

Change just one letter on each line to go from the top word to the bottom word. Do not change the order of the letters. You must have an English word at each step.

FORGE

_____

_____

_____ things in a front position or golfer's warnings

_____

_____

_____

MONEY

Answers on page 178.

FOR STAGE AND SCREEN

Every name below belongs to an actor who played the role of Watson in a Sherlock Holmes adaptation. Names can be found in a straight line horizontally, vertically, or diagonally. They may be read either forward or backward.

ALAN COX

BEN KINGSLEY

BRUCE MCRAE

COLIN BLAKELY

DAVID BURKE

DONALD PICKERING

EDWARD HARDWICKE

H. KYRLE BELLEW

HUBERT WILLIS

JUDE LAW

MARTIN FREEMAN

NIGEL BRUCE

PATRICK MACNEE

RAYMOND FRANCIS

ROBERT DUVALL

ROLAND YOUNG

```
D O N A L D P I C K E R I N G
A K K B N B R U C E M C R A E
V R A Y M O N D F R A N C I S
I Q Y X O C N A L A Q Q Y R R
D G N U O Y D N A L O R W O F
B E N K I N G S L E Y H F B B
U I N I G E L B R U C E X E V
R T R H T F Q S C D Q J S R M
K W P O J X D Y R Y U V I T H
E K C I W D R A H D R A W D E
M A R T I N F R E E M A N U I
W E L L E B E L R Y K H C V T
H X E E N C A M K C I R T A P
S I L L I W T R E B U H M L V
W J M C O L I N B L A K E L Y
```

Answers on page 178.

INTERCEPTION

You've intercepted a message that is meant to reveal a location for an upcoming meeting between two criminal masterminds. The only problem is, the message shows many place names. Can you figure out the right location?

BANGKOK

ATLANTA

BOSTON

ARKANSAS

OTTAWA

HONDURAS

DOMINICAN REPUBLIC

TRIPOLI

RABAT

PARAGUAY

Answers on page 178.

OVERHEARD INFORMATION PART I

Read the story below, then turn the page and answer the questions.

A bystander heard two people talking at a coffee shop, only to realize they were counterfeiters! One said to the other, "The order is thirty-five $20 dollar bills, sixty $100 bills, and one hundred $10 bills. I've left it in the safe, and the temporary combination is 03-21-17. You need to pick it up by Thursday at 6 PM or the money is removed."

OVERHEARD INFORMATION PART 2

(Do not read this until you have read the previous page!)

1. How many bills of each denomination are being delivered? (For some, the answer may be zero.)

$5: _____

$10: _____

$20: _____

$50: _____

$100: _____

2. What is the combination for the safe?

_____

3. What is the deadline to pick up the delivery?

_____

Answers on page 178.

FINGERPRINT MATCH

Find the matching fingerprint(s). There may be more than one.

A. B. C.

D. E. F.

G. H. I.

Answers on page 178.

CRIME SCENE

ACROSS

1. No place for a roller skate
6. Football or badminton
11. One-named author of "A Dog of Flanders"
12. Jouster's protection
13. It's collected at a crime scene
15. Countess's counterpart
16. Ending with Siam or Japan
17. "But of course!"
20. "Naked Maja" painter
22. Sheriffs and marshals, e.g.
24. After-dinner treat
28. "Precious bodily fluid" that may be found at a crime scene
29. Telltale strand that may be found at a crime scene
30. Realtor sign add-on
31. Slangy physician
32. "Good gravy!"
34. It's above the horizon
35. Belonging to the Thing?
38. Metals in the raw
40. They provide a permanent record of a crime scene
45. Font feature
46. Fields of expertise
47. Jets, to Sharks
48. Garment size

DOWN

1. Fastest way to a new lawn
2. Large cask for wine
3. Org. for Saarinen
4. Concept for Colette
5. Devastated
6. "I'm sorry to say..."
7. Canada's Grand ___ National Historic Park
8. Everything: Lat.
9. Fabled giant birds
10. Sequoia or sycamore
14. Fe, to a chemist
17. Church robes
18. Metaphor for purity
19. Derelict GI
21. Between
23. Pop music's Depeche___
25. Bird of the Nile
26. Giraffe's trademark
27. Homer's besieged city
29. FBI part
31. "CSI" star Helgenberger
33. He was originally called Dippy Dawg
35. ___ dixit (unproven assertion)
36. Back in those days
37. Aching
39. "Love Song" singer Bareilles
41. Bob Cratchit's son
42. Miles ___ hour
43. Crone
44. Direction opposite NNW

Answers on page 178.

TREASURE HUNT

The investigator is tracking a jewelry thief's past trips in order to find and recover jewelry that was left behind in six cities. Each city was visited only once. Can you put together the travel timeline, using the information below?

1. The first and last locations were in the United States.
2. The thief went straight from Denver to Atlanta.
3. Seoul was one of the first three cities visited.
4. The thief went from Buenos Aires to a city in Europe.
5. Atlanta was one of the last three cities visited.
6. The thief did not go from Nashville to Athens, or vice versa.

Answers on page 179.

MOTEL HIDEOUT

A thief hides out in one of the 45 motel rooms listed in the chart below. The motel's in-house detective received a sheet of four clues, signed "The Logical Thief." Using these clues, the detective found the room number within 15 minutes—but by that time, the thief had fled. Can you find the thief's motel room more quickly?

1. The sum of the digits is less than 10.
2. The sum of the digits is greater than 5.
3. The first digit is larger than the second digit.
4. The second digit is divisible by 4.

51	52	53	54	55	56	57	58	59
41	42	43	44	45	46	47	48	49
31	32	33	34	35	36	37	38	39
21	22	23	24	25	26	27	28	29
11	12	13	14	15	16	17	18	19

Answers on page 179.

DON'T LEAVE A PRINT

Change just one letter on each line to go from the top word to the bottom word. Do not change the order of the letters. You must have a common English word at each step.

LEAVE

_____

_____

_____

_____

_____

_____

_____

_____

PRINT

70

Answers on page 179.

FINGERPRINT MATCH

There are 8 sets of fingerprints. Find each match.

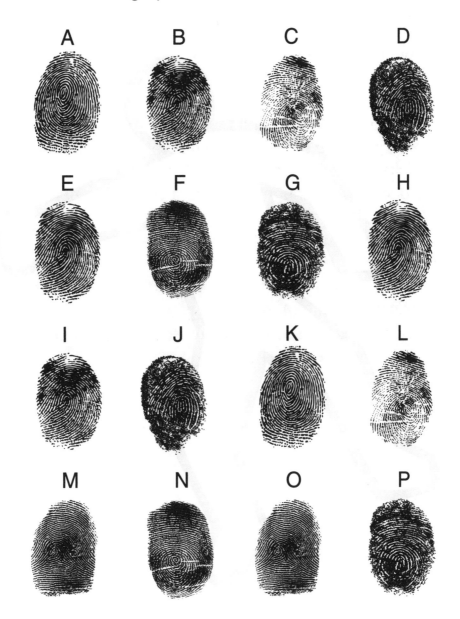

A B C D

E F G H

I J K L

M N O P

71

Answers on page 179.

CRIME RHYMES

Each clue leads to a 2-word answer that rhymes, such as BIG PIG or STABLE TABLE. The numbers in parentheses after the clue give the number of letters in each word. For example, "cookware taken from the oven (3, 3)" would be "hot pot."

1. When investigators are weighing whether to charge someone with a crime, it is said that they (5, 6): _____
2. The burglar who stole food from a variety of summer picnickers was known as the (10, 5): _____
3. The doctor who thought his patient was being poisoned could be said to have a (9, 9): _____
4. The detective who like this sweet wine was known as the (8, 6): _____
5. When the criminal left traces of an adhesive at the scene, it was known as the (4, 4): _____
6. When the captain's second in command seemed suspicious, the detective chose to (11, 5, 4): _____ (the)

   _____ _____
7. A murder next to a body of water (8, 8): _____
8. A person who wants to be an investigator (11, 9): _____

Answers on page 179.

OVERHEARD INFORMATION PART I

Read the story below, then turn the page and answer the questions.

While on a train, a bystander overheard a conversation between two men talking about how best to rob a restaurant.

The first man says, "They lock up their money in the safe each night, and Kerri's given me the combo. 05-36-29. They don't take it to the bank until Friday, so I think we go Thursday night after they close."

The second man says, "I've scoped out the video situation. They don't use their cameras to record—they just have them there to deter robberies. But the store on the left, the antique shop, does keep cameras running—so we have to approach and leave from the corner on the left."

OVERHEARD INFORMATION PART 2

(Do not read this until you have read the previous page!)

1. The bystander hears a conversation between these two people.
A. Two men
B. A man and a woman
C. Two teenagers
D. Two women

2. The combo for the safe is:
A. 36-29-05
B. 29-36-05
C. 05-29-36
D. 05-36-29

3. The theft is planned for this night.
A. Wednesday
B. Thursday
C. Friday
D. Saturday

4. The name of the accomplice inside the restaurant who gave the safe code is:
A. Kitty
B. Kerri
C. Kelli
D. Karen

Answers on page 179.

MOTEL HIDEOUT

"Trixter" has left another series of clues! Now he says the police will find him in one of forty-five different motel rooms. Each room has a different number, and "Trixter" has given a series of clues that will reveal that number. Can you find "Trixter" before he makes his escape?

1. It is not divisible by 7.
2. The sum of the digits is less than 10.
3. It is divisible by 3.
4. The product is greater than 15.
5. It is divisible by the cube root of 125.

12	13	14	15	16	17	18	19	20
22	23	24	25	26	27	28	29	30
32	33	34	35	36	37	38	39	40
42	43	44	45	46	47	48	49	50
52	53	54	55	56	57	58	59	60

Answers on page 180.

GRID FILL

To complete this puzzle, place the given letters and words into the shapes in this grid. Words and letters will run across, down, and wrap around each shape. When the grid is filled, each row will contain one of the following words: bolts, fools, liars, spoon, stamp, tawas.

1. O, S
2. AT, SS
3. OWL
4. FOOT, LAMP, SLIP, STAB
5. ARSON

Answers on page 180.

ALL SECRET PLOTS LEAVE CLUES

Change just one letter on each line to go from the top word to the bottom word. Do not change the order of the letters. You must have a common English word at each step.

PLOTS

_____

_____

_____

_____

_____

CLUES

Answers on page 180.

MOTEL HIDEOUT

A thief hides out in one of the 45 motel rooms listed in the chart below. The motel's in-house detective received a sheet of four clues, signed "The Holiday Thief." Using these clues, the detective found the room number within 15 minutes—but by that time, the thief had fled. Can you find the thief's motel room quicker?

1. It is not a prime number.
2. The first digit is odd, and the second even.
3. It is divisible by 6.
4. The sum of its digits is less than 9.

51	52	53	54	55	56	57	58	59
41	42	43	44	45	46	47	48	49
31	32	33	34	35	36	37	38	39
21	22	23	24	25	26	27	28	29
11	12	13	14	15	16	17	18	19

Answers on page 180.

OVERHEARD INFORMATION PART 1

Read the story below, then turn the page and answer the questions.

The detective overheard the thief tell her accomplice about the different places where she stashed the loot. She said, "I left the largest diamond taped to the drainpipe underneath the upstairs sink. The four smaller diamonds are tucked in a pair of pantyhose in the third drawer down in the dresser. The gold necklace is wrapped up in the rose-patterned pillowcase in the linen closet. The gold bars are in a locked trunk in the attic."

OVERHEARD INFORMATION PART 2

(Do not read this until you have read the previous page!)

The investigator overheard the information about where the stolen loot was stored, but didn't have anywhere to write it down! Answer the questions below to help the investigator remember.

1. What is found in the drainpipe?
A. The largest diamond
B. The four smaller diamonds
C. The gold necklace
D. The pearl

2. The gold necklace is wrapped in this.
A. Pantyhose
B. Plain pillowcase
C. Rose-patterned pillowcase
D. Sock

3. The gold bars are in this.
A. The linen closet
B. A locked trunk in the attic
C. A trunk in the crawlspace
D. A trunk in the basement

4. Which item or items are found in the top dresser drawer?
A. The largest diamond
B. The four smaller diamonds
C. The gold necklace
D. None of them

Answers on page 180.

LEAVING CLUES

Change just one letter on each line to go from the top word to the bottom word. Do not change the order of the letters. You must have a common English word at each step.

LEAVE

_____

_____

_____

_____

_____ synonym for burns

_____

_____

_____

_____

_____

CLUES

Answers on page 180.

BLUE BLOODS

Every word listed is contained within the group of letters. Words can be found in a straight line horizontally, vertically, or diagonally. They may read either forward or backward.

ARREST
ATTORNEY
BLUE
CHARGE
CITY
COMMISSIONER
COPS
DANNY
DETECTIVE
ERIN
FAMILY
FRANK

HENRY
JAMIE
JUSTICE
LINDA
MOYNAHAN (Bridget)
NYPD
OFFICER
POLICE
REAGAN
SELLECK (Tom)
WAHLBERG (Donnie)

```
A Y R E N O I S S I M M O C G
E R I N H J W A H L B E R G R
K B E E A M J S E L L E C K Z
Y A N M K E J E F A M I L Y D
H R I W E V E C I L O P A T P
Y E S E F I C O P S Y I T I Y
H A O G R T M T K T N R T C N
L G Y R A C O A D X A Z O J N
G A J A N E P T L G H V R U O
W N B H K T S Y N N A D N S F
I J B C A E F Y R O N L E T F
W U X L R D G C D D S V Y I I
Q U Q R U U N B S V Y J H C C
B J A O P E S I Z U Z H K E E
W N S O K M K D L X X Y T Q R
```

Answers on page 181.

DNA QUIZ

How much do you know about DNA?

1. What does DNA stand for?

A. Deoxyribonucleic acid
B. Dynamic nucleic acid
C. Derivative nucleotidic acid
D. Deoxynucleic acid

2. Cytosine is one of the four bases found in DNA. Name the other three.

_____

_____

_____

3. Which statement below is true?

A. DNA can be gathered from blood, skin, saliva, and hair.
B. DNA can be gathered from blood, skin, and saliva, but not hair.
C. DNA can be gathered from blood and hair, but not saliva or skin.

Answers on page 181.

WHAT WENT MISSING? PART I

The investigators were testing each other's attention to detail. Study this picture 1 minute, then turn the page.

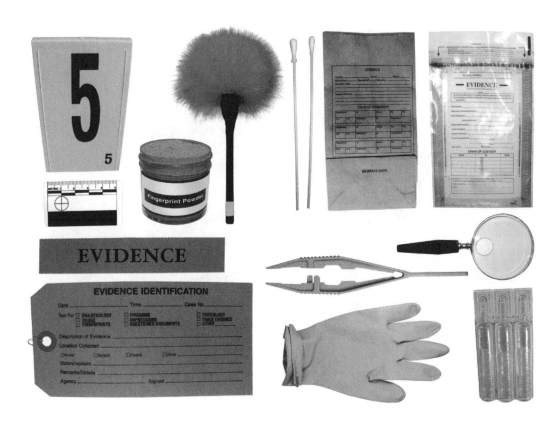

WHAT WENT MISSING? PART 2

(Do not read this until you have read the previous page!)

The investigators removed one object from their colleague's workspace, and asked what it was. From memory, can you work out which single object went missing?

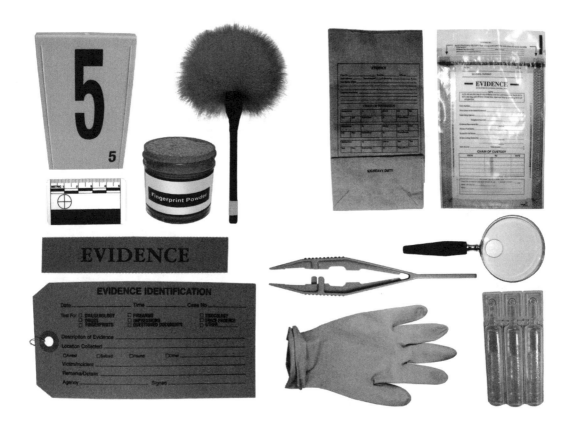

Answers on page 181.

FINGERPRINT MATCH

Find the matching fingerprint(s). There may be more than one.

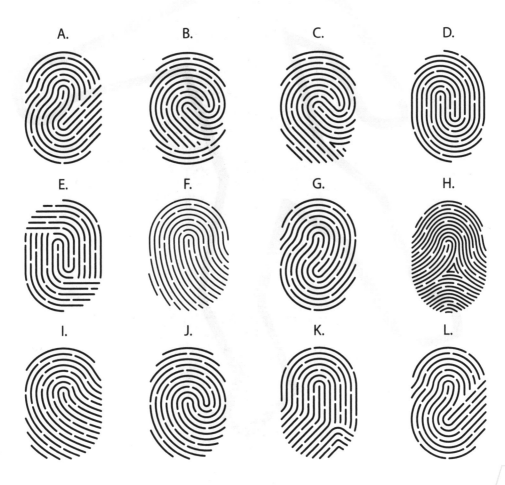

A. B. C. D.

E. F. G. H.

I. J. K. L.

87

Answers on page 181.

A LONG PATH FROM CRIME TO TRIAL

Change just one letter on each line to go from the top word to the bottom word. Do not change the order of the letters. You must have a common English word at each step.

CRIME

———————

———————

———————

———————

———————

——————— sets of two

———————

———————

———————

———————

———————

TRIAL

Answers on page 181.

MOTEL HIDEOUT

"Trixter" has left another series of clues! Now he says the police will find him in one of forty-five different motel rooms. Each room has a different number, and "Trixter" has given a series of clues that will reveal that number. Can you find "Trixter" before he makes his escape?

1. It is not divisible by 6.
2. No digit is greater than 5.
3. The hidden number is divisible by a 2-digit prime number.
4. It is divisible by 3.

12	13	14	15	16	17	18	19	20
22	23	24	25	26	27	28	29	30
32	33	34	35	36	37	38	39	40
42	43	44	45	46	47	48	49	50
52	53	54	55	56	57	58	59	60

Answers on page 181.

DNA SEQUENCE

Examine the two images below carefully. Are these sequences a match or not?

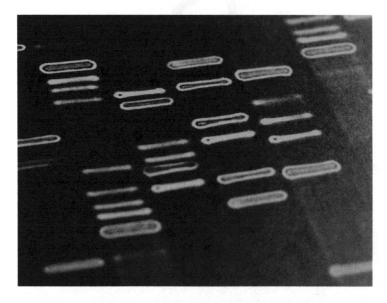

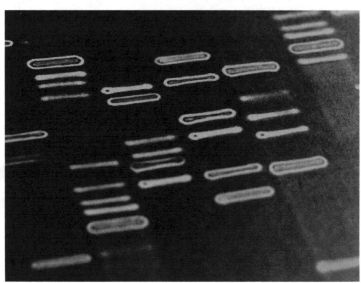

Answers on page 182.

WHAT CHANGED? PART I

Study this picture of the crime scene for 1 minute, then turn the page.

WHAT CHANGED? PART 2

(Do not read this until you have read the previous page!)

From memory, can you tell what changed between this page and the previous page?

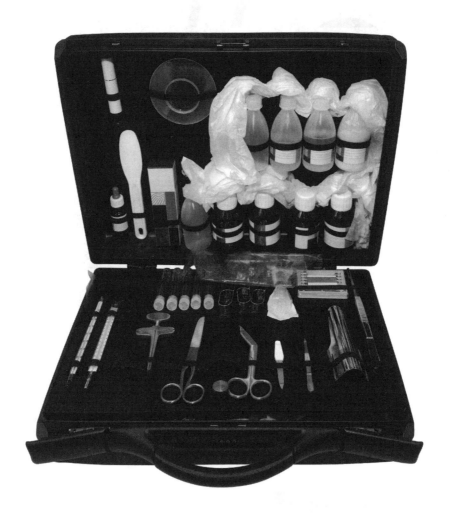

Answers on page 182.

A MYSTERY FROM HISTORY

Cryptograms are messages in substitution code. Break the code to read the message. For example, THE SMART CAT might become FVO QWGDF JGF if **F** is substituted for **T**, **V** for **H**, **O** for **E**, and so on.

GSP ITQMWOS NKMHFOCWXG WF K RKNTHF NKMHFOCWXG

GSKG SKF OSKDDPMUPV OCQXGTUCKXSPCF. GSP

NKMHFOCWXG FHXXTFPVDQ VKGPF BKOE GT GSP PKCDQ

RWRGPPM OPMGHCQ. WG OTMGKWMF VCKJWMUF TR

XDKMGF KMV TGSPC TBZPOGF KOOTNXKMWPV BQ GPLG,

BHG MT TMP SKF BPPM KBDP GT VPOWXSPC GSP GPLG.

Answers on page 182.

GRID FILL

To complete this puzzle, place the given letters and words into the shapes on this grid. Words and letters will run across, down, and wrap around each shape. When the grid is filled, each row will contain one of the following words: archer, arrest, cookie, on time, slight, Sparta, tamale.

1. C, G, I
2. ET, LI
3. HER, HIM, TEA
4. CART, REAM, SALE, TART
5. ARSON, SPOOK

94

Answers on page 182.

Change just one letter on each line to go from the top word to the bottom word. Do not change the order of the letters. You must have a common English word at each step.

CLUE

——————

——————

——————

——————

——————

——————

RAID

95

Answers on page 182.

STOLEN ART

ACROSS

1. Having to do with bees
6. A little bit of salt
10. 3-Down poet
11. Artery from the heart
12. Breaks in friendly relations
13. Even more adorable
14. First lady's home?
15. "The ___," Edvard Munch painting stolen in 1994 and 2004 and recovered
16. Kilimanjaro's cont.
17. "Annabel Lee" poet
18. '60s campus radical gp.
19. Da Vinci painting stolen in 1911 and recovered in 1913
22. "Hee Haw" honey Misty
23. Legendary puppeteer Tony
26. "___ Bridge, London," Claude Monet painting stolen in 2012
29. Like 7 and 11
32. Cheerless
33. C. Everett Koop and others: Abbr.
34. "The ___," Edgar Degas painting stolen in 2009 and recovered in 2018
36. Gillette razor brand
37. One in a lion cage
38. Larsson who created Lisbeth Salander
39. White poplar tree

40. Richards of women's tennis
41. Island near Venice
42. Congregation's affirmations

DOWN

1. End of "Row, Row, Row Your Boat"
2. Settled in full
3. 10-Across masterwork
4. "This is for," on an env.
5. "Super Mario Bros." console
6. Glum
7. Commedia dell' ___
8. Place
9. Injures
11. Gained entry to
15. ___-disant (self-styled)
17. Hedonist's goal
20. "How cute is that?"
21. Berne's river
24. Author of "Go Eat Worms!"
25. Make eco-friendly changes
27. Brit's "thank yous"
28. Indians or oranges
29. Base-eight system
30. Abu ___ (Arabian sheikdom)
31. Like the Capitol Building
35. Change addresses, in real estate lingo
36. "Up and ___!" ("Rise and shine!")
38. Casa lady: Abbr.

Answers on page 182.

LEGAL TV SHOWS

Every TV show title listed is contained within the group of letters. Titles can be found in a straight line horizontally, vertically, or diagonally. They may read either forward or backward.

ALLY MCBEAL	JAG
BOSTON LEGAL	JUDGING AMY
BULL	L.A. LAW
CIVIL WARS	MATLOCK
CONVICTION	NIGHT COURT
THE D.A.	PAPER CHASE (The)
DAMAGES	PERRY MASON
DEFENDERS (The)	PETROCELLI
ELI STONE	PRACTICE (The)
GOOD WIFE (The)	SHARK
GUARDIAN (The)	SUITS

```
C O N V I C T I O N E T F V L
J U D G I N G A M Y F S C W C
I L L E C O R T E P I R N A N
M V K Q X W K I L A W A P L I
P P B A I C A D I O D W J A G
N C O L O E P E S V O L R L H
O K S L G S R F T Q O I R L T
S D T Y U A A E O Q G V K Y C
A A O M A H C N N T O I Y I O
M M N C R C T D E P Z C T G U
Y A L B D R I E C K R A H S R
R G E E I E C R R W P Z U C T
R E G A A P E S L B Z I X J E
E S A L N A A D E H T N D H J
P W L M W P D N D S L L U B L
```

99

Answers on page 183.

POLICE STATION SHENANIGANS

It seems this "Trixter" guy just never gets tired of playing games with the police! This time he's hidden a stolen brooch in a vending machine right in the waiting room of Precinct 23! Each option in the vending machine has its own number, and "Trixter" has given the police a series of clues that will reveal its exact location. Can you retrieve the stolen brooch?

1. It is less than 40.
2. It is divisible by 3.
3. It is odd.
4. It is a 2-digit prime number.
5. It is not divisible by 11.

11	12	13	14	15	16	17	18	19
21	22	23	24	25	26	27	28	29
31	32	33	34	35	36	37	38	39
41	42	43	44	45	46	47	48	49
51	52	53	54	55	56	57	58	59

Answers on page 183.

INTERCEPTION

You've intercepted a message. You think it might be the date and location of a meeting, but it doesn't seem to make sense. Can you decipher the true message?

AGREED

HOP ROUND SKI LIFT AT HIGHEST ZUCCHINI

RUN AND NEVER GO ON THIN POSTS

VIA ROAD WALK MORE

BANDANNA IN TAN SIDEWAYS CART

READ THE EXCELLENT PAMPHLET

Answers on page 183.

ELEVATOR WORDS

Like an elevator, words move up and down the "floors" of this puzzle. Starting with the first answer, the second part of each answer carries down to become the first part of the following answer. With the clues given, complete the puzzle.

1. Crime _____

2. _____

3. _____ _____

4. _____

5. _____

6. _____ _____

7. _____ scene

1. An uptick in crime incidents

2. A graphic image of a wave's frequency

3. Companies send these

4. A company logo shows up on this

5. Holds hair back from your face

6. Grade school music classes might teach this

7. Groupies are part of this.

Answers on page 183.

QUICK CRIME QUIZ

How much do you know about the history of crime scene investigation?

Answer the following questions.

1. Long before they were used to identify criminals, fingerprints were sometimes used to "sign" documents in lieu of a signature.
_____ True
_____ False

2. In Mark Twain's books "Life on the Mississippi" and "Pudd'n Head Wilson," these were used to identify perpetrators of crimes.
_____ Hair
_____ Fingerprints
_____ Footprints

3. The Bertillion method, named after the French police officer who invented it, used body measurements to establish identity.
_____ True
_____ False

4. Bertillion was also the first person to standardize the use of:
_____ DNA testing
_____ Mug shots

5. America's first detective agency, the Pinkertons, was created in this year.
_____ 1850
_____ 1912

103

Answers on page 183.

CRIME ON TV

ACROSS

1. Aptly named forensics crime show on Fox
6. Milkmaid's needs
11. Byron or Keats
12. In ___ (agitated)
13. City visited by pilgrims
14. Beauty pageant crown
15. Ailing chemistry teacher turns to crime (AMC)
17. Leonardo ___, a.k.a. Fibonacci
18. They tempted Ulysses
21. "Bravo, torero!"
24. Captain in "The Caine Mutiny"
25. Cool red giant in the sky
27. Range of sizes, briefly
28. Donny or Marie, by birth
29. "8 Mile" rapper
32. Dark yet funny TBS mystery starring Alia Shawkat
37. "Who's there?" reply, perhaps
38. Bolivian city, former capital
39. Oscar actress Garson
40. Go ballistic, with "out"
41. Avian abodes
42. Dark-comedy crime drama with Billy Bob Thornton as a hitman in Minnesota (FX)

DOWN

1. Big flop
2. German/Czech river
3. "Good work!"
4. Object of a manhunt
5. Supporting, as tomato plants
6. City on the Ganges (or Lord Jim's ship)
7. Not ___ of (no trace of)
8. Where diner patrons may prefer to sit
9. Former Italian money
10. End of many Dutch town names
16. NASA orbiter
18. Four-sided figs.
19. Chemical suffix.
20. Puts out, as a record
22. Anaheim baseball team, in box scores
23. Fish-catching eagle
25. Debark
26. John O'Hara's "Appointment in ___"
28. The Wildcats of the NCAA, for short
30. Shea Stadium mascot
31. Cake decorators
32. Communicate by hand
33. Being, in Paris
34. One who's sorry
35. "King Lear" or "Hamlet": Abbr.
36. Lennon's wife

Answers on page 183.

CRIME SCENE

Use the clues to change just one letter on each line to go from the top word to the bottom word. Do not change the order of the letters. You must have a common English word at each step.

CRIME

_____

_____

_____

_____

_____ a communication device

_____

_____

_____

_____

_____

_____ not large

_____

_____

_____ a type of wheat

_____

SCENE

Bonus: Can you do this word ladder with only five words between CRIME and SCENE, using a Scottish verb meaning "shrivel" and a noun referring to a cut of meat that includes the backbone?

Answers on page 184.

OVERHEARD INFORMATION PART I

Read the story below, then turn the page and answer the questions.

The detective overheard the jewelry thief tell her accomplice about the different places where she stashed the loot. She said, "The gold bars are in a sack in the treehouse at the farm. The diamonds are taped to a closed vent in the front room of the Chicago two-flat. The ruby choker is in a sack of flour in the pantry at the condo. The emeralds are in the safety deposit box at the bank on Fourth Street."

OVERHEARD INFORMATION PART 2

(Do not read this until you have read the previous page!)

The investigator overheard the information about where the stolen loot was stored, but didn't have anywhere to write it down! Answer the questions below to help the investigator remember.

1. What is found in a treehouse?
A. Gold bars
B. Diamonds
C. Rubies
D. Emeralds

2. What is found in a sack of flour?
A. Ruby bracelet
B. Ruby choker
C. Ruby ring
D. Emeralds

3. The diamonds are found in this building.
A. Farmhouse
B. Two-flat
C. Condo
D. Bank

4. The bank is found here.
A. Fourth Street
B. Fourth Avenue
C. Fourth Drive
D. We are not told.

Answers on page 184.

MOTEL HIDEOUT

A thief hides out in one of the 45 motel rooms listed in the chart below. The motel's in-house detective received a sheet of four clues, signed "The Logical Thief." Using these clues, the detective found the room number within 15 minutes—but by that time, the thief had fled. Can you find the thief's motel room quicker?

1. Multiply the first digit by 2 to get the second digit.
2. The first digit is a prime number.
3. The second digit is not prime.
4. It is not divisible by 9.

51	52	53	54	55	56	57	58	59
41	42	43	44	45	46	47	48	49
31	32	33	34	35	36	37	38	39
21	22	23	24	25	26	27	28	29
11	12	13	14	15	16	17	18	19

Answers on page 184.

TREASURE HUNT

The investigator is tracking a jewelry thief's past trips in order to find and recover jewelry that was left behind in six cities. Each city was visited only once. Can you put together the travel timeline, using the information below?

1. The thief did not go from Albany to Newark or vice versa.
2. The trip to Los Angeles took place after the trip to Toronto, but not immediately.
3. Madison was either the first or last location visited.
4. From Dallas the thief fled directly to Newark.
5. The thief did not begin in a province or state that borders a Great Lake.

Answers on page 184.

SEEN AT THE SCENE PART I

Study this picture of the crime scene for 1 minute, then turn the page.

(Do not read this until you have read the previous page!)

Which image exactly matches the picture from the previous page?

1.

2.

3.

4.

Answers on page 184.

CODE-DOKU

Solve this puzzle just as you would a sudoku. Use deductive logic to complete the grid so that each row, column, and 3 by 3 box contains the letters NO GLUM REV. When you have completed the puzzle, read the shaded squares to reveal a name and 2 words.

Hidden name and words: _____

	N	U	O					
L		G						N
V					N	O		
				G				U
					R	E		
	G	O		M				
R			L	V			U	
		E			O	N		
	L							

MISSING WORDS

This word search has a twist. Instead of a list of words to find, we've given you a list of TV show titles with missing words. First, figure out the word(s) missing from each title, then search for the missing word(s) in the grid. Words can be found in a straight line horizontally, vertically, or diagonally. They may read either forward or backward.

1. _____ Most Wanted

2. American _____

3. _____ Nine-Nine

4. _____ & Lacey

5. Crossing _____

6. _____: Murder

7. Forensic _____

8. Hill _____ Blues

9. _____, P.I.

10. Murder, _____

11. _____ Blue

12. _____ Suspect

13. The _____ Files

14. _____, Texas Ranger

15. Without a _____

```
V B F U C H T Q G U O D S U P
R D Q S T R E E T C Q G I L U
B R E U V H Y F H R J A S D Z
D O P D P Y N S L P X J O U U
A F W K H E H Q R A F O N E T
X K I A M E R I C A S R G R G
M C T K W D M J N B C D A N D
F O L R X E Z G D B Q A I C W
B R O O K L Y N E Z O N D A W
Y T P I B E H W T R A C E A C
E M T L M S Q Q H C B Q L I A
W W M U N G A M P I D K Q L G
E C I T S U J J Z J E S U W N
R F I L E S P W A R R Z D H E
C L S C G T M Z B K H F H P Y
```

115

Answers on page 185.

MULTIPLES OF SIX NUMBER MAZE

Find your way through the maze. Start with the hexagon containing a 6 on the left, and finish with the hexagon containing a 6 on the right. Move from hexagon to hexagon only if there is a line connecting them, and only pass through hexagons containing multiples of 6.

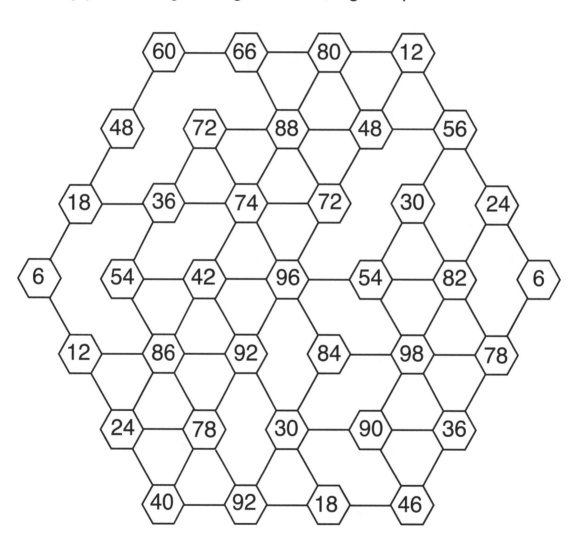

116

Answers on page 185.

MOTEL HIDEOUT

A thief hides out in one of the 45 motel rooms listed in the chart below. The motel's in-house detective received a sheet of four clues, signed "The Holiday Thief." Using these clues, the detective found the room number within 15 minutes—but by that time, the thief had fled. Can you find the thief's motel room quicker?

1. The first digit is larger than the second.
2. The second digit is not 3 or 4.
3. It is not divisible by 3 but is divisible by 4.
4. The sum of the digits is less than 7.

51	52	53	54	55	56	57	58	59
41	42	43	44	45	46	47	48	49
31	32	33	34	35	36	37	38	39
21	22	23	24	25	26	27	28	29
11	12	13	14	15	16	17	18	19

117

Answers on page 185.

QUICK CRIME QUIZ

How much do you know about forensic science?
Answer the following questions.

1. If the crime scene technicians did not find a person's fingerprint at the scene of a crime, does that prove they couldn't have been there?

____ Yes

____ No

2. Is "body farm" another word for morgue?

____ Yes

____ No

3. Can a guilty person fool a polygraph test?

____ Yes

____ No

4. Can an innocent person fail a polygraph test?

____ Yes

____ No

5. What does the acronym AFIS stand for?

____ Arson Federal Investigator at the Scene

____ Automated Fingerprint Identification System

____ Automatic Facial Identification System

Answers on page 185.

ACRONYM QUIZ PART I

Read the following information about acronyms used in forensic science, then turn the page for a quiz.

AAFS: American Academy of Forensic Sciences

ABO: ABO blood group system

ADME: absorption, distribution, metabolism, and excretion

ALS: alternate light source

ASTM: American Society for Testing Materials

BAC: blood alcohol concentration

CE: capillary electrophoresis

FID: flame ionization detector for gas chromatography

GLP: good laboratory practice

GSR: gunshot residue

MO: modus operandi

NASH: natural, accidental, suicidal, homicidal (cause of death)

PDQ: paint data query

RMNE: random man not excluded

ACRONYM QUIZ PART 2

(Do not read this until you have read the previous page!)

    1. In the context of forensic investigation, PDQ stands for:
a) pretty darn quick
b) paint data query, a database of vehicle paint colors
c) people deserve quality

    2. GLP stands for:
a) gunshot
b) guided laser probe
c) good laboratory practice

    3. The professional society for people in the forensic professions is:
a) American Academy of Forensic Sciences (AAFS)
b) Academy of American Forensic Investigators (AAFI)
c) American Society for Forensic Professionals (ASFP)

    4. Light sources such as ultraviolet and fluorescent light are
       referred to as:
a) unfamiliar light sources (ULS)
b) alternate light sources (ALS)
c) non-standard light sources (NSLS)

    5. Pharmaceutical compounds go through four phases:
a) absorption, distribution, metabolism, and excretion (ADME)
b) ingestion, distribution, affect, excretion (IDAE)
c) ingestion, metabolism, distribution, absorption (IMDA)

Answers on page 185.

GEMSTONE MATH

There are 6 types of gems. There is 1 gem of the first type, 2 of the second type, 3 of the third type, 4 of the fourth type, 5 of the fifth type, and 6 of the sixth type. From the information given below, can you tell how many gemstones there are of each kind?

There is more than 1 amethyst, and more than 3 garnets. There are twice as many amethysts as there are pieces of jade. There are twice as many sapphires as there are rubies. There is an even number of pieces of topaz. There are more sapphires than amethysts.

Answers on page 185.

VISUALIZE THIS!

Can you determine the order of the restaurants on the street based on the information below?

There are seven restaurants on the street that you're walking down. The Korean barbeque is neither the first place you pass nor at the end of the street. The pizza place, the ice cream parlor, and the sandwich place are all in a row, in that order. There is one other restaurant between the sushi place and the Mexican restaurant. After the burger joint, you pass two restaurants before you reach the pizza place. The sushi restaurant is one of the first three restaurants.

Answers on page 186.

Read the story below, then turn the page and answer the questions.

While on a train, a bystander overheard a conversation where one person was giving another the passwords for a set of underground gambling clubs. The bystander heard that the password for the downtown club was, "Do you have the zucchini lasagna on the menu tonight?" At the near north location, the password was, "You have the most delicious brownies for dessert, pass my compliments to the chef!" At the east side location, the password is, "Is Lon in the kitchen tonight? He makes the best burgers." At the west side location, the password is, "Do you know if the salad dressing has MSG?"

OVERHEAD INFORMATION PART 2

(Do not read this until you have read the previous page!)

As the undercover investigator charged with going into the clubs, you'll need to know the passwords. How many do you remember?

West side: _____

Downtown: _____

Near north: _____

East side: _____

Answers on page 186.

TREASURE HUNT

The treasure hunter found six treasures in a row. At each find, she found a clue for the next treasure. Can you put the list of the six treasures she found in order, using the information below?

1. The amethysts were one of the first two finds, and were found earlier than the diamonds, the rubies, or the sapphires.

2. The diamonds were not the final find.

3. The silver coins were found immediately after the gold bars, and sometime before the diamonds, but not immediately before.

4. Exactly two other finds separated the amethysts and the rubies.

Answers on page 186.

MOTEL HIDEOUT

A thief hides out in one of the 45 motel rooms listed in the chart below. The motel's in-house detective received a sheet of four clues, signed "The Logical Thief." Using these clues, the detective found the room number within 15 minutes—but by that time, the thief had fled. Can you find the thief's motel room quicker?

1. Both digits are odd.
2. The second digit is divisible by 3.
3. The first digit is not divisible by 3 or 5.
4. The second digit is not a prime number.

51	52	53	54	55	56	57	58	59
41	42	43	44	45	46	47	48	49
31	32	33	34	35	36	37	38	39
21	22	23	24	25	26	27	28	29
11	12	13	14	15	16	17	18	19

Answers on page 186.

FLEEING THE SCENE

Change just one letter on each line to go from the top word to the bottom word. Do not change the order of the letters. You must have a common English word at each step.

FLEES

_____

_____

_____

shent (brought shame or discredit on)

_____

SCENE

Answers on page 186.

TRUE CRIME DRAMAS

ACROSS

1. "American Buffalo" playwright David
6. "Buffy the Vampire Slayer" spinoff
11. Classic violin
12. Chip dip
13. Two female investigators attempt to crack old murder cases (on Oxygen & TNT)
15. Mesozoic or Paleozoic
16. Big coffee server
17. Colonial descendants' grp.
18. Investigative journalism podcast from the creators of "This American Life"
20. Back-to-school mo., for many
21. ICU attendants
22. Birch or beech
23. "Coming of Age in ___" (Mead book)
26. Detective's load
27. "Hardly ___ is now alive..."
28. It alerts you when "You've got mail"
29. Buntline and Beatty
30. Real-life homicide cases that were ___ (on ID, Investigation Discovery)
34. "Soft & ___" antiperspirant
35. Down and back, in a pool
36. Exaggerated sense of self

37. Documentary series about missing persons cases (on ID)
40. Eventual oak tree
41. "Get Shorty" actress Rene
42. Judges' seats
43. Baseball card data

DOWN

1. Medieval war clubs
2. "That's ___" (Dean Martin classic)
3. Cheek-related
4. Flight takeoff fig.
5. San Diego neighbor
6. ABA or ALA part
7. Crooner ___ "King" Cole
8. Kin of porch swings
9. Manhunt quarry
10. Hamlet's killer
14. Addresses on the Net
19. Clubs for approach shots
20. Buy some time
23. Pacific flatfish
24. Song that begins "My country, 'tis of thee"
25. Wisconsin's capital
26. Barrel makers
28. "Immediately!" on a memo
31. Vice ___ (conversely)
32. Discharge, as lava
33. Birds extinct since 1681
35. 21-Across helpers
38. Anything bow-shaped
39. Self: Prefix

129

Answers on page 186.

QUICK CRIME QUIZ

How much do you know about fingerprint testing?
Answer the following questions.

1. The first fingerprint classification system was created by a police officer working in this country.

_____ United States

_____ Great Britain

_____ Argentina

2. Do identical twins have identical fingerprints?

_____ Yes

_____ No

3. Can someone be born without fingerprints?

_____ Yes

_____ No

4. Can you lose or erode fingerprints?

_____ Yes

_____ No

5. Can you lift fingerprints from fabric?

_____ Easily

_____ Sometimes, but it is difficult

_____ Never

Answers on page 187.

CODE-DOKU

Solve this puzzle just as you would a sudoku. Use deductive logic to complete the grid so that each row, column, and 3 by 3 box contains the letters from the words OAF ETHICS. When you have completed the puzzle, read the shaded squares to reveal a well-known saying.

Hidden saying: _____

		A		O		C	H
		S	C			E	
						O	
O			I	A		T	
H		F	E				
					O		
T	O		F				E
C			E				I
A				T			

131

ADDING INSULT TO INJURY

Cryptograms are messages in substitution code. Break the code to read the message. For example, THE SMART CAT might become FVO QWGDF JGF if **F** is substituted for **T**, **V** for **H**, **O** for **E**, and so on.

1994 RVW SBF SBFAS LAVUFPRCLI LAFKUVPK HTINB'R MVCISCIJ

SBF RNPFVH APLH V JVGGFPY CI LRGL. SBF SBCFUFR GFAS

QFBCIK V ILSF SBVIECIJ SBF HTRFTH ALP MLLP RFNTPCSY.

SBF GVRS GVTJB WVR LI SBF HTRFTH, SBLTJB, VR MLGCNF

PFNLUFPFK SBF MVCISCIJ VIK NVTJBS SBF SBCFUFR.

Answers on page 187.

CODE-DOKU

Solve this puzzle just as you would a sudoku. Use deductive logic to complete the grid so that each row, column, and 3 by 3 box contains the letters from the word SEARCHING.

G	N		H					
		H			E		G	
	A							C
N		S		I				
	C		S		A		R	
				R		S		G
S							A	
	E		R				I	
					C		H	R

133

SUSPENSE NOVELS

ACROSS

1. "Better late than never" is one
6. Catches, as fly balls
11. Chuck who sang "Maybellene"
12. Fulcrum
13. Show's host
14. Bowl game setting
15. 2000 James Patterson's thriller
17. Copier powders
18. Actor De Niro
21. Ending with Juan or senor
24. Become worn away
25. Like Humpty Dumpty
27. "Runaway" rocker Shannon
28. Completely destroyed
29. Dimwits
32. 2003 Dan Brown blockbuster, with "The"
37. Non-earthling
38. Handrail post
39. Old Wells Fargo transport
40. Like the Parthenon
41. Show respect for
42. Bygone Vegas hotel

DOWN

1. But, to Brahms
2. Audition platter, for short
3. Arrow trajectories
4. Said hello to
5. Decrepit building, e.g.
6. "Donut" in a car trunk
7. Employer, often
8. Intense dislike
9. "___ Girl," 2012 psychological thriller by Gillian Flynn
10. Large town, in Dutch
16. Colony member
18. "___ Dragon," 1981 Thomas Harris suspense novel
19. Bauxite or magnetite
20. Sucre native
22. Make a granny knot
23. Calculate a total
25. Picnics, e.g.
26. Innards
28. Huge bird of myth
30. Mexican muralist Rivera
31. Exclusive, as a "circle"
32. A little bit of salt
33. A choir voice
34. John Irving's "A Prayer for ___ Meany"
35. Closing document
36. American wapitis

1	2	3	4	5		6	7	8	9	10
11						12				
13						14				
15					16					
			17							
18	19	20						21	22	23
24						25	26			
27					28					
		29	30	31						
32	33							34	35	36
37						38				
39						40				
41						42				

Answers on page 187.

MOTEL HIDEOUT

A thief hides out in one of the 45 motel rooms listed in the chart below. The motel's in-house detective received a sheet of four clues, signed "The Logical Thief." Using these clues, the detective found the room number within 15 minutes—but by that time, the thief had fled. Can you find the thief's motel room quicker?

1. The number is divisible by 4.
2. The second digit is larger than the first.
3. The second digit is divisible by 4.
4. The first digit is not a prime number.

51	52	53	54	55	56	57	58	59
41	42	43	44	45	46	47	48	49
31	32	33	34	35	36	37	38	39
21	22	23	24	25	26	27	28	29
11	12	13	14	15	16	17	18	19

Answers on page 187.

TREASURE HUNT

The investigator is tracking a jewelry thief's past trips in order to find and recover jewelry that was left behind in six cities. Each city was visited only once. Can you put together the travel timeline, using the information below?

1. From Minneapolis the thief immediately flew further north.

2. Washington, D.C., was one of the final two cities.

3. Winnipeg was visited sometime before Orlando.

4. From Guadalajara the thief went directly to Seattle.

5. The first city was in the United States.

6. At least one city was visited between the city in Florida and the nation's capital.

Answers on page 188.

AL CAPONE

ACROSS

1. Gorbachev's wife
6. "___ directed" (Rx order)
11. Possessing melody and harmony
12. Beach locale
13. Britannica, e.g.: Abbr.
14. Consume dog style
15. Native of Japan's "second city"
17. Channel surfer's gizmo
19. 30 Rock's architectural style
23. Suffix for press or text
24. Grapples with, slangily
26. ___ good example (is a role model)
28. Mattress springs
29. African-American festival with candles
31. Bullfight shout
32. Like many head-turners
33. "Am not!" rejoinder
35. Bombard with noise
37. Floral shop receptacles
40. Alaskan native's language
43. Decorative pitchers
44. Jai alai basket
45. Apartment rental agreement
46. '50s Ford fiasco

DOWN

1. 1 or 66, briefly
2. L.A.'s ___ Center: second-tallest building in California
3. 20-Down finally got Al Capone on ___ evasion
4. Authority: Colloq.
5. Al Capone's home from 1934–39
6. Home of the Bruins
7. Unnamed person
8. "The Raven" author's monogram
9. Home of the Sun Devils
10. Auto additive brand
16. Hawaii's Mauna ___
17. Hard crisp breads
18. "Maid of Athens, ___ part": Byron
20. Capone's nemesis
21. Casals' instrument
22. Bone: Prefix
25. Capone's nickname
27. Pretzel brand, ___ of Hanover
30. Auto club inits.
34. Fished for congers
36. To be, in Latin class
37. MPH (Abbr.)
38. Amazed feeling
39. Mariner's milieu
41. 434 vehicle, for short
42. Former chess champ Mikhail

139

Answers on page 188.

WACKY WORDY

Can you "read" the phrase below?

BLOUNECMOEON

Answers on page 188.

GEMSTONE MATH

There are 5 types of gems. There is 1 gem of the first type, 2 of the second type, 3 of the third type, 4 of the fourth type, and 5 of the fifth type. From the information given below, can you tell how many gemstones there are of each kind?

There are 3 more emeralds than there are aquamarines. There is an even number of opals and an odd number of peridots. There are fewer agates than aquamarines.

Answers on page 188.

COLUMBO

Every word listed is contained within the group of letters. Words can be found in a straight line horizontally, vertically, or diagonally. They may read either forward or backward.

ARREST

BUMBLE

CATCH

CIGAR

COLUMBO

CONFESS

CRIMES

CRIMINAL

CRUMPLED

DETECTIVE

DISHEVELED

FUMBLING

GUILT

HOMICIDE

INCRIMINATE

LAPD

LIEUTENANT

PETER FALK

RAINCOAT

SHABBY

SUSPECT

THE MRS.

```
D R A I N C O A T A R R E S T
P Q W W H L I E U T E N A N T
A W I N C R I M I N A T E K O
L C A C T H E M R S I V C X T
T D C W A E K K J U Z Y D Z L
I P A I C W E V I T C E T E D
V C O K G V T C E P S U S P I
D O L K L A F R E T E P B R W
E N A K M Q R G E K U U U Q V
L F N I T S U J W O J L M S M
P E I T E I T C O L U M B O G
M S M M L D I S H E V E L E D
U S I T S H A B B Y Q I E V O
R R R H S F U E D I C I M O H
C E C B G N I L B M U F U W L
```

Answers on page 188.

CODE-DOKU

Solve this puzzle just as you would a sudoku. Use deductive logic to complete the grid so that each row, column, and 3 by 3 box contains the letters from the word CHEMISTRY.

			S	M				
					Y		H	
S	C		R			I		
	H	T			E			
			M					
	M				C	H		
	S		E				M	T
I		Y						
			T	I				

Answers on page 188.

LIAR'S LOGIC!

Use the following information to figure out who is lying and who is telling the truth. There are 2 truth tellers and 2 liars.

Person A says, "If you ask person B, he'll tell you I'm a truth teller."

Person B says, "If you ask person C, he'll tell you I'm a truth teller."

Person C says, "If you ask person D, he'll tell you I'm a liar."

Person D says, "If you ask person B, he'll tell you I'm a truth teller."

Answers on page 189.

CRIME STINKS

Change just one letter on each line to go from the top word to the bottom word. Do not change the order of the letters. You must have a common English word at each step.

CRIME

———

———

———

———

———

———

STINK

Answers on page 189.

CRIME RHYMES

Each clue leads to a 2-word answer that rhymes, such as BIG PIG or STABLE TABLE. The numbers in parentheses after the clue give the number of letters in each word. For example, "cookware taken from the oven (3, 3)" would be "hot pot."

1. Murder amongst Neanderthals (10, 7): _____

2. Person who wants to be a PI (11, 9): _____

3. When the police officer likes to play hockey in spare time (6, 12): _____

4. An investigator who specializes in crimes involving dental work (5, 6): _____

5. A line of people waiting at the detective's door (7, 5): _____

6. The detective called the fingerprint found on the candy cane this (10, 5): _____

7. The local ornithological society was horrified when a member was killed in what was later called this (6, 6): _____

8. The case of the poison being found in the toothpaste was called this (8, 8): _____

Answers on page 189.

MIXED-UP MARRIAGES

On Saturday, 6 marriages are due to be performed throughout the day at the local church. However, the details of the brides and grooms have been inadvertently mixed up in the planner. Although each name is in the correct column, only one name in each column is correctly positioned. The following facts are certain about the correct order:

1. Yates is two places below Goliath.
2. Colin is one place below Idi.
3. Fred is three places below Nina, who is two above Underwood.
4. Vitori is somewhere below Olive, who is somewhere below Kite.
5. James is one place above Pauline, who is two places above Doug.
6. Rosie is one place above Abe, who is one above Stephens.

Can you give the first and last names of the groom and bride for each position?

	Groom 1st	Groom 2nd	Bride 1st	Bride 2nd
1	Abe	Goliath	Minnie	Stephens
2	Bill	Holderness	Nina	Tallis
3	Colin	Idi	Olive	Underwood
4	Doug	James	Pauline	Vitori
5	Eddie	Kite	Alice	Wells
6	Fred	Leonard	Rosie	Yates

Answers on page 189.

HAN VAN MEEGEREN

Cryptograms are messages in substitution code. Break the code to read the message. For example, THE SMART CAT might become FVO QWGDF JGF if **F** is substituted for **T**, **V** for **H**, **O** for **E**, and so on.

PBCO MQPZB KWCIPRN DRAWI WO WI WNPCOP JT JNCACIWG

UJNF, AWCICIA OJHR OQZZROO. BJURSRN, BCO UJNF

UWO OJHRPCHRO ZNCPCLQRM WO MRNCSWPCSR WIM

QIJNCACIWG. BR RSRIPQWGGX PQNIRM PJ TJNARNCRO,

CIZGQMCIA JT MQPZB KWCIPRN EJBWIIRO SRNHRRN.

MQNCIA UJNGM UWN CC, JIR JT PBR TJNARN'O KWCIPCIAO

RIMRM QK CI PBR BWIMO JT IWYC BRNHWI AJNCIA.

SWI HRRARNRI UWO WNNROPRM WTPRN PBR UWN TJN

ZJGGWDJNWPCJI UCPB PBR RIRHX—QIPCG BR RVKGWCIRM

PBWP BR BWMI'P OJGM W NRWG SRNHRRN, DQP W

TJNARNX. BR UWO ACSRI W GROORN ORIPRIZR TJN TNWQM,

PBJQAB BR MCRM DRTJNR BR ORNSRM PCHR CI KNCOJI.

149

MOTEL HIDEOUT

A thief hides out in one of the 45 motel rooms listed in the chart below. The motel's in-house detective received a sheet of four clues, signed "The Logical Thief." Using these clues, the detective found the room number within 15 minutes—but by that time, the thief had fled. Can you find the thief's motel room quicker?

1. Each digit is a prime number.
2. The number itself is not prime.
3. The second digit is larger than the first digit by 2.
4. The sum of the digits is less than 10.

51	52	53	54	55	56	57	58	59
41	42	43	44	45	46	47	48	49
31	32	33	34	35	36	37	38	39
21	22	23	24	25	26	27	28	29
11	12	13	14	15	16	17	18	19

150

Answers on page 189.

QUICK CRIME QUIZ

How much do you know about the timeline of forensic science? Answer the following questions.

1. A Chinese book from the 13th century, Hsi DuanYu (the Washing Away of Wrongs) described this:

____ how to tell drowning from strangulation
____ how to tell drowning from natural death
____ how to tell heart attack from strangulation

2. The first instance of bullet comparison being used to solve a murder occurred in this century:

____ 1600s
____ 1700s
____ 1800s
____ 1900s

3. In the U.S., the first use of DNA evidence to solve a crime occurred in this decade.

____ 1970s
____ 1980s
____ 1990s

4. Scientist Karl Landsteiner established that there were different blood types in this decade.

____ 1830s
____ 1900s
____ 1970s

5. The FBI was founded in this year.

____ 1888
____ 1908
____ 1932

Answers on page 190.

151

GEMSTONE MATH

There are 6 types of gems. There is 1 gem of the first type, 2 of the second type, 3 of the third type, 4 of the fourth type, 5 of the fifth type, and 6 of the sixth type. From the information given below, can you tell how many gemstones there are of each kind?

There are 3 times more pearls than peridots. There are 2 more agates than there are garnets. There are 3 more pieces of turquoise than there are rubies. There are more agates than pearls.

Answers on page 190.

LIAR'S LOGIC!

Use the following information to figure out who is lying and who is telling the truth. There are 2 truth tellers and 2 liars. You know that A is telling the truth.

Person A says person C is lying.

Person B says person D is lying.

Person C says person B is telling the truth.

Person D says person A is telling the truth.

Answers on page 190.

JACK THE RIPPER

ACROSS

1. Bridal netting
5. Football Hall of Famer Lynn
10. Like many a shoppe
11. Brian of "A Night to Remember" (1942)
12. London district where Jack the Ripper committed his grisly murders
14. Fraternity with a sweetheart of a song
15. Hot time, in Paris
16. Blend gradually
20. With 28-Across, two-word description of Jack the Ripper
23. Kentucky Derby month
24. Frighten off
25. American Indian corn
27. Colorado NHL team, to fans
28. See 20-Across
29. Hang on to
31. Johann who opposed Martin Luther
32. Dubai and Abu Dhabi, e.g.
37. Study of Jack the Ripper's unsolved crimes
40. Big name in tableware
41. Persian Gulf state
42. Farm buildings
43. Answers, for short

DOWN

1. Wedding ceremony exchange
2. Concerning grades K-12
3. "Got it!"
4. Big Bad Wolf's demand
5. Librarian's interjection
6. "___ to please"
7. "Dada" artist Jean
8. D.C. to N.Y. heading
9. "Volare (___ Blu Dipinto di Blu)"
11. Speed up, in music: Abbr.
13. Bother over time
17. Actor Jannings who received the first Oscar ever presented
18. Be idle
19. Easter egg colorer
20. Mt. Rushmore's state
21. Home's overhang
22. Bit of subterfuge
25. It means very little
26. Acid neutralizers
28. Knightley of "Pride & Prejudice"
30. Charlemagne's father, dubbed "the Short"
33. Drugs, informally
34. Barcelona bull
35. Equal, in Paris
36. Roget entries, briefly
37. Actor/director Reiner
38. One-million link
39. For each

155

Answers on page 190.

FINGERPRINT MATCH

Find the matching fingerprint(s). There may be more than one.

A.   B.   C.   D.

E.   F.   G.   H.

I.   J.   K.   L.

M.   N.   O.   P.

Answers on page 190.

GAME BOARD PART I

Study this game board for one minute, particularly the shapes and their placement. Then turn the page for a memory challenge.

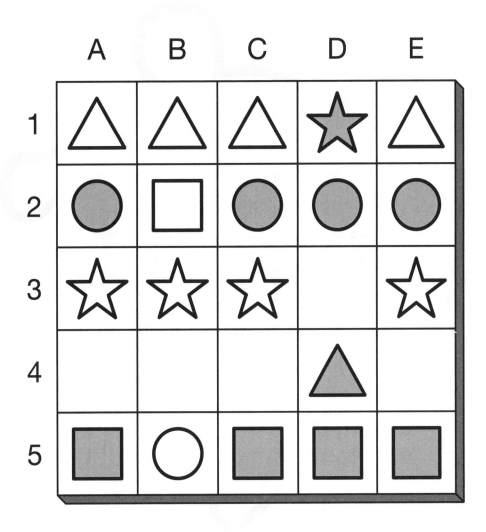

GAME BOARD PART 2

(Do not read this until you have read the previous page!)

Duplicate the board as seen on the previous page.

	A	B	C	D	E
1					
2					
3					
4					
5					

Answers on page 190.

LIAR'S LOGIC!

Use the following information to figure out who is lying and who is telling the truth. There are 2 liars and 2 truth tellers.

Person A says, "If you ask person B, he'll call me a truth teller."

Person B says, "If you ask person D, he'll call person C a liar."

Person C says, "Person B is a liar."

Person D says, "Person A is a liar."

159

POLICE STATION SHENANIGANS

It seems this "Trixter" guy just never gets tired of playing games with the police! This time he's hidden a stolen brooch in a vending machine right in the waiting room of Precinct 23! Each option in the vending machine has its own number, and "Trixter" has given the police a series of clues that will reveal its exact location. Can you retrieve the stolen brooch?

1. It is not divisible by 3.
2. It is less than 40.
3. The sum of the digits is less than 10.
4. It is divisible by 2 different prime numbers (excluding 1).
5. It is not even.

11	12	13	14	15	16	17	18	19
21	22	23	24	25	26	27	28	29
31	32	33	34	35	36	37	38	39
41	42	43	44	45	46	47	48	49
51	52	53	54	55	56	57	58	59

Answers on page 191.

TALKING TERMINOLOGY

How much do you know about the vocabulary of crime scene investigation? Answer the following questions.

1. What is the difference between a coroner and a medical examiner?

a) No difference. These are two different terms for the same role.

b) Coroners are elected and may not be physicians; medical examiners are physicians appointed to the job.

c) Medical examiners can only perform exams like blood tests and visual examinations, while autopsies must be performed by coroners.

2. In American law, the terms robbery, burglary, and theft are used to describe three slightly different crimes. Which statement below describes each crime?

a) This term refers to the act of wrongfully taking property from someone without their consent.

b) If you use force or the threat of force to take someone else's property without consent, this term is used.

c) If you enter a structure or dwelling with the intent of committing a crime, this term is used.

3. A forensic dentist is also called by this term.

a) Entomologist

b) Odontologist

c) Pathologist

4. This word is used by arson investigators to describe a substance that promotes or spreads a fire.

a) Accelerant

b) Combustant

c) Flammable

Answers on page 191.

MOTEL HIDEOUT

A thief hides out in one of the 45 motel rooms listed in the chart below. The motel's in-house detective received a sheet of four clues, signed "The Logical Thief." Using these clues, the detective found the room number within 15 minutes—but by that time, the thief had fled. Can you find the thief's motel room quicker?

1. It is a prime number larger than 20.
2. The second digit is larger than the first.
3. The second digit is divisible by 3.
4. The first digit is not divisible by 2.

51	52	53	54	55	56	57	58	59
41	42	43	44	45	46	47	48	49
31	32	33	34	35	36	37	38	39
21	22	23	24	25	26	27	28	29
11	12	13	14	15	16	17	18	19

Answers on page 191.

DO IT YOURSELF PART I

Study these basic tools for a minute, then turn the page for a memory challenge.

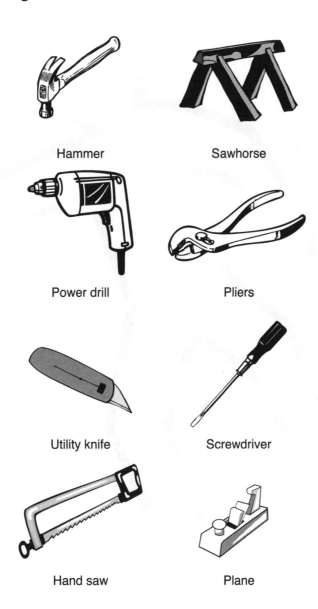

Hammer

Sawhorse

Power drill

Pliers

Utility knife

Screwdriver

Hand saw

Plane

DO IT YOURSELF PART 2

(Do not look at this until you have read the previous page!)

Check off the tools you saw on the previous page.

CIRCULAR SAW

PLIERS

PIPE WRENCH

LATHE

PLANE

SAWHORSE

LEVEL

RULER

CROWBAR

CHISEL

HAMMER

HAND SAW

UTILITY KNIFE

Answers on page 191.

POLICE STATION SHENANIGANS

It seems this "Trixter" guy just never gets tired of playing games with the police! This time he's hidden a stolen brooch in a vending machine right in the waiting room of Precinct 23! Each option in the vending machine has its own number, and "Trixter" has given the police a series of clues that will reveal its exact location. Can you retrieve the stolen brooch?

1. It is not a multiple of 5.
2. It is greater than 30.
3. It is a multiple of 7.
4. The sum of the digits is less than 10.

11	12	13	14	15	16	17	18	19
21	22	23	24	25	26	27	28	29
31	32	33	34	35	36	37	38	39
41	42	43	44	45	46	47	48	49
51	52	53	54	55	56	57	58	59

Answers on page 191.

FIND THE WITNESS

You want to interview a witness in a cold case, Ken Rawlins. He and his wife have moved since the case was active. From their fomer neighbor, you know they now live on Perkins Avenue, which has five houses, but you don't know which house they live in. They do not have any children. The staff at the bakery around the corner and your own observations give you some clues. From the information given, can you find the right house?

1. There are married couples in two of the houses.
2. Kids live in the middle house and one of the houses next door.
3. An elderly widower lives in one of the corner houses.
4. A single mom with custody of her kids lives in house D.
5. A widow lives next door to the widower and they have recently begun dating.

Answers on page 192.

WHAT CHANGED? PART I

Study this picture of the crime scene for 1 minute, then turn the page.

WHAT CHANGED? PART 2

(Do not read this until you have read the previous page!)

From memory, can you tell what changed between this page and the previous page?

Answers on page 192.

FIND THE WITNESS

On Riverdell Street, there are 5 houses. You need to follow up with a witness, Harriet Chin, but without any address on the doors you are not sure which house to approach. You know from the previous interview that Chin is a single mother with a daughter. The staff at the corner bakery and your own observations give you some clues. From the information given, can you find the right house?

A. The two corner houses are green, while the others are blue. There is a child or children living in one green house and two blue houses.
B. An elderly widower lives alone in the middle house.
C. The nanny for the couple in house E regularly brings her charge by for a treat at the bakery.
D. Sometimes she brings in the daughter of her next door neighbor, but the nanny doesn't like the boy further down the street.

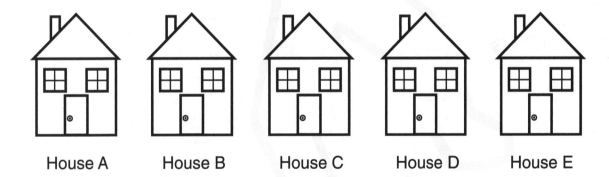

House A   House B   House C   House D   House E

169

Answers on page 192.

ANSWER PAGE

Detectives (page 4)

The leftover letters spell: "Sherlock Holmes and Doctor Watson (Doyle)."

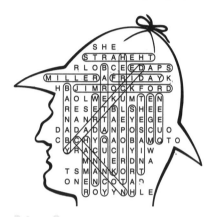

Prime Suspect (page 6)

	Nationality	Hair	Coat	Build
1	Italian	none	green	round
2	English	red	blue	thin
3	Chinese	gray	purple	slim
4	Spanish	white	cream	medium
5	African	dark	yellow	hunched
6	Mexican	brown	mauve	fat

The Yellow-Brick Road (page 7)

B. The blue road. If the liar tells us the truth-teller would say to take the red road, we know that we should take the blue road. If the truth-teller tells us the liar would tell us to take the red road, he's telling the truth that the red road would be lied about as the right way to go. So if we are told to take the red road, we should take the blue road and vice versa, regardless of who we ask.

Identity Parade (page 8)

A   B   C   D

Game Board Part 2 (page 10)

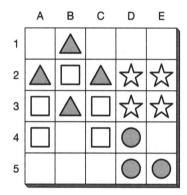

Code-doku (page 11)

A	P	N	O	I	M	E	C	L
E	O	M	N	C	L	I	P	A
C	L	I	P	A	E	N	M	O
O	I	A	E	N	C	M	L	P
N	C	P	M	L	I	A	O	E
M	E	L	A	P	O	C	I	N
L	M	E	I	O	A	P	N	C
P	A	O	C	M	N	L	E	I
I	N	C	L	E	P	O	A	M

ANSWER PAGE

Motel Hideout (page 12)
The thief is in room 42.

Bank Mayhem (page 13)
The answer is 14.

Criminals (page 14)
BANDIT
BURGLAR
CROOK
GANGSTER
MUGGER
OUTLAW
ROBBER
THIEF

High Fives (page 15)

	Name	Surname	Subject	University
1	Daisy	Gopher	history	MIT
2	Ben	Jelly	physics	Caltech
3	Arnold	Harris	philosophy	Yale
4	Ellen	Fate	mathematics	Harvard
5	Cathy	Ink	economics	Princeton

Eavesdropping Logic (page 16)
The answer is A, as the idea that nobody "could" have heard her suggests that she is denying the accusation, and the idea that nobody "would" have heard it suggests a condition under which it would not have happened, perhaps implying a sentence in which the woman defends the fact that she overheard something. Whereas "should" suggests that it was improper for the conversation to be overheard, and is most compatible with an admission of guilt.

Find the Witness (page 17)
Mr. Jones lives in House D.

ANSWER PAGE

She's a Cop! (page 18)

Cold Case; CSI; In Plain Sight; Law and Order: SVU; Missing; Police Woman; Saving Grace; T.J. Hooker; The Closer; The Mod Squad; Without a Trace

```
C T M D N R E L T O T I C E W
L S H P O L E J S D I O L I P
R A A G W M H S R C D A T W O
P C W T I O I S O A C H U I L
I O Q A O S V S U L O S E T I
S H L K N S N Q S U C C O S C
T H E I P D S I T I A E C O E
E R C I C D O A A R N G H U W
P S A P O E T R G L S G T T R
O E A M H R W G D P P W H M T
L H E C A O N O U E Q N E I H
I H W C D I L C M O R C I S O
T C E H V L T J H A N S A S U
I I I A I C O T E C N S V I S
A C S L N P L C W I T H O U W
```

Chemical Reaction (page 20)

C. We know the first chemical (Chem1) and the second chemical (Chem2) will total 40 ounces. We also know that 40 ounces times $70 is $2,800. So:

Chem1 + Chem2 = 40
90 X Chem1 + 40 X Chem2 = 2800
Multiply the first equation by -90.
-90 Chem1 -90 Chem2 = -3600
 90 Chem1 + 40 Chem2 = 2800
              -50 Chem 2 = -800
Chem2 equals 16 ounces, which means
Chem1 = 24 ounces

Back Up Your Memory Part 2 (page 22)

Backboard; backpack, back flip, backgammon

Find the Suspect (page 23)

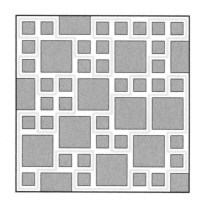

Bank Mayhem (page 24)

The answer is 99.

Eavesdropping Logic (page 25)

A is untrue. B and C are correct.

ANSWER PAGE

Word Trio (page 26)

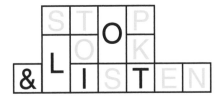

Sequence (page 27)

D. The sequence consist of the repeated symbols:

Riddle (page 28)

Alice drove the car down the driveway in reverse.

Famous Detective Scramble (page 29)

1. Sherlock Holmes, E. Arthur Conan Doyle; 2. Miss Marple, C., Agatha Christie; 3. C. Auguste Dupin, D. Edgar Allan Poe; 4. Nero Wolfe, A. Rex Stout; 5. Kinsey Millhone, B. Sue Grafton

Visualize This! (page 30)

The order is: notepad, magnifying glass, pencil, fingerprint kit, flashlight, measuring tape

Train Station Terrors (page 31)

The answer is 27.

ANSWER PAGE

Sequencing (page 32)
A. Ulan Bator. The pattern is that the first vowel in the gem's name is the first letter in the city's name.

From Clues to Trial (page 33)
Answers may vary. CLUES, flues, flies, fries, tries, tried, triad, TRIAL

Crime Rhymes (page 34)
1. eel steal; 2. bleu clue; 3. beef thief; 4. lime crime; 5. aperitif thief; 6. yacht plot; 7. reflective detective; 8. mint print

Crime Cryptogram (page 35)
The actor's costar accused him of a dastardly crime, but the police refused to investigate. What did he do?

He stole the scene!

Come Together (page 36)

| S | U | S | P | E | C | T | E | D |

| E | X | A | M | I | N | E | R | S |

| B | A | L | L | I | S | T | I | C |

Motel Hideout (page 37)
The thief is in room 28.

Find the Witness (page 38)

Mr. Linus lives in House E.

Planted Evidence at the Scene (page 39)

Answers may vary. PLANT, slant, scant, scent, SCENE

Treasure Hunt (page 40)

The order is: Los Angeles, California; Chicago, Illinois; Austin, Texas; St. Louis, Missouri; Dallas, Texas; Portland, Oregon; Boston, Massachusetts; Tallahassee, Florida.

Crime Rhymes (page 41)

1. stolen colon; 2. yuletide homicide; 3. subliminal criminal; 4. indict knight; 5. swaps cops; 6. steal oatmeal; 7. illegal beagle; 8. mime crime

Bank Mayhem (page 42)

The answer is 64.

Crack the Password (page 43)

The missing letter is O.

noise, primrose, loaner, mosaic

ANSWER PAGE

Homicide: Life on the Streets (page 44)

```
B E P T A H A H T S Y Y A Y B
Z K S E E V I T C E T E D H L
T L Q S M C Q U O M C C O P G
P C I S G B A H C Z E I W O N
A E I I H C L R C L P L I S G
R C A L D Z I E U N S O N O I
T E K Y F M B O T H U P T L A
N V U A E N S X P O S M E I R
E I V B M J O Q O G N I R H D
R D V V Y L H C G P B J V P E
S E C I T S U J J L E W I S L
I N E Q U A L I T Y V I E I L
U C B A L T I M O R E L W E O
O E X Y M W M T R O A V T E P
R E E R A C A J U D G M E N T
```

Motel Hideout (page 46)
The thief is in room 14.

Overheard Information Part 2 (page 48)
1. B; 2. C; 3. D; 4. C

Fingerprint Match (page 49)
The matching pairs are: A and G; B and H; C and E; D and F

Train Station Terrors (page 50)
The answer is 35.

Can a Clue Set You Free? (page 51)
Answer may vary. CLUE, glue, glee, flee, FREE

Crime Rhymes (page 52)
1. Fry alibi; 2. lyre fire; 3. steeplechase case; 4. melon felon; 5. knock hemlock; 6. supplied cyanide; 7. gem mayhem; 8. mortician suspicion

Mealtime Crime (page 53)
What did the headline read for the bakery theft that took place during the solstice in June?

The Summertime Key Lime Crime.

The Law (page 54)

```
A E A Y B M V X H Q F W Y Z Y
T E U E V K S H D D P V V R S
R M L A V E A P P E A L U X S
U A G P G I H X T V W J A G I
O R A A J I D J R A E U N F M
C R M P B R U E A C Z D L E S
L A D O C U M E N T I G O L I
D I I A W T Q E S C V E Z O D
R G S E H F T S C Y E T T N E
R N C L D N V F R A S L Q Y V
E J O I E N D I I D R O C E R
Y A V S R E H N P R U L I N G
W O E U P P Q E T C Z I B Y J
A G R T F Y F N R U C I V I L
L L Y H O M F G N I R A E H S
```

Treasure Hunt (page 56)
The order is: Charleston, South Carolina; Topeka, Kansas; Oklahoma City, Oklahoma; Baltimore, Maryland; Milwaukee, Wisconsin; San Diego, California; Boise, Idaho; Atlanta, Georgia.

AKA (page 57)
1. B; 2. F; 3. D; 4. A; 5. E; 6. C

Motel Hideout (page 58)
The thief is in room 48.

ANSWER PAGE

Forging Money (page 59)

Answers may vary. FORGE, forte, forts, fores, bores, bones, hones, honey, MONEY

For Stage and Screen (page 60)

```
D O N A L D P I C K E R I N G
A K K B N B R U C E M C R A E
V R A Y M O N D F R A N C I S
I Q Y X O C N A L A Q Q Y R R
D G N U O Y D N A L O R W O F
B E N K I N G S L E Y H F B B
U I N I G E L B R U C E X E V
R T R H T F Q S C D Q J S R M
K W P O J X D Y R Y U V I T H
E K C I W D R A H D R A W D E
M A R T I N F R E E M A N U I
W E L L E B E L R Y K H C V T
H X E E N C A M K C I R T A P
S I L L I W T R E B U H M L V
W J M C O L I N B L A K E L Y
```

Interception (page 62)

Take the last letter of each place name to reveal: Kansas City

Overheard Information Part 2 (page 64)

1. Zero $5 bills, 100 $10 bills, 35 $20 bills, zero $50 bills, 60 $100 bills
2. 03-21-17
3. Thursday at 6 PM

Fingerprint Match (page 65)

F is the matching fingerprint.

Crime Scene (page 66)

```
S T A I R . S P O R T
O U I D A . A R M O R
D N A E V I D E N C E
. . . E A R L . E S E
A H A . G O Y A . . .
L A W M E N . M I N T
B L O O D . F I B E R
S O L D . M E D I C O
. . . E G A D . S K Y
I T S . O R E S . . .
P H O T O G R A P H S
S E R I F . A R E A S
E N E M Y . L A R G E
```

Treasure Hunt (page 68)

The order is: Nashville (United States); Seoul (South Korea); Buenos Aires (Argentina); Athens (Greece); Denver (United States); Atlanta (United States)

Motel Hideout (page 69)

The thief is in room 54.

Don't Leave a Print (page 70)

Answers may vary. LEAVE, heave, heavy, heady, heads, hears, heirs, hairs, pairs, paint, PRINT

Fingerprint Match (page 71)

The matching pairs are: A and K; B and I; C and L; D and J; E and H; F and N; G and P; M and O

Crime Rhymes (page 72)

1. might indict; 2. watermelon felon; 3. physician suspicion; 4. vermouth sleuth; 5. glue clue; 6. investigate the first mate; 7. lakeside homicide; 8. prospective detective

Overheard Information Part 2 (page 74)

1. A. Two men; 2. D. 05-36-29; 3. B. Thursday; 4. B. Kerri

ANSWER PAGE

Motel Hideout **(page 75)**
The answer is 45.

Grid Fill **(page 76)**

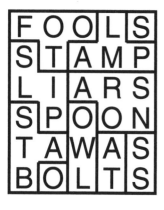

All Secret Plots Leave Clues **(page 77)**
Answers may vary. PLOTS, slots, slits, flits, flies, flues, CLUES

Motel Hideout **(page 78)**
The thief is in room 12.

Overheard Information Part 2 **(page 80)**
1. A; 2. C; 3. B; 4. D

Leaving Clues **(page 81)**
Answers may vary. LEAVE, lease, cease, chase, chasm, charm, chars, chaps, chips, clips, flips, flies, flues, CLUES

Blue Bloods (page 82)

```
A Y R E N O I S S I M M O C G
E R I N H J W A H L B E R G R
K B E E A M J S E L L E C K Z
Y A N M K E J E F A M I L Y D
H R I W E V E C I L O P A T P
Y E S E F I C O P S Y I T I Y
H A O G R T M T K T N R T C N
L G Y R A C O A D X A Z O J N
G A J A N E P T L G H V R U O
W N B H K T S Y N N A D N S F
I J B C A E F Y R O N L E T F
W U X L R D G C D D S V Y I I
Q U Q R U U N B S V Y J H C C
B J A O P E S I Z U Z H K E E
W N S O K M K D L X X Y T Q R
```

DNA Quiz (page 84)

1. A; 2. Adenine, guanine, thymine; 3. A

What Went Missing? Part 2 (page 86)

The cotton swabs went missing.

Fingerprint Match (page 87)

A and L are the matching fingerprints.

A Long Path from Crime to Trial (page 88)

Answers may vary. CRIME, grime, gripe, grips, grins, gains, pains, pairs, hairs, hairy, dairy, daily, drily, drill, trill, TRIAL

Motel Hideout (page 89)

The answer is 33.

ANSWER PAGE

DNA Sequence (page 90)

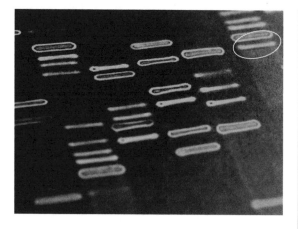

What Changed? Part 2 (page 92)

A pair of tweezers disappeared. Look to the right of the scissors in the bottom half of the suitcase.

A Mystery from History (page 93)

The Voynich manuscript is a famous manuscript that has challenged cryptographers. The manuscript supposedly dates back to the early fifteen century. It contains drawings of plants and other objects accompanied by text, but no one has been able to decipher the text.

Grid Fill (page 94)

```
A R C H E R
S L I G H T
O N T I M E
S P A R T A
C O O K I E
A R R E S T
T A M A L E
```

Find a Clue on a Raid (page 95)

Answers may vary. CLUE, glue, glum, slum, slim, slid, said, RAID

Stolen Art (page 96)

¹A	²P	³I	⁴A	⁵N		⁶D	⁷A	⁸S	⁹H

(Crossword solution grid)

Across/Down letters:
- APIAN, DASH
- DANTE, AORTA
- RIFTS, CUTER
- EDEN, SCREAM
- AFR, POE, SDS
- MONALISA
- ROWE, SARG
- WATERLOO
- ODD, SAD, SGS
- CHORUS, ATRA
- TAMER, STIEG
- ABELE, RENEE
- LIDO, AMENS

182

Legal TV Shows (page 98)

```
C  O  N  V  I  C  T  I  O  N  E  T  F  V  L
J  U  D  G  I  N  G  A  M  Y  F  S  C  W  C
I  L  L  E  C  O  R  T  E  P  I  R  N  A  N
M  V  K  Q  X  W  K  I  L  A  W  A  P  L  I
P  P  B  A  I  C  A  D  I  O  D  W  J  A  G
N  C  O  L  O  E  P  E  S  V  O  L  R  L  H
O  K  S  L  G  S  R  F  T  Q  O  I  R  L  T
S  D  T  Y  U  A  A  E  O  Q  G  V  K  Y  C
A  A  O  M  A  H  C  N  N  T  O  I  Y  I  O
M  M  N  C  R  C  T  D  E  P  Z  C  T  G  U
Y  A  L  B  D  R  I  E  C  K  R  A  H  S  R
R  G  E  E  I  E  C  R  R  W  P  Z  U  C  T
R  E  G  A  A  P  E  S  L  B  Z  I  X  J  E
E  S  A  L  N  A  A  D  E  H  T  N  D  H  J
P  W  L  M  W  P  D  N  D  S  L  L  U  B  L
```

Police Station Shenanigans (page 100)

The answer is 39.

Interception (page 101)

Take the first letter of the first word, the last letter of the second word, the first letter of the third word, and the last letter of the fourth word. Continue, alternating between the first letter of one word and the final letter of the next word, until you have the whole message: April third, noon, park, Main Street

Elevator Words (page 102)

1. CRIME wave; 2. waveform; 3. form letter; 4. letterhead; 5. headband; 6. band music; 7. music SCENE

Quick Crime Quiz (page 103)

1. True. Fingerprints were used as signatures as far back as ancient Babylon; 2. Fingerprints; 3. True. Bertillion's system produced a set of measurements for each person (for instance, the length of their head, their middle finger, and their foot) that were, in theory, unique to that person. 4. Mug shots; 5. 1850

Crime on TV (page 104)

Across/Down crossword solution:

```
B O N E S  P A I L S
O D I S T  A S N I T
M E C C A  T I A R A
B R E A K I N G B A D
      P I S A N O
S I R E N S    O L E
Q U E E G  S S T A R
S M L    U T A H A N
      E M I N E M
S E A R C H P A R T Y
I T S M E  O R U R O
G R E E R  F R E A K
N E S T S  F A R G O
```

ANSWER PAGE

Crime Scene (page 106)

Answers may vary. CRIME, prime, prise, prose, prone, phone, shone, stone, stole, stale, stall, small, smell, spell, spelt, spent, scent, SCENE. Variation: CRIME, crine, chine, shine, shone, scone, SCENE

Overheard Information Part 2 (page 108)

1. A; 2. B; 3. B; 4. A

Motel Hideout (page 109)

The thief is in room 24.

Treasure Hunt (page 110)

The order was: Dallas (Texas); Newark (New Jersey); Toronto (Ontario); Albany (New York); Los Angeles (California), and Madison (Wisconsin). The states of Wisconsin and New York, and the province of Ontario, all border a Great Lake.

Seen at the Scene Part 2 (page 112)

Picture 4 is a match.

Code-doku (page 113)

MR. GREEN, REVOLVER, LOUNGE

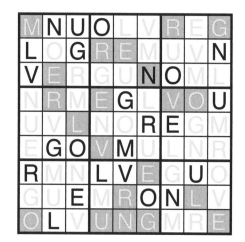

ANSWER PAGE

Missing Words (page 114)

1. America's; 2. Justice; 3. Brooklyn;
4. Cagney; 5. Jordan; 6. Diagnosis;
7. Files; 8. Street; 9. Magnum;
10. She Wrote; 11. NYPD; 12. Prime;
13. Rockford; 14. Walker; 15. Trace

```
V B F U C H T Q G U O D S U P
R D Q S T R E E T C Q G I L U
B R E U V H Y F H R J A S D Z
D O P D P Y N S L P X J O U U
A F W K H E H Q R A F O N E T
X K I A M E R I C A S R G R G
M C T K W D M J N B C D A N D
F O L R X E Z G D B Q A I C W
B R O O K L Y N E Z O N D A W
Y T P I B E H W T R A C E A C
E M T L M S Q Q H C B Q L I A
W W M U N G A M P I D K Q L G
E C I T S U J J Z J E S U W N
R F I L E S P W A R R Z D H E
C L S C G T M Z B K H F H P Y
```

Multiples of Six Number Maze (page 116)

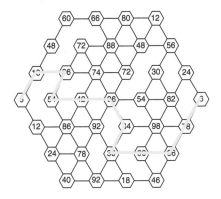

Motel Hideout (page 117)

The thief is in room 32.

Quick Crime Quiz (page 118)

1. No. They may have been there but worn gloves, for example. 2. No. A body farm describes a place where forensic investigators test to see what happens to corpses under different conditions. 3. Yes. 4. Yes. Many courts do not admit polygraph evidence, because they can show both false negatives and false positives. 5. Automated Fingerprint Identification System

Acronym Quiz Part 2 (page 120)

1. B; 2. C; 3. A; 4. B; 5. A

Gemstone Math (page 121)

The count is: 1 piece of jade, 2 amethysts, 3 rubies, 4 pieces of topaz, 5 garnets, 6 sapphires.

Visualize This! (page 122)

The order is: sushi, burger joint, Mexican, Korean barbeque, pizza, ice cream parlor, sandwich place.

Overheard Information Part 2 (page 124)

West side: "Do you know if the salad dressing has MSG?" Downtown: "Do you have the zucchini lasagna on the menu tonight?" Near north: "You have the most delicious brownies for dessert, pass my compliments to the chef!" East side: "Is Lon in the kitchen tonight? He makes the best burgers."

Treasure Hunt (page 125)

The order is: amethysts, gold bars, silver coins, rubies, diamonds, sapphires.

Motel Hideout (page 126)

The thief is in room 19.

Fleeing the Scene (page 127)

Answers may vary. FLEES, fleet, sleet, sheet, shent, scent, SCENE

True Crime Dramas (page 128)

M	A	M	E	T		A	N	G	E	L
A	M	A	T	I		S	A	L	S	A
C	O	L	D	J	U	S	T	I	C	E
E	R	A		U	R	N		D	A	R
S	E	R	I	A	L		S	E	P	T
		R	N	S		T	R	E	E	
S	A	M	O	A		C	A	S	E	S
A	M	A	N		A	O	L			
N	E	D	S		S	O	L	V	E	D
D	R	I		L	A	P		E	G	O
D	I	S	A	P	P	E	A	R	E	D
A	C	O	R	N		R	U	S	S	O
B	A	N	C	S		S	T	A	T	S

Quick Crime Quiz (page 130)

1. Juan Vucetich of Argentina created the first fingerprint classification system for police. 2. No. 3. Yes. It is rare, but it does happen. 4. Yes. Wear, certain chemicals, and certain chemotherapy drugs can erode fingerprints, but it is difficult to do. 5. Researchers have been developing techniques to lift fingerprints off fabric, but it is more difficult than lifting them from other materials.

Code-doku (page 131)

Set a thief to catch a thief

S	E	A	T	I	O	F	C	H
I	H	O	S	C	F	A	E	T
F	C	T	H	A	E	I	O	S
O	S	C	I	H	A	E	T	F
H	T	F	E	O	C	S	I	A
E	A	I	F	T	S	O	H	C
T	O	H	A	F	I	C	S	E
C	F	S	O	E	T	H	A	I
A	I	E	C	S	H	T	F	O

Adding Insult to Injury (page 132)

1994 saw the theft of a version of Edvard Munch's painting The Scream from a gallery in Oslo. The thieves left behind a note thanking the museum for poor security. The last laugh was on the museum, though, as police recovered the painting and caught the thieves.

Code-doku (page 133)

G	N	I	H	C	R	A	E	S
C	S	H	A	N	E	R	G	I
R	A	E	I	G	S	H	N	C
N	R	S	G	I	H	E	C	A
I	C	G	S	E	A	N	R	H
E	H	A	C	R	N	S	I	G
S	G	R	N	H	I	C	A	E
H	E	C	R	A	G	I	S	N
A	I	N	E	S	C	G	H	R

Suspense Novels (page 134)

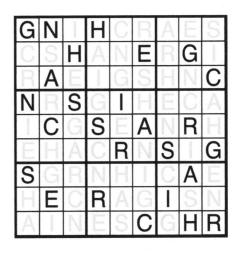

Motel Hideout (page 136)

The thief is in room 48.

ANSWER PAGE

Treasure Hunt (page 137)

The order is: Minneapolis (Minnesota); Winnipeg (Canada); Orlando (Florida); Guadalajara (Mexico); Seattle (Washington); Washington, D.C.

Al Capone (page 138)

R¹	A²	I³	S⁴	A⁵	⬛	U⁶	S⁷	E⁸	A⁹	S¹⁰
T¹¹	O	N	A	L	⬛	C¹²	O	A	S	T
E¹³	N	C	Y	C	⬛	L¹⁴	A	P	U	P
⬛	⬛	O¹⁵	S	A	K¹⁶	A	N	⬛	⬛	⬛
R¹⁷	E¹⁸	M	O	T	E	⬛	D¹⁹	E²⁰	C²¹	O²²
U²³	R	E	⬛	R²⁴	A	S²⁵	S	L	E	S
S²⁶	E	T	S²⁷	A	⬛	C²⁸	O	I	L	S
K²⁹	W	A	N	Z	A³⁰	A	⬛	O³¹	L	E
S³²	E	X	Y	⬛	A³³	R	E³⁴	T	O	O
⬛	⬛	⬛	D³⁵	E³⁶	A	F	E	N	⬛	⬛
V³⁷	A³⁸	S³⁹	E	S	⬛	A⁴⁰	L	E	U⁴¹	T⁴²
E⁴³	W	E	R	S	⬛	C⁴⁴	E	S	T	A
L⁴⁵	E	A	S	E	⬛	E⁴⁶	D	S	E	L

Wacky Wordy (page 140)

Once in a blue moon

Gemstone Math (page 141)

The count is: 1 piece of agate, 2 aquamarines, 3 peridots, 4 opals, and 5 emeralds.

Columbo (page 142)

D	R	A	I	N	C	O	A	T	A	R	R	E	S	T
P	Q	W	W	H	L	I	E	U	T	E	N	A	N	T
A	W	I	N	C	R	I	M	I	N	A	T	E	K	O
L	C	A	C	T	H	E	M	R	S	I	V	C	X	T
T	D	C	W	A	E	K	K	J	U	Z	Y	D	Z	L
I	P	A	I	C	W	E	V	I	T	C	E	T	E	D
V	C	O	K	G	V	T	C	E	P	S	U	S	P	I
D	O	L	K	L	A	F	R	E	T	E	P	B	R	W
E	N	A	K	M	Q	R	G	E	K	U	U	U	Q	V
L	F	N	I	T	S	U	J	W	O	J	L	M	S	M
P	E	I	T	E	I	T	C	O	L	U	M	B	O	G
M	S	M	M	L	D	I	S	H	E	V	E	L	E	D
U	S	I	T	S	H	A	B	B	Y	Q	I	E	V	O
R	R	R	H	S	F	U	E	D	I	C	I	M	O	H
C	E	C	B	G	N	I	L	B	M	U	F	U	W	L

Code-doku (page 144)

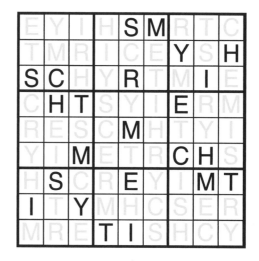

			S	M				
						Y		H
S	C			R				I
	H	T				E		
				M				
		M					C	H
	S			E				M
	I		Y					
				T	I			

Liar's Logic! (page 145)

The truth tellers must be B and C. If A is telling the truth, then B must also be telling the truth, then C must also be telling the truth, which is too many truth tellers. If A is lying, B wouldn't call him a truth teller, he'd truthfully call him a liar. If B is telling the truth then C must be as well, in which case D is a liar, which fits his statement given B is a truth teller.

Crime Stinks (page 146)

Answers may vary. CRIME, prime, pride, bride, brine, brink, blink, slink, STINK

Crime Rhymes (page 147)

1. prehistory mystery; 2. prospective detective; 3. skater investigator;
4. tooth sleuth; 5. gumshoe queue;
6. peppermint print; 7. birder murder;
8. fluoride homicide

Mixed-up Marriages (page 148)

	Groom 1st	Groom 2nd	Bride 1st	Bride 2nd
1	Eddie	Kite	Nina	Tallis
2	Bill	James	Rosie	Wells
3	Abe	Goliath	Pauline	Underwood
4	Fred	Holderness	Olive	Stephens
5	Doug	Idi	Alice	Yates
6	Colin	Leonard	Minnie	Vitori

Han van Meegeren (page 149)

This Dutch painter began as an artist of original work, gaining some success. However, his work was sometimes critiqued as derivative and unoriginal. He eventually turned to forgeries, including of Dutch painter Johannes Vermeer.

During World War II, one of the forger's paintings ended up in the hands of Nazi Herman Goring. Van Meegeran was arrested after the war for collaboration with the enemy—until he explained that he hadn't sold a real Vermeer, but a forgery. He was given a lesser sentence for fraud, though he died before he served time in prison.

Motel Hideout (page 150)

The thief is in room 35.

ANSWER PAGE

Quick Crime Quiz (page 151)

1. How to tell drowning from strangulation. 2. 1800s. 3. 1980s. 4. 1900s. 5. 1908.

Gemstone Math (page 152)

The count is: 1 peridot, 2 rubies, 3 pearls, 4 garnets, 5 pieces of turquoise, and 6 agates.

Liar's Logic! (page 153)

Since A is telling the truth, we know C is lying when saying that B is a truth teller. Therefore D must be the second truth teller.

Jack the Ripper (page 154)

Fingerprint Match (page 156)

E is the matching fingerprint.

Game Board (PART 2) (page 158)

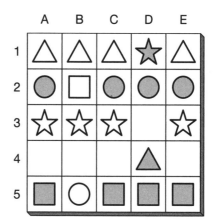

Liar's Logic! (page 159)

A and B are liars. C and D are truth tellers. If C is telling the truth, then B is a liar. If B is a liar, then D would really call C a truth teller, which would make D a truth teller. That means A would have to be the second liar. If A is a liar, then B would actually call him a liar, which fits. If C is lying, then B is a truth teller. If B is a truth teller, then D would indeed call C a liar, but D doesn't, therefore making B a liar and C a truth teller.

Police Station Shenanigans (page 160)

The number is 35.

Talking Terminology (page 161)

1. B; 2. A describes theft, B describes robbery and C describes burglary. 3. B; 4. Accelerant

Motel Hideout (page 162)

The thief is in room 59.

Do It Yourself Part 2 (page 164)

Pliers, plane, sawhorse, hammer, hand saw, utility knife

Police Station Shenanigans (page 165)

The answer is 42.

ANSWER PAGE

Find the Witness (page 166)
Ken Rawlins and his wife are found in house E.

What Changed? Part 2 (page 168)
The gun moved closer to card 2.

Find the Witness (page 169)
Chin lives in house D.